PRAISE FOR USA TO AUTHOR JAN MORAN

Coral Cottage and Seabreeze Inn series

"Jan Moran is the new queen of the epic romance." — Rebecca Forster, *USA Today* Bestselling Author

"The women are intelligent and strong. At the core is a strong, close-knit family." — Betty's Reviews

"The characters are wonderful, and the magic of the story draws you in." Goodreads Reviewer

The Chocolatier

"A delicious novel, makes you long for chocolate." – *Ciao Tutti*

"Smoothly written...full of intrigue, love, secrets, and romance." – *Lekker Lezen*

The Winemakers

"Readers will devour this page-turner as the mystery and passions spin out." – *Library Journal*

"As she did in *Scent of Triumph*, Moran weaves knowledge of wine and winemaking into this intense family drama." – *Booklist*

The Perfumer: Scent of Triumph

"Heartbreaking, evocative, and inspiring, this book is a

powerful journey." – Allison Pataki, *New York Times* Bestselling Author of *The Accidental Empress*

"A sweeping saga of one woman's journey through World War II and her unwillingness to give up even when faced with the toughest challenges." — Anita Abriel, Author of *The Light After the War*

"A captivating tale of love, determination and reinvention." — Karen Marin, Givenchy Paris

"An epic journey with the most resilient of heroines as our guide. It is a book to savor, like the most beautiful of perfumes…riveting from start to finish." — Samantha Vérant, Author of *Seven Letters from Paris*

"A stylish, compelling story of a family. What sets this apart is the backdrop of perfumery that suffuses the story with the delicious aromas – a remarkable feat!" — Liz Trenow, *New York Times* Bestselling Author of *The Forgotten Seamstress*

"Courageous heroine, star-crossed lovers, splendid sense of time and place capturing the unease and turmoil of the 1940s; HEA." — *Heroes and Heartbreakers*

"A thoroughly engaging tale, rich in all five senses." — Michelle Gable, Author of *A Paris Apartment*

"Jan rivals Danielle Steel at her romantic best." — Allegra Jordan, Author of *The End of Innocence*

BOOKS BY JAN MORAN

Contemporary

Summer Beach: Coral Cottage Series

Coral Cottage

Coral Cafe

Coral Holiday

Summer Beach: Seabreeze Inn Series

Seabreeze Inn

Seabreeze Summer

Seabreeze Sunset

Seabreeze Christmas

Seabreeze Wedding

The Love, California Series

Flawless

Beauty Mark

Runway

Essence

Style

Sparkle

20th-Century Historical

Hepburn's Necklace

The Chocolatier

The Winemakers: A Novel of Wine and Secrets

The Perfumer: Scent of Triumph

Life is a Cabernet: A Wine Country Novella

JAN MORAN

Coral CAFÉ

THE CORAL COTTAGE AT SUMMER BEACH
BOOK TWO

CORAL CAFE

CORAL COTTAGE AT SUMMER BEACH, BOOK 2

JAN MORAN

SUNNY PALMS

PRESS

Library of Congress Cataloging-in-Publication Data

Moran, Jan.

/ by Jan Moran

SBN 978-1-951314-15-6 (epub ebook)

ISBN 978-1-64778-004-3 (hardcover)

ISBN 978-1-64778-005-0 (paperback)

ISBN 978-1-64778-006-7 (audiobook)

ISBN 978-1-64778-016-6 (large print)

Published by Sunny Palms Press. Cover design by Sleepy Fox Studios. Cover images copyright Deposit Photos.

Sunny Palms Press

9663 Santa Monica Blvd STE 1158

Beverly Hills, CA 90210 USA

www.sunnypalmspress.com

www.JanMoran.com

For all my beach-loving readers.

1

*S*ummer Beach, California

THE SEA BREEZE WAS CRISP, though the morning sun warmed Marina's shoulders as she arranged fresh-baked bread on a table in her specialty food stall. She waved at a retired couple threading their way through the busy farmers market toward her. Anne and Charles had been her first customers—thanks to her sister Kai, who had insisted on handing out samples that day.

While the initial decision to transform herself from San Francisco television news anchor to entrepreneur might have been forced upon her, Marina couldn't imagine going back to the stress-filled job she'd held for years.

"I have the rosemary-garlic focaccia bread you ordered," Marina said, greeting the pair. With their stylish silver hair, deck shoes, and navy cotton sweaters draped around their necks, Anne and Charles looked as if they'd just stepped out of a commercial for high-end wealth management. *Almost too perfectly cast.*

Marina had once called them the yacht couple—and she'd been correct. Their gleaming white yacht—far too large for most of Summer Beach's boat slips—loomed at the end of the marina beyond Mayor Bennett's modest craft. They'd told her they were friends of local celebrity Carol Reston, and they'd docked there to visit Carol and other friends visiting from Los Angeles for the summer.

Marina had worked late last night on the large order, making sure she served nothing short of perfection to her best customers.

This summer, she had to succeed, not only for herself but also for her children. The twins were turning nineteen this summer. Heather was finishing college, and Ethan was trying to figure out his life. Young adults perhaps, but still kids in so many ways. And she was the only parent they had.

But Marina had a plan. This wasn't the first time she'd faced a tough challenge.

"I can always count on you," Anne said. Diamond studs twinkled at the older woman's earlobes as she inspected her order. "Smells marvelous, my dear. Our chef thought it perfect for our party."

Kai lifted a plate of samples. "Marina is adding Quiche Lorraine to the menu this summer. I call it sophisticated comfort food. Try a bite."

Marina and Kai had argued over the quiche. In a world of kale and quinoa and avocado toast, a savory egg custard seemed almost quaint. "I disagree," her sister said. "Martinis made a comeback, and so will quiche."

And so, quiche was the specialty of the day.

Anne sampled one. "Marina, darling, this is divine. You've done it again." The older woman motioned to her husband. "Charles, you must try Marina's quiche. It reminds me of that little cafe on the Croisette, overlooking the Mediterranean."

"Save me a bite," Charles said as his phone rang. Answering it, he stepped to one side in the aisle.

Kai nudged Marina and whispered, "Told you the quiche would be a hit. People indulge on vacation."

"These are selling fast," Marina said, stretching the truth just a little. "I created this based on another one of Julia Child's classic recipes—though I lightened it a little. Still just as tasty, though." As she handed Anne a paper napkin, she recalled how she'd learned to make this recipe.

When their grandmother, Ginger Delavie, lived in Boston as a young woman, she had become friends with Julia Child, the renowned chef and cookbook author, through their mutual government work. Some of Marina's fondest memories were of Ginger gathering her and her sisters in the kitchen to teach them how to make her friend's recipes.

This was one of Julia's favorites, Ginger would say. Or, *this was Julia's special omelet—the first one she made on television.* After their parents died, these kitchen gatherings became even more important to Marina, Kai, and Brooke. Always brilliant in math, Ginger taught Marina and her sisters measurements and fractions in the kitchen before they started first grade.

Anne's husband joined her, and she handed him a sample of Marina's quiche. "As delicious as I've ever had," he said, nodding.

"Don't forget the cookies," Charles said, though his smile didn't reach his eyes.

"We should both forget the cookies," Anne shot back. "But we simply can't. We'll take a dozen. Half oatmeal and half chocolate chip." She paused, shifting her gaze to her husband, who was uncharacteristically quiet. "Who was that on the phone?"

"Jean-Luc," Charles said. "His mother was in an accident. He's leaving immediately."

"Oh, no." Anne furrowed her brow. "Is it quite serious?"

"I'm afraid so."

Anne nodded. "Of course, he must go at once. Well, there goes the party we'd planned. I'll call our guests to cancel.

Without a chef, it's all that we can do. Unless we serve cocktails and focaccia," she added, her gaze resting on the bread that Marina had prepared for the party. Anne brightened. "We have plenty of caviar, though."

"No reason to cancel," Charles said. "We can take everyone out to a restaurant."

"That's not the point of this dinner party. Besides, I doubt if we can find reservations for that many people tonight." Anne sighed. "What a shame. It was such a lot of work finding a date that worked for everyone. I hate to disappoint people."

Marina didn't mean to eavesdrop, but the couple was standing an arm's length from her. *A party tonight.* She shot a look at Kai, who angled her head in the couple's direction and arched a brow. Marina shook her head. She wouldn't have much time to prepare, and it could be a disaster. "Kai, would you help Anne and Charles with the cookies while I wrap their quiche?"

"I'm so glad you came early this morning," Kai said to Anne and Charles, springing into her role. "We often sell out, but we try to accommodate everyone. Even on very short notice."

Early this morning, Kai had left their grandmother's beach cottage to meet Shelly at the Seabreeze Inn for yoga. Kai still wore leopard-patterned yoga gear under a loose top, and her thick strawberry blond hair was caught in a ponytail. Whether on stage with her musical theater troupe or at the farmers market, Kai always stood out.

"We've learned to beat the rush here," Anne said. "Last week, Marina had sold out of our favorites. So we called in our order ahead of time."

Kai scooped up the cookies that Anne pointed out. "It won't be long before you can visit Marina's new cafe on the beach." She threw another pointed look at Marina.

"I've heard about that from Mitch at Java Beach," Charles

said, nodding at the logo on her new apron. "The Coral Cafe, I take it. Good name."

Marina smiled as she slid their order into a bag. "My grandparents bought their cottage on the beach decades ago, not long after they married. They called it the Coral Cottage. You've probably seen it from the beach."

"Can't miss the place," Kai said. "It has a fresh coat of coral paint on it."

"We've been serving casual suppers on a new deck with a view of the ocean," Marina added. She did a quick calculation of the time. Maybe she could put together something simple for them on the patio. A salad and pasta wouldn't take long, even for a crowd.

Marina had paid for the new deck with her severance settlement from the television station. Ginger's insurance had also covered repairs after a waterspout had hurtled onshore just a few weeks ago. The twister had sheared the roof from the guest cottage and made a mess of the yard. They had just finished installing new shrubs and flowers. Fortunately, the new patio escaped damage.

Jack Ventana, a writer who'd been renting the cottage from Ginger for a short sabbatical, had moved to a room at the Seabreeze Inn with his overgrown Labrador retriever puppy, Scout. As irksome as Jack and Scout could be, Marina missed taking the occasional morning walk on the beach with the pair.

But that was before Jack had pulled a disappearing act. After she'd joined him for what turned out to be a romantic swim at the Seabreeze Inn—the historic house that her old friend Ivy Bay had restored—he'd promised to call her. They'd even shared a kiss. But a week had passed, and then another, and he'd made no effort to contact her again.

She was too busy for a relationship anyway.

As Marina secured the bag with tape, her mind whirred. She probably had time to create more than salads and pasta.

She could do this. "I couldn't help but overhear your conversation. You have a dinner party planned for this evening?"

"We did," Anne said, looking glum.

"We could host you and your friends on the deck," Marina began.

Anne shook her head. "The whole point was that our friends wanted a tour of the yacht." As her gaze fell on Marina's apron, she pressed a finger to her lips. "Charles, you don't suppose…"

Here's my chance, Marina thought. Lifting her chin, she started to ask a question—but Kai beat her to it.

"As luck would have it, we had a cancellation for tonight, so we're available to cater a dinner party. How many are you expecting?" Kai had been handling the pop-up dinner marketing and reservations.

"We'll have twelve," Anne said, smiling. "Why, I think that might work. Carol told me your crab-stuffed salmon and mango cheesecake are to die for."

"That's perfect," Charles said, brightening. "Jean-Luc told me that the food has been delivered, so all you have to do is throw it together." Charles made sweeping motions with his hands as if a little juggling is all it would take.

"Marina can do anything," Kai said, turning bright eyes in Marina's direction.

Twelve people, Marina thought. She could manage that. And the supplies were already there. "I'm sure I can sort out supper for you. What did your chef plan?"

"Lobster of some sort," Anne said. "Jean-Luc is a magician with crustaceans."

Marina smiled. "That's one of my specialties as well." She'd often made Julia Child's Lobster Thermidor recipe with her grandmother. It was one of Ginger's favorites. *Dry white wine, parmesan cheese, mushrooms, cognac.* She could do this.

"We have a few errands in town, and we'll be back on board at 2 p.m.," Anne said. "That should give you enough time." She reached out to Marina. "Thank goodness you're available. All that work coordinating twelve couples and their dietary preferences nearly drove me mad. I'm glad the effort isn't wasted."

"Twelve *couples*?" Marina asked, suddenly concerned. "Then, you mean twenty-four *people*?" She cast a worried glance toward Kai, who gave her a brave smile and a little thumbs-up sign behind Anne and Charles.

"And us, so I suppose that's twenty-six if you're counting," Charles said. "Jean-Luc always buys extra food to allow for the extra last-minute house-guests people must bring along. Say about thirty-ish. Should be fine weather to dine on the deck."

A shiver coursed through Marina. She'd never cooked for that many at once. Most of the dinners she'd catered had been six or eight people. "Not a problem. Kai will be my sous-chef tonight."

Kai's eyes bulged in protest, and she shook her head, but Marina ignored her.

"We appreciate this," Charles said. "We'll pay you well, especially on such short notice." He picked up their purchases.

Marina watched the couple weave through the crowd. The dinner party would be an event to remember. Ever since she'd kicked off the pop-up brunches, lunches, and dinners a few weeks ago, she'd been busy, but this was an important job.

Marina needed the income—and it would give her the credentials she needed to approach other restaurant owners in town about her idea for a new event she was calling Taste of Summer Beach. With increased competition from major restaurant chains in the neighboring community, they needed to attract new business.

She turned to her sister. "I'm counting on you, Kai. Whatever you had planned, cancel it. Given the size of that vessel and the number of people, this soiree will be a lot to handle. I can't do it alone."

"All right, it's not like I have a date or anything," Kai said, leaning on the display table that they'd draped with a new coral cloth that matched Marina's apron. "Besides, I'm dying to see what that yacht looks like inside. I wonder who is on the guest list?"

"Never mind that. I wish we could get inside the galley sooner. We'll have to organize the menu and ingredients as quickly as we can." Marina sliced another piece from their sample quiche and lifted it onto a cutting board. "Speaking of dates, have you heard from Dmitri?"

"He's busy flying from one meeting to another," Kai replied. "New York, Chicago, Miami. Raising money for a new theater production is a lot of work."

"Think he'll manage to come here? Ginger sure would like to meet the man you're engaged to marry." Marina cut the quiche into sample bites, arranging them on the platter they used for sampling. As she did, she thought about tonight's job, hoping that Jean-Luc's menu wouldn't be too difficult.

"About that…" Kai's voice drifted off, and she twisted the ends of her hair around a finger.

Marina sensed a note of uncertainty in her sister's voice. "That didn't sound like a vote of confidence."

"I just want to be sure."

"I can understand that. You've only known each other a few months, and you've spent half of that time here." Marina was worried about this, too. Still, she was trying to support her sister.

Kai pursed her lips. "I'm going to push out the wedding."

"I thought you had. Didn't you tell Dmitri?" Marina placed an apple cinnamon muffin with a puffy top on the board and began to slice it into bite sizes. Kai had yet to wear the impressive ring Dmitri had given her, saying that it was too much for beachwear.

"I did, but I meant even farther out," Kai said. "We have so much in common, but the more Dmitri pushes, the more I draw away. Or maybe it's because we're apart. Is that crazy or normal?"

"Ginger always tells us to listen to our instincts," Marina said, arranging the muffin bites beside the quiche. "Dmitri is perfect on paper, and your clock is ticking. But you need to spend more time together. Kai, this will be a long-playing role, not a weekend marquee in Cleveland. Get to know each other better—beyond the first crush stage."

"And that's another thing," Kai said, replenishing the cookies on display under the glass domes Marina had found in their grandmother's china cabinet. "Dmitri wants me to quit this theater company. He says I've outgrown it, and I need to land larger roles in New York."

"Isn't that what you wanted?" Her sister was on break from her usual musical theater tour for the summer.

"It is, so there's truth in what he says, but I want that to be my decision." Kai clasped her hands and leaned on the table. "The theater company is like family. Still, Dmitri and I will probably live in New York after we're married, so maybe it's time to get on with our future." A pensive expression shadowed Kai's face. "Sure will miss spending summers here, though."

Marina picked up the platter and paused. "This wouldn't have anything to do with our friend Axe, would it?" The contractor and his crew were working on the damaged guest cottage.

"He's not interested in me," Kai said, dipping her chin. "We're just friends."

"Many of the best relationships began as friendships."

"Like you and Jack?"

"Try again," Marina said, pursing her lips. That fluttery feeling she had in her chest when she thought of him was now annoying. Marina wasn't ready to upend her life for any man. At forty-five, she was past that. He'd probably sensed that, which would explain why she hadn't heard from him. Still, he could have called. She supposed she could have been the one to call, but she wanted it to be his idea.

She wiped fingerprints from a glass dome. Maybe they'd both gotten the proverbial cold feet after that evening.

Unlike Kai, Marina knew how marriage worked. She'd followed her husband from one military base to another before he died. Now, her life was in flux, and her children still depended on her. To their credit, Heather and Ethan were preparing to be more responsible out of necessity. After Marina had lost her job, they'd had the honest family talk about finances.

Now, Marina didn't have long to ramp up, so a relationship would only take time away from the new cafe. She had to be smart and give everything she had to this new venture.

And then there was Jack's predicament. She twisted her lips to one side and frowned.

"Hey, what's that look?" Kai asked.

"What look?"

Kai folded her arms and nodded. "The Jack look."

"I do not have a Jack look," Marina said, wiping her hands on a dishtowel and snapping on a fresh set of food handling gloves. "And stop diverting the conversation."

Kai shrugged. "Ginger says their work on the book is going well. And Jack's been spending a lot of time with Leo."

"As a father should," Marina said evenly. "Jack has ten years to catch up on."

"And with Leo's mom."

Marina pressed her lips together. "This is not a competition. Jack should appreciate the time he has with Vanessa before..." She paused, thinking of the poor woman's health crisis. "There's a lot he needs to learn about his son. It's only right."

Kai sighed. "Do you think there's any hope for Vanessa's condition?"

"I wish...for Leo's sake." Marina couldn't quite understand why Vanessa hadn't told Jack about Leo until now. From the way Vanessa looked at Jack, she clearly adored him.

Or maybe Jack had been the problem.

More red flags.

Kai touched Marina's shoulder. "Hey, Grady was a jerk and never deserved you. And it's been eighteen years since Stan died. It's okay to let yourself be attracted to someone and try again."

"Jack's situation is too complicated for me," Marina said. "I'm busy, and he can deal with his life just fine without me." She pushed the sample tray into Kai's hands. "Go work your magic. We need customers now. The sooner we sell out, the sooner we can leave and plan for this evening. And I have a food order to pick up."

Marina passed a hand over her eyes. Despite her words, she truly felt for each of them—Jack, Vanessa, and especially young Leo. Jack should be spending time with them. This wasn't jealousy she was feeling, was it?

Kai grinned. "We'll be sold out in no time." Humming the opening notes to a show tune, she raised the platter and stepped into the aisle as if she were stepping into the spotlight.

Watching her sister, Marina laughed. Only Kai could pull this off. She thought about how long it had been since she and Kai had spent time together like this. And if Kai were to marry soon, this would probably be their last summer, except for the occasional vacation. A wistful knot formed in her throat. Just as Marina was finding her freedom, Kai was on the opposite path. Marina pursed her lip. *Their last summer.*

"Fresh-baked goodies," Kai called out. "Free samples right here."

Marina truly appreciated Kai's efforts. Since arriving in Summer Beach, Marina had been nursing her wounded pride over Grady. It hadn't been long since she'd discovered her fiancé had become engaged to a pop star—while she was delivering the morning news on KSFB, a San Francisco Bay area television station. She'd lost her composure on the air and quit before her boss could fire her in front of the crew.

By the end of the day, Marina's shocked, bumbling reaction had become an instant meme hit on social media, while late-night talk shows ran endless clips to roaring laughter. Even worse, Grady was the first man she'd seriously dated since Stan had died.

Marina brushed her hands and lifted her chin. That was all behind her, and she had a lot more to worry about than the Gradys and Jack Ventanas of the world.

Such as thirty lobsters. And what could Anne's comment about dietary preferences mean? Probably gluten-free or dairy-free. Maybe vegan or shellfish allergies. Or preference-driven.

That she could handle, but until she saw Chef Jean-Luc's pantry supplies, she had no idea what she could substitute. Had he made arrangements?

Marina drew a breath and considered her options.

When she had been a morning news anchor, she knew her routine. After reviewing the written newscast, reading the script, and confirming pronunciations of names and places, she'd carefully put on makeup, dress, and style her hair—her appearance was the source of the most frequent comments. She'd clip on her microphone and adjust her earpiece to receive cues from the producer or director. The control room could be in chaos, but she would remain calm.

Marina exhaled. That's how she would run her kitchen. She would prepare for the unexpected. *Risotto*, she thought. *Or pasta. Steamed vegetables.* Marina considered easy dishes she could prepare and have on standby for requests. She could do this. What could go wrong?

Suddenly, someone yanked her apron ties, pulling her off balance. She stumbled backward. Surprised and angered, Marina swung around. "Hey, what gives you the right—"

A yellow Labrador retriever held the apron ties in its

mouth and tilted its head. Its tail beat against the plastic cooler bins stacked to one side. A leash hung from the collar around its neck, and its paws were wet and sandy.

"Wrong, Scout," she cried, tugging the fabric from the dog's mouth, but he took this as a sign to play and tightened his jaw grip. She tried to keep from laughing as the overgrown puppy dug in and pulled back. "Where's your dad?"

A tall man in a faded T-shirt and jeans rushed through the crowd. "Hey, boy, cut it out." Towering over the pup, Jack pointed to the damp apron ties. "Drop it. Sit."

With doleful eyes, Scout obeyed, though the dog could hardly contain his enthusiasm. His tongue hung from one side of his mouth, and his tail wagged against Marina's calves. She reached down and rubbed Scout's head and neck. "Haven't seen you in a while, buddy."

"Or you." Jack ran a hand over thick brown hair in need of a haircut.

Marina glanced up and caught his gaze that sparkled with interest. Or was that her imagination? "Because of you, I have to scrub up again." She could simply change her gloves, but this would give her an excuse to get away from Jack.

She paused. Why did she want to flee from him?

Because he's dangerous, that's why. Her heart might overwhelm her common sense around Jack. And she had no certificate of guarantee that he wouldn't go all Grady on her and show up with a bikini-clad twenty-something. Plenty of them on the beach and everywhere you looked in town. The drawback to a beach village was the youthful, well-toned competition.

Not that she was in a competition with anyone. Marina stood and leveled her gaze at Jack. She was past the race for a husband, past the competition from younger women angling for her job at a news desk. And certainly past men who disappeared like holograms.

"How is the book?" Marina asked lightly.

"Coming along. Ginger is amazing."

"We've always thought so." Marina shifted, trying not to stare into eyes so blue they took her breath away. "And Leo?"

"Great kid—all thanks to Vanessa, of course. I don't deserve him."

An awkward silence ensued.

Marina thought about the situation and wondered if Vanessa had truly exhausted all treatment, though it wasn't any of her business.

Scout pawed at Marina's apron and wagged his head.

"He has your cheesy grin," Marina said, scratching Scout behind the ears, which were also damp and smelled of saltwater. Scout rolled into her arms. He was irresistible, especially with his awkward gait from an injury that never slowed him down.

"Look, I've been awfully busy, but I thought you might like to join me tonight for dinner—"

"Tonight? Sorry, I have major plans." Marina bristled at his last-minute invitation, especially considering his lousy follow-up history. She didn't need this kind of distraction.

"Then how about—"

"Awfully busy," Marina said, echoing his excuse. She picked up Scout's leash and handed it to Jack. "You should use this. Or is that how you get the girls?"

"Guess I deserved that." Jack took the leash. "Come on, Scout. We've got work to do."

Maybe she'd been too sharp with him, even he deserved it. After all, he was working with her grandmother. She threw up her hands. "Jack," she began.

He swung around, hope etched on his face.

"You should spend time with Vanessa."

Stymied again, Jack blinked heavily and nodded before moving on with Scout.

Marina stepped from her post and made her way toward Kai, who was handing out samples farther down the aisle.

"Would you mind the store? I've got to wash up." Marina

held out her hands and angled her chin in Scout's direction. "Eau de wet dog."

Kai's eyes lit. "You talked to Jack?"

"Nothing new there. Be right back." Marina made her way toward the community facilities on the beach next to the farmers market. Even if she hadn't been busy tonight, she couldn't believe the nerve of Jack asking her out tonight. Maybe she was old-school, but she had no intention of being anyone's date-of-convenience.

Marina shook her head, banishing Jack from her mind. She had a critical job tonight that could solidify her reputation in Summer Beach—or destroy it. No one was going to deter her from that.

Certainly not Jack Ventana, the master of disappearance.

2

*M*arina heaved an industrial-sized bag of flour onto the counter in Ginger's mid-century kitchen. She and Kai had sold out of her baked goods and quiche at the farmers market in record time—just as Kai had forecast. Afterward, they stopped to pick up a food order. Marina was now buying supplies in bulk, improving her profit margin, not to mention her upper body strength.

As they were unloading, Kai said, "We have to ask Anne and Charles for a tour of their floating mansion before we start dinner."

"I don't know if we'll have time," Marina said, frowning. "I'm worried about the supplies on hand and prep work, let alone finding everything we'll need in a new kitchen."

Kai made a face. "Oh, come on. This might be our only chance to check out such a large boat."

"Yacht," Marina said, correcting her. "There's a smaller runabout craft tucked inside. You can call that a boat. Although it's actually called a tender."

Marina had bought Italian rice for risotto, along with butternut squash that could keep if she didn't use it all. She hoped that her clients' chef would have more on hand, but at least she'd have the basic ingredients for a dish that she could serve to those with dietary restrictions.

"We'll leave the rice in the car, but let's bring the vegetables inside," Marina said. "I don't want the heat to spoil them."

Kai lugged in a carton of squash and placed it inside the kitchen door. "That's the last of it. I'm going to shower and change. See you in a bit."

Marina leaned against the counter to catch her breath. She hadn't been this physically active since the twins were young. It felt good to challenge muscles she hadn't used much sitting behind an anchor desk. Now, she woke every morning looking forward to another day—rather than dreading it. At this stage in her life, that meant everything to her.

"You're creating quite the production line," Ginger said as she walked into the kitchen.

Marina grinned. She didn't know anyone who ironed their jeans anymore, but with Ginger's imperious carriage, she wore them well.

Her grandmother had high standards that were as exacting as her mathematical calculations. She often dressed in crisp white shirts and polished loafers, even if she were only strolling into town. Sometimes, she wore flowing ensembles she'd bought on her travels—or yoga gear with a puffy jacket to hike the cliffside for her meditation. Ginger had a style of her own, and she could be as flamboyant as classic, depending on her mood. Today, she had added a chunky red coral necklace and earrings to her outfit.

"Trying to keep up with demand," Marina said. "We had a great day. We sold out at the farmers market today, and we picked up a dinner party for thirty on board the giant yacht in the marina."

Ginger arched a brow. "Be careful there."

"Why do you say that?" Marina inclined her head at the comment. "The owners are clients from the farmers market."

"Great wealth sometimes spells danger. Haven't I taught you to exercise your full awareness?"

While some might think this an odd comment, coming from Ginger, who'd put Marina and her sister in self-defense training at young ages, it wasn't out of character. Especially since Marina had recently learned that Ginger had been a top code-cracker during the Cold War. Ginger still downplayed her involvement, but Jack interviewed others who praised her efforts.

Marina didn't have much time to talk about this. She gazed around the kitchen, where supplies filled every surface. "Kai is upstairs in the bath, but I'll have this organized and put away shortly."

"I've given this cafe idea a great deal of thought," Ginger said, placing her hands on her hips.

"And I'd love to hear those thoughts." Marina blew a wisp of hair from her forehead as she unloaded supplies. "Maybe later?"

"We can talk while I help you put these away." Ginger opened another cabinet to shift items to make room, falling in sync with her granddaughter.

"I won't say no to that." Marina smiled to herself. Her grandmother was efficient—and persuasive.

"While I've enjoyed having the most interesting guests in residence every summer," Ginger began, "I've decided to put that structure to better use. I'm sure Bennett can help Jack can find another place to live for the remainder of his sabbatical. Besides, now that Jack has young Leo, he should stay on in Summer Beach. See the boy through school and be a real father to him."

Marina bit her lip at that thought. She had thought a relationship with Jack was developing, but she was mistaken. Who knew what went on in the minds of men?

"About Jack…" A faraway look filled Ginger's eyes. "Why, when Bertrand was in the diplomatic corps, there was an irresponsible young man who took in a nephew he'd never met. That shaped up the scoundrel in a hurry. Even he said it was the best thing that could have happened to him. Not so much for the boy, of course. Still, with Jack—"

"Excuse me," Marina said. Ginger loved reminiscing, and while Marina usually enjoyed hearing her stories, she didn't have the time or inclination to listen to her grandmother go on about Jack. She and Kai planned to be at the marina before Anne and Charles in case they were early. They'd need every minute to prepare.

"You said you've been thinking about the cafe," Marina said. "I can get by with the patio this summer, but I hope to move into a proper facility next year. While I appreciate it, I can't use your kitchen forever."

Ginger smiled. "Then I should tell you that I visited City Hall this week and had a long chat with Boz in the planning department. Bertrand and I purchased this house first, then the lot for the guest cottage, which we had built. That lot is outside of the Summer Beach city limits and zoning. Technically, I can do whatever I want on that property. That's why I plan to enlarge the kitchen in the guest cottage for the cafe. You can work from there."

"Really?" Marina could hardly believe what Ginger was saying. That might be the answer to her dilemma. Excitement bubbled through her, but then her pragmatic side surfaced. Marina wrinkled her brow with concern. "More space would be welcome, but what about the cost and inconvenience to you?"

Ginger lifted her chin. "According to my calculations, the insurance funds will cover most of it. However, you might want some kitchen upgrades."

"I'll cover that cost," Marina said quickly, thinking about the equipment and increased capacity she would soon need to grow the business. Investing limited funds was risky, but didn't every new venture carry an element of risk? She drew a breath to quell her nerves. "I still have funds from my settlement."

As long as Marina made a reasonable profit this summer, she'd have money for the portion of Heather's tuition not covered by school loans at Duke University. The investment in a new business was necessary to replace her old income, as her agent hadn't managed to find another anchor position for her.

Marina had to be realistic. At her age, her options in front of the camera were growing more limited every year—even though she felt like she was at the top of her game.

However, a cafe was more than a second-place option— it's what she'd dreamed of doing for years. And she'd be the boss, not some trust-fund hipster who was playing television producer at one of his billionaire father's acquisitions.

Her former boss Hal had been more interested in on-air eye candy than reporting the news. Yet as a single parent with two children, Marina had needed the security of a paycheck at the time. In the end, that illusion of security had been subject to Hal's whims. It might have taken her years to realize it, but now Marina was determined to create more reliable security on her own.

She'd already taken the first steps toward her dream— perfecting her recipes, creating a vision, and building a clientele at the farmers market. Except for a couple of small disasters—including her debut at the Seabreeze Inn—her business was off to a fairly good start. Still, she'd had to be careful not to make mistakes or get derailed.

"We can discuss the finances later," Ginger said, checking her watch. "Let's look at the guest cottage. I thought you'd like to start planning your workspace before you have to leave."

"I don't have much time, Ginger." Just then, Marina heard Kai's soprano voice soaring into show tunes.

"Kai takes a long bath. And she's only just beginning the *Sound of Music*." Ginger checked her watch. "Axe Woodson is also due here shortly."

"Lead the way then."

The two women made their way past freshly planted bougainvillea plants, replacements for the voluptuous, ruby-flowering vines the tornado had shredded and unearthed. As they reached the front door, a late-model pick-up truck eased to a stop in the driveway. A tall, rugged-looking man in a plaid shirt stepped out. His cowboy boots stood out in Summer Beach, though probably not in his home state of Montana.

"We're out here, Mr. Woodson," Ginger called out with a wave.

With a roll of plans under his arm, Axe strode toward them. His sandy, sun-bleached hair contrasted with a face weathered from the outdoors. "I brought the plans so we can make notes of any changes you want."

Kai's vocals drifting from the bathroom's open window drew Axe's attention. He paused, nodding thoughtfully. "That's quite the song."

"Isn't it?" A smile touched Ginger's face with pride.

Smoothing a hand over his chin, he said, "I didn't realize Kai was so talented." His rich voice rumbled in his barrel chest.

"With her gift and flair, she could easily play on Broadway." Ginger nodded toward the plans, drawing his attention back. "Marina will also have input on the new design."

Marina greeted Axe, whose crew had been repairing the damaged roof. They walked inside the guest cottage, which had been cleared of furnishings. The old stuffed sofa had been drenched, and the wooden desk warped. A musky aroma hung in the air.

"It was time to redecorate anyway," Ginger said, tapping the damaged desk.

"Summer Beach can use a restaurant this close to the beach. You should draw a crowd."

"That's the idea," Marina said. "But when I spoke to Boz a few weeks ago, he mentioned that chain restaurants in the next town were running a lot of specials to attract Summer Beach visitors. That's hurting a lot of restaurants in town." That was the unknown part of her venture that disturbed her. "Do you know Rosa at the fish taco stand in the village?"

Axe grinned. "I buy take-out from her place a couple of times a week, at least. My crew—even more often. It's good, homemade food."

"Did you know that a national taco chain just down the beach is hurting her business? She had to reduce employee hours."

Marina had talked to Rosa, a long-time proprietor in Summer Beach who was part of the fabric of the community. Rosa purchased fresh fish every morning at the dock from the fishing vessels, her family grew organic vegetables, and they made salsa and tortillas without any additives. They offered plenty of vegan options as well. Marina thought Rosa's fare was far superior to the fast-food chain's dry excuse for tacos— and it was less expensive for what you got.

"I didn't know that, but I'm not surprised," Axe said, shaking his head. "People often opt for what they know. It will be up to you and restaurant owners in Summer Beach to figure out how to get visitors to stay here. You'll need good marketing and PR."

"Kai does that quite well," Ginger said.

"I've seen her in action at the farmers market." Axe rubbed the back of his neck and chuckled.

"We should position Summer Beach as a destination for foodies," Marina said. "I plan to produce an annual Taste of Summer Beach to attract visitors. With Kai's help, of course."

"Kai mentioned that," Axe said thoughtfully. "It's a good idea—if you can shake up some of the restaurant owners in town."

"I think they're already shaken." Marina motioned toward the kitchen. "Let's start here."

Glancing around the space, Marina imagined the equipment she'd need. "I'll have to give it more thought, but at the least, I'll need a lot more counter space." She tapped a wall that separated the kitchen from a small dining area. "If we can remove this wall, we can open this space and extend the kitchen. I'll need a larger cooktop, more ovens, and room for a large refrigerator." The old apartment-sized refrigerator couldn't hold enough.

"Sure, that's possible." Axe indicated an option on the plans and made notes on a pad he withdrew from his pocket. "Here's the name of a restaurant supply store. They get a lot of good used equipment from high-end restaurants that have failed. You can find some deals there, and sometimes they have auctions."

Marina brightened. "I'll check that out right away." She gestured outside. "You did such a good job on the deck, so I thought about building another one to join the two together. That would double the seating space and give us better access." Since rain was infrequent, especially in the high-season summer months, she could save the cost of enclosed space. Many people preferred eating outside on the beach.

"Good idea. Outdoor seating is a cheaper option." Axe made another note. "I'll take some measurements later." He clicked his pen. "What are your plans for the living area?"

Marina studied the space. A large adobe fireplace that she knew provided the only heat in the cottage anchored the room. Generally, the weather in Summer Beach was mild, although she knew unexpected cold weather did occur. Just last winter, Ginger told her they'd had a rare dusting of snow on Christmas, even though it melted the moment it touched the sand.

Marina ran her hand over the old fireplace. "I want to keep this, and I could use the living room as flex space for a chef's table or cooking classes." She could serve friends and family with the open layout and share new dishes she was trying out.

Ethan could bring his hungry friends, and Ginger and Heather could catch up while Marina cooked and served them. The thought filled her with happiness, and she could just imagine how it would look.

"A chef's table is an excellent idea," Ginger said, pressing her hands together.

"Would it be possible to replace the large window with doors we could open? That would open the kitchen to the patio." That would be easier to manage and entertaining for customers.

"Sure, we can do that," Axe replied.

While Marina watched, Axe surveyed the room. He asked a few questions, and they discussed safety measures and the need for a larger electrical panel to handle the new equipment.

Once Axe had everything he needed, he returned to his truck. Just as he was leaving, Kai emerged, fresh from the bath. Her makeup was expertly applied, and her hair looked stage-perfect. She turned toward Axe's truck, looking crestfallen at having missed him. Axe waved as he left.

Kai turned back to Marina and Ginger. "Why didn't one of you tell me Axe was here?"

"I didn't know we were supposed to," Marina replied.

Kai rolled her eyes. "A lot of help you two are."

"So when will Dmitri grace us with his presence?" Ginger asked, raising her brow.

"I'll ask him," Kai replied, though she sounded vague.

Ginger touched her shoulder. "If he's going to be part of the family, it's only proper. Tell him I'm looking forward to meeting him. Long overdue, don't you think?"

Kai nodded, though she glanced over her shoulder, still watching Axe.

Marina knew Kai was vacillating between the ideal life she envisioned with Dmitri and the attraction she felt for Axe. She

wondered if Kai really had a deep connection with Dmitri—
or if her infatuation was dimming.

"I'll get ready," Marina said. She had no idea what to
expect in the kitchen galley. She turned to Ginger. "Anne and
Charles assured me that the food had been delivered, so I
think we'll have everything we need on board. And Kai, don't
forget to change into deck shoes. Make sure the soles are
clean, too."

"Aye, aye," Kai said.

As Marina packed supplies and tools she might need for
the evening, she couldn't help wondering what awaited them
aboard the *Princess Anne*.

3

*S*eated at a patio table at the seaside Seabreeze Inn, Jack stared across the sand at the ocean, willing the right words into his mind and onto the screen. His hands poised motionless over the keyboard, waiting for a cue from his brain.

He was accustomed to investigative reporting with its in-depth research, interviewing, and detailed writing. Writing and illustrating a series of children's books with Ginger Delavie—a legend in her right among top-secret coding circles —required a rewiring of the gray matter.

This certainly wasn't how he'd imagined spending his six-month sabbatical.

But then, Jack hadn't counted on discovering he had a son, either. Or even getting a dog.

Next to him, Scout whimpered at a seagull cruising over-head. Jack reached down to scratch the dog's neck.

Just then, his phone buzzed on the table. He'd meant to turn it off while he wrote, trying to edit and add to Ginger's original text and make notes for his drawings. With a sigh, he reached for the phone, noting the name of a fellow reporter and friend whose name appeared on the screen.

"Hank, what's going on?" Jack grinned. This was the prankster who'd told the puppy rescue organization that their office offered doggie massages and a pet park in the middle of Manhattan.

"Aren't you tired of that sabbatical yet?"

Jack held the phone toward the ocean. "Hear the waves? Can't beat working in Summer Beach."

Hank laughed. "Figured you'd be getting bored. Can't imagine you'd find many stories there. Don't you miss ducking whizzing bullets?"

"Only sometimes. What's up?"

"I got a new assignment approved. Sure could use you on the team."

"Yeah?" The hair on the back of Jack's neck bristled. Hank sounded pumped up. A familiar frisson of excitement gathered in his chest. He should say no, but he was curious.

"Packing my bags for an overnight flight. You could board your dog and meet me tomorrow. This is big, Jack. Could be another Pulitzer for your mantle."

"I don't have a mantle."

"This might help get that mantle then."

Jack chewed his lip and thought about that. "Where are you heading?"

Hank named a country that had been a hotbed of activity. Dangerous, too. Jack's heart rate accelerated. "Got sources?"

"Enough to start. Jennifer can book your flight. This story is critical, Jack. We'll have unprecedented access, too."

"Who else do you have on the team?"

"No one as good as you. See you tomorrow?"

"I need to think about it." Jack flexed his fingers. "Have to check on something first."

"You got an hour. I'll need to call someone else if you can't do it." Hank paused. "What's going on there? You usually beat me to the front lines. Don't tell me you're going soft, dropping out."

Jack wasn't ready to confide in Hank. "It's complicated. I'll call you back."

He hung up and pressed his hand to his chest, which was pounding in anticipation. He glanced around the terrace. Behind him, he saw Vanessa's friends, Denise and John, with Leo and Samantha. They were talking to Ivy Bay, the proprietor of the inn.

Jack didn't have much time.

How Ginger had shifted his idea of writing a book about her to collaborating on children's stories was beyond him. Not that he wasn't enjoying the new project, but he wondered if Hank was right. Was Jack squandering the professional reputation he'd worked so hard to achieve?

This was his livelihood, after all.

Leo caught his gaze and waved at him. At ten years old, the boy was a near replica of Jack at his age. There was no denying that Leo was his son. Jack should count himself lucky the boy didn't hate him for not being in his life until now. That had been Vanessa's choice, and in her condition, he couldn't blame her for anything.

"Hey, Dad," Leo called out. "Brought my stuff." Leo was carrying a snorkel, mask, fins, and a float vest.

"You've got the right gear." Jack ran a hand through his hair. He'd promised his son they'd go snorkeling this afternoon after he finished writing.

His son. Jack wondered if the word *Dad* came easily to Leo or if it still seemed as foreign to him as it did to Jack.

An hour to decide.

Would he break his promise to Leo or break his commitment to his profession?

Jack closed his laptop and shoved it into his backpack. Charging out is what Jack did—what he'd always done. Pack on a moment's notice and head wherever he needed to be. That's how he and Vanessa had met. Comrades with pens—shining a light on truth and strife in the world.

Someone had to do it.

Jack slung his backpack over his shoulder and rose. There would be other days to snorkel. He'd have to catch Denise and John before they left. They'd understand. He was sure Ginger would, too.

Scout was jumping around Leo as he came up the walkway. The boy broke into a run and collided with Jack, throwing his arms around him and letting his equipment clatter to the ground.

"Hey, hey," Jack said, feeling a lump rise in his throat.

"Can Samantha come snorkeling, too? Her parents have to go to Los Angeles."

"About that," Jack began, as a wave of guilt overtook him.

Denise and her husband hurried toward them. After greeting Jack, John pulled him to one side and lowered his voice. "Vanessa hasn't been feeling well. We're taking her to Los Angeles to see her doctor. Would you mind if we left Samantha here with Leo?"

Jack's heart sank. "I just got a call, too. Actually, I was hoping that…" He cast a glance in Leo's direction. Jack had told himself that Leo would understand, that there would be other days. That wasn't always true, though. And he'd already missed a lot of those days.

"We wouldn't ask, except—"

"That's fine," Jack said, perhaps a little too abruptly. He swallowed his disappointment.

John frowned. "You were saying that you got a call. From Vanessa, too?"

"From an old colleague. It's nothing." Jack shrugged. "Really. Go on. The kids will be fine with me."

"It might be a few hours." John nodded toward his wife. "Denise brought extra clothes and snacks for them for after snorkeling."

"I'll take care of the kids." What had Jack been thinking? Being a father had real responsibilities. It wasn't only about buying Leo a new bike or talking about sports. He'd committed to being there for Leo, and this is what that promise meant.

Maybe Hank shouldn't have called because Jack had corralled his time off, but Jack knew he would have done the same thing. That was the nature of media work.

John and Denise hugged the kids and hurried away, leaving Jack with a canvas bag of clothes and supplies for the children.

"Wait here with Scout," Jack said to Leo and Samantha. "I'll change, and then we'll go to a rental place for my equipment. I'm counting on you two to tell me what I need for snorkeling."

Jack walked back to his room, dropped off the bag and his laptop, and made the call. He could tell Hank was disappointed, too.

"This isn't like you," Hank said. "You haven't fallen in love or anything, have you?"

"It's not that, but it's important," Jack replied. With a jolt, he realized what he'd just said was wrong. He had fallen in love. With Leo, with Summer Beach…maybe even with a woman. "I'll tell you later, Hank. Good luck out there, and keep your head down."

He'd have to talk to his boss first. The reality of being a parent finally dawned on him. He might not be able to return to his old job when his sabbatical was over. Sure, he could take Leo back to New York with him, but Denise and John were like family to Leo. Now wasn't the time to break those bonds.

Bennett Dylan, the Summer Beach mayor who also worked in real estate sales and rentals, had offered to help him find another seasonal rental that would give him more room with Scout. And Ginger was urging him to take a position as editor of the town's small, struggling newspaper.

Jack considered his options. Whether he was ready to step

out of the big city excitement or not, he realized Leo needed him.

He couldn't remember the last time he'd had that feeling. If he could continue writing freelance stories along with Ginger's book series, maybe he could manage to stay in Summer Beach.

While Leo might be the impetus behind this decision, Jack couldn't deny another strong pull to Summer Beach. From the first time he'd seen Marina, hobbling on a sprained ankle at the Seabreeze Inn, he'd felt an almost indescribable draw to her. He, a man of letters, was at a loss to describe this inexplicable feeling—save resorting to the language of romance, which he had a hard time believing after writing about tragedies between people who professed love.

And yet, that growing sense of destiny, weird as it sounded, seemed to have taken hold of him. He shook his head.

No, as much as Jack was growing to care for Marina—there, he'd admitted it—he couldn't allow her to complicate the decision he would have to make when his sabbatical was over. He closed his eyes. Yet he couldn't forget the touch of her fingers twined in his in the pool, the warmth of her kiss—or his promise to call her.

How many times had he said that to a woman and failed to follow through?

Becoming a father overnight was one thing, but embarking on a relationship that could turn serious was quite another. Jack imagined that Marina wasn't the type of woman that men dated casually—she was too smart for that. Plus, she'd just come out of a bad relationship. He hoped that hurtful meme of her would die out soon.

Complicating the matter was Leo, who liked Marina a lot. Yet considering the tragedy ahead for his son, Jack couldn't stand to break Leo's heart twice. If a relationship with Marina didn't work out—and Jack's track record wasn't stellar—Leo would feel the loss, too.

Jack might have run from romantic commitment most of his life—important stories had always taken precedence—but after looking into a young face that mirrored his own, this was one commitment he decided he could not break.

After changing into swim trunks and packing their gear, Jack drove Leo and Samantha to the rental shop. Suitably armed with snorkeling equipment, they continued to a sheltered cove a few miles away that Mitch at Java Beach had told him about. The kids had fun snorkeling in the cool, shallow water and watching fish dart beneath the surface. Scout scampered in the waves, and Jack enjoyed himself, too.

Scout ran to Jack and dropped a piece of driftwood on his feet. "Ow, in front of me, you silly goon." Scout panted, his tongue hanging from his mouth, which curved into a perpetual grin.

Leo and Samantha laughed and waved, and Jack hurled the wood toward them.

Scout took off after it. He ran so fast that instead of stopping, he skidded and tumbled over his prize.

"Silly old pup." Jack laughed.

When he picked up his phone to take photos of Leo to send to Vanessa, he noticed that Denise had called. He rang her back, and she picked up right away.

"Thank heavens, Vanessa will be okay," Denise said. "But the doctor wants more tests, so we have to stay longer. Can you take care of the kids for supper? Traffic will be heavy out of Los Angeles by then."

"Stay and have dinner there. No need to fight the traffic." Jack would have to cancel the dinner party he'd been invited to. On such short notice, he felt terrible, but what could he do?

"Good idea," Denise said. "I should have left you the keys to the house."

"No worries. We can have a slumber party if the kids get tired."

Denise laughed. "They can stay up late. It's summer break. Vanessa would probably like going to one of her favorite restaurants, even though she won't eat much."

"Do that," Jack said, and the thought made him feel good. He was fond of Vanessa, and he'd always admired her talent and courage—now more than ever.

While Leo and Samantha played, Jack called his dinner hosts. He'd met the couple one morning at Java Beach, and Mitch had introduced them. Summer Beach was the sort of town where people easily socialized. They'd immediately invited him to a dinner party they'd planned. Jack knew that when a man of his age was single and could regale guests with stories from around the world, he was often welcome. He enjoyed meeting people, but he could only handle a few of these parties a year.

And yeah, he'd been a jerk to think he could invite Marina at the last minute.

Jack tapped the phone to call his host.

When Charles answered, Jack said, "Sorry to call so late, but I've had a development." In the background, Leo and Samantha yelled as they threw sticks for Scout.

"Hope it's nothing serious," Charles said. "Is that a woman screaming?"

Jack chuckled. "It's my young son and his friend. I hadn't expected to have them tonight, but his mother had an emergency."

"Bring them along," Charles said with a hearty laugh. "It's a casual evening, and another friend is bringing her nanny and daughter. We have a playroom on board and plenty of food. They'll like the lifeboat drill."

"Are you sure it wouldn't be any trouble?" Jack glanced at the children. They were a happy mess of sand and saltwater. They would all have to clean up, but they'd have to do that anyway. Besides, they had to eat, and he'd been looking forward to the evening.

"Anne loves children. We'll be disappointed if you don't bring them."

Jack finally agreed and hung up. It wasn't often he had a chance to go on a yacht that size. He waved to Leo and Samantha. "Your parents are going to be a little later tonight. But I have a surprise. Who wants to explore a great big yacht tonight?"

"Cool," Leo said. He whirled around.

Samantha's eyes widened. "The one at the marina? My mom and dad said it's one of the biggest they've ever seen."

"We'll have supper on board with some new friends, but we'll have to cycle through my shower. Samantha, you'll be first. Now, you two help me with all this gear. And someone's going to have to spray off that filthy pup."

As if recognizing his cue, Scout trotted to them and shook. The kids screamed and scampered away.

Jack laughed. "Show off," he said to Scout.

While they loaded the van, Jack thought about how much his life had changed in a couple of months. As exciting as it had been to get Hank's call and think about a new assignment, he had to admit that he was glad he'd stayed. As for a long-term lifestyle change, Jack still wasn't sure. A lot could happen in one summer.

4

"Welcome to *Princess Anne*," Charles said, guiding Marina and Kai onto the yacht docked at a slip at the far end of the marina. "We call this our getaway vehicle."

"Oh, Charles, you make it sound so dramatic," Anne replied. She slipped off her shoes and deposited them in a basket at the end of the gangplank, and her husband followed suit.

"Shall we remove our shoes?" Kai asked.

"I respect the conventions, but it might not be wise in the galley." Marina was concerned about cooking barefoot. "We cleaned the soles before we came." Many accidents could happen in a kitchen, from dropped knives to scalding pots that slipped out of hand.

"You'll be fine with your deck shoes in the kitchen," Charles said. "But first, a safety briefing." He pointed out lifeboats and life vests. "Don't be surprised if we have a safety drill. Captain's orders. He's a stickler for maritime law and insurance requirements," he added with a wink.

Marina couldn't imagine how many millions this yacht might be worth or the operating budget required to maintain it. A captain, a chef—she wondered how many others were aboard. She adjusted her heavy supply bag over her shoulder.

As Charles led them on board, they skirted an outdoor seating area and a hot tub. Once inside, they passed a bar and screening room decorated with exotic woods and creamy white shades. Highly impractical for a vessel, she thought. But practicality didn't seem to matter here. Everywhere she looked were displays of wealth, from high-tech gadgetry to mood lighting and artwork.

"We enjoy our playground at sea," Anne said with an airy wave of her hand. A stack of gold and diamond bracelets clinked as she did. "This way to the galley."

As she stepped inside the galley kitchen, Marina took in great, modern swaths of stainless appliances, counters, and glass cabinets. Sunlight poured through windows lining the side of the kitchen.

"Where are the supplies for the party?" Marina asked.

"Provisions are in the walk-in refrigerator and freezer units," Charles said, motioning to twin doors at the end of the galley. "You'll find everything you need." Eyes twinkling, he lowered his voice. "We're well-stocked for fast getaways."

"In the middle of the night, I'll bet," Kai said, joining in the fun.

"Spot on," Charles said, grinning.

That phrases reminded her of Ginger. "Have you ever lived in England?"

Charles seemed surprised. "The occasional vacation. Funny you ask."

Marina brought the conversation back to business. "And the menu and recipes?"

A blank look filled Anne's face. "Chef Jean-Luc handles that. I've never seen him write anything down. He simply tells me what he has planned."

"It's lobster night," Charles added.

"Can you be a little more specific?" Marina's nerves were

sizzling, a clear signal of imminent danger. She shot a look at Kai, who seemed blissfully unaware of the dilemma. "How do you prefer your lobster prepared? Maybe you have a favorite recipe."

Charles chuckled. "Anne swears she's never made a meal in her life. But she's adventurous, and she'll try anything."

"It's true. I like surprises." Anne gave another twirl of her hand. "Jean-Luc knows what we like, so simply use whatever he ordered. We're fairly relaxed on board."

"May I contact him to see what he had planned?" Marina's pulse raced. She didn't consider herself a chef; she wasn't even a restaurateur yet. At best, a solid cook.

"We wouldn't want to bother him while he's at his mother's bedside," Anne said. "I'm sure you'll be fine with Jean-Luc's supplies. Simply put them together." As Charles had done, Anne made a sweeping motion with her hands as if she were scooping together ingredients before finishing with a flourish. Clearly, this was all the direction they deemed necessary. Marina thought maybe that's the way it was done on board a yacht such as this.

Anne beamed as if she'd been helpful. "Now, if you'll excuse us, we have to get ready for our guests."

After the couple left, Marina leaned against a cool stainless counter and swept a hand over her face. Without a menu to guide her, or even a lifeline from the elusive chef, Marina felt overwhelmed. "What have we gotten ourselves into?"

Kai's eyebrows shot up. "What do you mean? Look at this place. Should be a piece of cake for you."

"It's not the cake I'm worried about." Marina drew her apron from her bag, fidgeting with the tangled ties. "Kai, I'm not really a chef. I'm a home cook with aspirations. We have to prepare and plate thirty fairly complicated dinners at once."

"Then why did you agree to do this?" Kai sounded

perplexed. "Don't let this floating palace intimidate you. You've made lobster before, right?"

"Of course." Marina straightened her shoulders, willing her courage to return, though her heart was hammering. What was wrong with her? In the last couple of weeks, she'd prepared several dinners for parties of eight. But she'd used the recipes she knew well, and the parties were casual. She hadn't felt the pressure that was suddenly constricting her chest. And the drifting motion of the craft wasn't helping. Though it was gentle, it was still enough to make her feel a little off-kilter.

Kai took her hands. "Remember how nervous you were the first time you went on air?"

"My tongue felt like cardboard."

"Like my first time on stage," Kai said. "I could hardly sing, let alone dance. But after a few beats, I got into it. Really, what's the worst that could happen?"

"They dump everything and call for pizza."

Kai grinned. "So, save them the trouble. Make lobster pizza."

"I'm serious."

"So am I. Did I tell you about the time that Wolfgang Puck's team catered one of our grand openings? People went wild over his seafood pizzas. The smoked salmon with caviar was to die for."

"Maybe that's not a bad idea." Marina managed a nervous laugh. "They did say they were casual on board." She gestured toward an open brick oven. "They do have a pizza oven."

Kai turned around. "And a rotisserie. Look at all these culinary toys. Any other day you'd be in heaven. We're not going to abandon ship." She peered at Marina with concern in her eyes. "But I think we need to do some yoga breathing. You're having a moment. Here, take my hand."

Marina did; she remembered what Ginger had once told

her when she was a child to alleviate the seasickness and panic she'd felt the first time they'd been at sea. *Focus on the horizon. Find a point and breathe.*

She turned her attention toward the horizon through the porthole. She hadn't been seasick since, but this felt a little like that. Maybe it was an anxiety attack, though she'd faced much worse in her life. What was this really about?

Kai squeezed her hand. "These past few weeks, you've had a lot of sudden changes in your life. It's normal to feel overwhelmed."

Marina nodded. From leaving her job and her profession, moving from San Francisco to Summer Beach, starting a new business—and worrying about how these changes would impact Heather and Ethan—her brain was as full as a stuffed pepper. As she thought about it, she realized that her feelings were probably the culmination of all of that. Still, she had to forge ahead.

Kai peered at her. "Remember what Ginger says. Feel the fear and do it anyway."

"From her friend Eleanor Roosevelt," Marina added.

"Sometimes I wonder if there is anyone Ginger hasn't met," Kai said. "Grandma is pretty remarkable. And so are you. Give yourself some credit for being a single mom and a successful anchorperson. You made it look easy, but I know it wasn't. No reason to think you can't handle a few lobsters."

"Thanks for the reminder, Kai," Marina said, turning back to face her sister. "Maybe I should start joining you for Shelly's morning yoga classes at the inn."

Kai grinned. "That's the spirit. Now, I'm going to wash up and check out the fridge. We should see what we've got to work with."

Feeling her heart rate slowing to normal and a sense of control returning, Marina nodded. "I'm with you. Let's do this."

Inside the walk-in refrigerator, Marina and Shelly looked

around. The delivery boxes had been placed inside, so it was easy to find the supplies for the evening.

"There's enough in here for months," Marina said as she took in the provisions in the refrigerator, freezer, and larder. "Guess you have to be prepared if you're out on the high seas."

Just then, a young man who looked hardly older than a teenager arrived with a cardboard box. He was tall and wiry with a sun-darkened face that showed the unmistakable delineation of sunglasses. "Hi, you must be the temporary chef. I'm Len, junior deckhand here. Where do you want these lobsters?"

Marina eyed a box, which had air holes in it. A hairy antenna poked out. "They're not frozen?"

"Chef wouldn't allow that. These were flown in from back east for tonight. Fresh Atlantic Maine lobsters."

"I say we release them," Kai said. "I'm not prepping those."

Len shifted uncomfortably. "Pardon me, ma'am, but they've been out of saltwater, so they're in shock anyway, and the Pacific is a lot colder than the Atlantic. And they'd be aliens in these waters. I'm afraid the future doesn't look good for them either way."

Kai sighed and wagged a finger at Marina. "Last time I do this. I swear I'm finishing my change into a vegetarian."

"I didn't make the menu or order the supplies," Marina said, holding up a hand.

Len glanced shyly at Kai. "I can help you, ma'am. My parents own a restaurant in Maine, and I worked in the kitchen growing up. I've prepared lobsters and shucked oysters for as long as I can remember."

"All right, but only if you don't call me ma'am," Kai said. "I'm not much older than you are."

Marina rolled her eyes. "Figure it out, Kai. I have to decide on a menu."

"So why aren't you working in the kitchen?" Kai asked Len.

"I wanted to do something different. But the chef pulls me in when he needs help. The captain sent me here to ask if you needed help."

"You don't have anything else to do?" Marina asked.

Len shook his head. "Not until later. Captain told me I'm to help serve tonight. We each have a job to do, but we pitch in to help others, too. We're like a family on board."

Marina liked that. "Have you traveled all over the world?"

"Quite a lot. But we've never been to such a small port. The owners usually like the usual busy places." He nodded toward a cabinet. "The chef has bamboo steamers in there."

Marina breathed a sigh of relief. "Welcome to the team, Len."

While Len and Kai prepared the lobsters, Marina took inventory. Parmigiano Reggiano, mozzarella, and fontina. Fresh romaine, arugula, mushrooms, and mounds of freshly clipped basil. Rummaging in the larder, Marina located extra virgin olive oil, flour, yeast, and salt. She found individual ramekins and serving dishes and spied a bottle of Grand Marnier.

"A simple menu," Marina announced, glancing at the clock. "Rustic lobster or mushroom pizza along with Caesar salad. We can begin with an assortment of vegetable kebobs and prosciutto-wrapped melon balls. It will be easy to adapt the pizza for those who are vegetarian, vegan, lactose intolerant, or don't eat shellfish."

"Sounds like you have it all covered," Kai said. "What about dessert?"

Marina checked the time on the stove. "Tiramisu would be nice, but it should chill about six hours. That would be cutting it too close, and we have a lot of other prep work. Maybe a choice of Grand Marnier soufflé, fruit, or ice cream."

"Fancy," Kai said, her face lighting. "Soufflés on a boat—you're brave. I knew you could pull this off."

"On second thought, I'll think of something else." Marina slung her arm around Kai. "Thanks for being here. We make a good team."

"So, does that make me the best sister?"

Marina laughed. "Brooke might have something to say about that. She tried to reach me this morning, but we've been trading calls."

Len listened with interest. "Excuse me, ma'am. You're sisters?"

"That's right," Marina said.

Kai jerked a thumb toward Marina. "She's the older one. And definitely in charge."

"That's cool," Len said. "My brother and I fought a lot, but I sure miss him now."

"And he probably misses you," Marina said. "Now, here's the plan for this evening. Kai, you'll assist me in the galley. And Len, you can serve?"

"Yes, ma'am."

Unlike Kai, Marina didn't mind the *ma'am*. Or maybe she was more accustomed to it since she was older. Kai still looked much younger than she was.

"Kai, as long as things are under control here, then I'd like for you to help Len serve. That's a lot of plates to get out there." She thought about the table settings. "Len, do you know where they will dine and how to set the tables?"

"Yes, ma'am. We had a server, but she quit when we came to port. She showed me how to do everything."

"Thank goodness." Marina rubbed her hands together. "Len, if you'll steam and crack the lobsters, Kai can help me prepare the dough."

While Len took charge of the lobster, Marina and Kai made the pizza dough. Following that, Marina put Kai on slicing vegetables for a marinade while she made notes of ingredients and organized the work area. The evening would move fast, so everything had to be in order. If they were missing ingredients, she had to make changes now.

THE AFTERNOON FLEW, and soon Marina could hear the chatter and laughter of guests arriving. So far, she and her small team were running on time. Kai had prepared vegetable kebobs, Len was on lobster duty, and Marina made the Caesar salad. All she had to do was toss the romaine with her home-made dressing, and they could quickly serve that after the appetizers.

She would have reversed the order had the guests been Europeans or others who traditionally preferred salad after the main course. Marina was guessing that as Americans, Charles and Anne were accustomed to salads early in a multi-course meal.

Marina had also prepared the dough and set up each station in advance—her *mise en place*—with ingredients measured and standing ready there or in the walk-in refrigerator. She smiled to herself.

They had this.

Suddenly, a loudspeaker crackled overhead, causing Marina to jump. "Attention, this is your captain speaking."

Len leapt from his stool. "Lifeboat drill." He gestured toward a cupboard. "Life vests are in there."

"Now?" Marina looked up and frowned in consternation. This change would throw them off schedule.

"Captain's orders." Len sprang into action, pulling out bright, fluorescent padded jackets.

"Surely he doesn't mean us," Marina said. It wasn't as if they were leaving port.

Frowning, Len bit his lip. "If I don't get you out on deck, I'll be in trouble."

"I guess Charles wasn't kidding," Kai said, washing her hands. "Let's put these fashion pieces on."

"And get it over with," Marina added.

While the captain gave orders, Len helped Marina and Kai slide on life vests and secure the straps.

"I have to have a picture," Kai said, laughing. "We didn't see this coming."

"Hurry up," Len said. "We can't be late."

Kai snapped a few photos before pocketing her phone. They hustled onto the deck, and Len led them to a spot where other crew members were gathered.

"Here comes the captain," Len said. "Get ready for inspection."

"You've got to be kidding," Kai said before Len silenced her with a stern look.

"Actually, we should be pleased that the captain is taking such care," Marina said. Although she wasn't happy about the interruption, she understood how important this was.

"Dinner is going to be delayed," Kai said.

"What's that?" The captain stepped in front of Kai. He spoke with an accent.

She tilted her chin. "I said, dinner will be delayed. Just so you know."

Clearing his throat, he lifted slightly on his heels. "Wouldn't you agree that the safety of the passengers and crew is more important?"

Len coughed, and the line grew quiet. Marina flicked her fingers against her sister's in warning.

"Yes, sir," Kai said quietly.

The captain moved on, and he appeared to find the rest of the crew in compliance, although Marina couldn't tell from the language they were speaking. Russian, she thought. Then the captain shifted back to English and said a few words about safety. He pointed out a route and lifeboats.

Satisfied, the captain released them and moved on to the

guests assembling haphazardly on the deck. Charles and Anne were taking photos for guests while a few sipped cocktails.

Marina paused and glanced over her shoulder to see who they might be serving tonight. "Looks like a happy crowd."

Kai nodded. "Your lobster pizza should go over well with them."

"Look how cute the kids look in their life jackets." Marina peered into the sun. A little girl seemed familiar. "Say, isn't that Samantha? Denise and John must be here."

Kai nudged her, though her elbow bounced off Marina's thick life vest. "Jack and Leo are here, too."

Next to Jack stood a young, slender blond woman. Leo was shyly shaking her hand. And then Marina realized that this was the event Jack had asked her to this morning. The younger woman obviously didn't mind a last-minute date.

Marina turned away. She had an important job to do. She unfastened her life vest and tugged at the straps.

"Are the kebobs ready?" Marina asked, annoyance creeping into her voice.

"Almost," Kai replied. "Hey, what did that life vest ever do to you?"

Marina pushed the vest into Len's arms, maybe a little too hard. "Oh, sorry," she added quickly as a startled Len caught his balance. She couldn't let Jack cloud her thoughts. "Would you put that back for me? I have to cook."

Striding ahead, Marina threw back her shoulders. The last time she'd let a man get to her, it had cost her a job she'd had for years. She wouldn't allow that to happen again.

"Let's get those appetizers out during cocktail hour," Marina said to Len. "Once they're seated, deliver the Caesar salads." Turning to Kai, she added, "We'll have to hurry with the kebobs. Are the melon and prosciutto balls ready?"

"Aye, aye," Kai said.

Marina went to work finishing the kebobs. She and Kai worked quickly, spearing the zucchini, mushrooms, and red and yellow cherry tomatoes that Kai had marinated in extra virgin oil olive and lemon juice. They added small, round, ciliegine mozzarella on the skewers with basil leaves and vegetables.

"Is that it?" Kai asked.

"Let's sprinkle on a little fresh basil for color," Marina replied.

Working together, they dusted the kebobs with bits of basil. Marina stepped back and turned to Len. "The first course is up. These are Caprese vegetable kebobs. Serve one per guest." When Len looked hungrily at the dish, Marina smiled. "I have a few left over for us."

"What shall I do next?" Kai asked.

"You'll follow behind with the prosciutto melon balls," Marina said. Next time, she might reverse the order, but she had no time to think about that now. They were behind schedule. While Charles had said they were fairly casual on board, Anne had been firm on the dinner time.

Suddenly, the vessel lurched, and Marina caught the bowl of melon balls before it careened onto the floor. "The kebobs," she called out.

Len was wavering, and Kai was scrambling toward him. While Kai slammed against a counter, Len gracefully regained his balance with clearly practiced movements. "We're getting underway," he said.

"I thought we were staying in port," Marina said. Charles and Anne hadn't said anything about this.

"Probably cruising the coastline," Len said. "They like to do that when they have guests."

Kai pushed back from the counter. "Good thing we didn't have soufflés in the oven. I don't think they'd like the waves very much."

"Seasick soufflés would never do," Marina said, trying to find the humor in the situation.

"Every sailor gets seasick at least once in life." Len gave

them a lopsided grin and repositioned the kebobs. He walked smoothly from the galley as Marina awkwardly made her way across the room, touching counters to maintain her balance.

Her sister steadied herself. "This is like dancing. You just shift and move with the motion. Kind of fun, actually."

"I never learned the kitchen waltz." Marina wasn't sure she agreed, but she had little choice. Here they were, and she had thirty guests to feed. After sweeping stray hairs from her face and securing them with a clip, she turned back to the neat balls of dough and began to press them out, working as an assembly line.

She brushed olive oil onto the rounded dough and sprinkled fontina, mozzarella, and Parmigiano Reggiano cheeses on top. Next, she added caramelized, sweet Maui onions she'd already prepared, along with chunks of lobster sautéed in garlic butter.

After she removed the pizzas from the open oven, she carefully added small dollops of caviar. The saltiness of the caviar would balance the sweetness of the caramelized onions. Russian beluga caviar was expensive, though the chef had cases in the refrigerator—probably for parties. That stash alone represented thousands of dollars.

Kai hurried back into the galley. "That other woman isn't with Jack." Her eyes flashed with excitement. "She's a nanny for another couple on board, so all the kids are with her."

"No gossiping about the guests," Marina said, pushing back the irritation she felt. She had to focus on the food and keep her balance—mentally and physically. "How did you get this intel?"

"It's not like he's someone we don't know," Kai said, grinning. "I just asked him. And we served the kids, too. They have a children's room on board."

Marina rolled her eyes. She couldn't stop Kai from talking to Jack. They had all become friends. "That's nice," she said dismissively. From the corner of her eye, she could see Kai giving her a funny look, but Marina had no time for this.

As the pizzas came out, she sliced them for presentation. Kai added the caviar, and Len began to take them out.

While that course was being delivered, Marina turned her attention to dessert. In keeping with the Italian theme, she'd decided on sweet *crespelle*, or Italian crepes. When Kai returned, she quickly explained.

"Flavored with Grand Marnier, drizzled with chocolate, topped with whipped cream and berries. Easy, but a beautiful presentation."

"Easy for you," Kai said.

Marina laughed. "You can still make a chocolate sauce, right? Like we used to put on our ice cream."

"Ginger taught us that," Kai said, checking out the last grouping that Marina had organized. "Is that what all this is for?"

Marina nodded. "Start melting the chocolate. While that is going, you'll find raspberries in cold storage. Oh, and some ricotta and honey. I'll show you what to do with it."

As Marina turned her attention to mixing a thin batter with a splash of orange liqueur for crepes, Len cycled in and out of the galley fetching special requests and carrying dishes. They'd also made a few alternative versions—kebobs without mozzarella, pizza with vegan cheese, mushrooms, and caramelized onions. So far, everyone seemed pleased, and Marina could hear peals of laughter from the deck.

She caught herself thinking about how she might have been a guest this evening with Jack instead. But that wasn't meant to be. She'd already committed to Anne and Charles, and she wouldn't have gone out with Jack as a last-minute date. She'd done that with Grady, and look where that had landed her. As for her husband Stan, his manners were impeccable, and he conducted himself with the honor of his position in the military.

While Marina poured thin layers of batter into a pair of skillets, she wondered if early stumbles in potential relationships might be a signal or message not to pursue.

She recalled the laughs that she and Jack had shared. He had seemed so genuine. Would they have had a long-term chance? Probably not. At least she was in agreement now with the universe, or whatever powers there were in the world.

And that's all there is to it, she decided, watching the crepes form tiny bubbles and enjoying the sweet aroma they released.

Marina worked quickly, flipping the crepes with practiced ease as she instructed Kai on making the crepe filling. Once Marina had a plate of crepes, she joined Kai and showed her how to assemble the desserts.

"You make that look easy," Kai said.

Len leaned on the counter, watching. "What is that dessert called?"

"Our grandmother taught me how to make this. Sweet crepes with ricotta cheese and honey. When you serve, call them *Princess Anne crespelle.*"

While Len and Kai hurried out with dessert, Marina sank onto a chair, her energy spent. A smile spread across her face, and a feeling of accomplishment suffused her chest with warmth.

Despite not realizing what she was getting into, having no menu or recipes, Marina had risen to the occasion and cooked for the largest party she'd ever had. But then, cooking was about knowing your ingredients, not always following a recipe as she would do in baking.

Marina stretched her arms overhead. She couldn't have done this without Kai and Len. A celebration was definitely in order.

After turning on some music on her phone, she brought out the kebobs that she'd put aside, along with an extra lobster pizza they could share. Kai and Len had worked hard, and they would have a few minutes before they had to clear the plates from the table.

Marina was pouring a small split of champagne she'd brought when she heard footsteps behind her. With a glass in her hand and a smile on her face, she turned around.

Marina's smile dimmed at the sight of Jack. "What are you doing in here?"

5

"Hi there." Jack grinned and shifted from one foot to another as if he'd suddenly found himself in the galley.

Marina glared at him. "Did you take a wrong turn? The head is to your left."

"I'd like for us to talk, Marina."

"As you can see, I'm pretty busy," she said, lifting the glass of champagne she had just poured to celebrate the dinner with Kai and Len. And she was hot, tired, and in no mood to talk to Jack. Plus, damp tendrils of hair hung around her face, which was probably bright red from cooking crepes over the stove.

Running a hand through thick brown hair that had grown longer since he'd been in Summer Beach, Jack took a step toward her. "Look, I had no idea you were working as a chef for Charles and Anne. When I found out you had made this meal, I felt like a double idiot—first, for asking you out tonight."

He held up a hand before she could say anything. "Too short notice, I realize that. I'm not completely without manners, even though it might seem like that. And second, for enjoying such a delicious dinner—and then learning you'd made it."

"Would have been kind of hard to attend and cook at the same time." Marina pressed the cool champagne flute against her warm cheek. She sipped the bubbly, trying to ease the heat that flared in her chest. That Jack could have that effect on her was disturbing.

"I meant no disrespect to you. And I'd like to explain what was going on in my mind. Maybe we could get a cup of coffee next week."

Marina ticked off her fingers. "Between building my clientele at the farmers market, working pop-up dinners, starting a cafe, and organizing Taste of Summer Beach, I don't see how I can fit you in."

"I'm a jerk. I get it."

"I don't think you do. I'm a working mother and a businesswoman. I'm not waiting for a man to whisk me off my feet." As soon as the words were out of her mouth, Marina winced. She didn't mean to imply that. Far from it, in fact.

Jack drew a hand over his face. "Not what I was trying to do, but that's good to know. In case any guy asks me."

"That's it. You need to leave."

"Hey, I'm sorry. That slipped out." Jack spread his hands in an appeal. "I wanted to talk to you because I can't continue working with your grandmother knowing that there is animosity between us. I never intended to slight you, and I didn't want to ignore you."

Marina blinked back angry tears that inexplicably sprang to her eyes. She hated when that happened. "Then why did you?"

"My situation is complicated. I have to think of Leo."

"As you should. You're his father. Welcome to parenthood."

"Why is this so difficult?" Jack smacked his forehead. "We're both trying to look out for our children, and some of our decisions are based on that. Let's start with that common ground, okay?"

Marina shrugged. Beyond Jack, she could see Kai, who had stopped Len from charging into the galley. "Granted."

Jack blew out a breath. "I really want to clear the air between us. I know you don't have time for coffee, but—"

"I'll make time. For Ginger." She didn't want to cause angst for her grandmother.

"Okay. Your choice. Java Beach, the Seabreeze Inn. Or a new place, the Coral Cafe. The new deck is pretty nice."

Marina couldn't help but smile at that. "Okay, you got me. But not Java Beach. Too many eyes and ears there."

Jack's startling blue eyes sparkled. "We're not hiding anything."

"Thirty minutes. That's all I can spare." Marina nodded toward Kai, who led Len into the galley, their arms full of dishes. She turned to Kai. "You shouldn't have to clear tables, too."

"I don't mind," Kai said brightly. She bumped Jack on the shoulder. "This one didn't even notice me. I didn't know whether to be insulted or impressed."

"My attention was on the children." Jack cleared his throat and stepped aside. "And as I was saying, I need to check on Leo and Samantha again. It's getting late for them, so we'll need to leave as soon as we dock."

He hadn't said that, but Marina could tell he was nervous.

Kai's eyes grew wide as she watched him leave. "What was that all about?"

"Nothing," Marina said, gazing after him. "He just made a wrong turn." She gave a glass of champagne to Kai and turned to Len. "Are you old enough to drink?"

"I'm nineteen, but it's against the captain's rules."

Marina handed him a glass of water. She lifted her glass. "Here's to the best crew I could've asked for. Congratulations, we did it." She clinked her glass against theirs and hugged her sister. "Couldn't have done it without you."

"Wouldn't have let you." Kai grinned and sipped the champagne.

Len glanced hungrily at the food Marina had brought out. "I sure would like to try some of that."

While Marina scooped a healthy portion onto Len's plate, the young man told her that Anne and Charles had asked for her.

"Sounds like a curtain call to me," Kai said.

"Might not be." Marina thought about what might not have been to their liking. Was it the lobster pizza? That was a risky choice, she allowed. Maybe that had been too casual for their taste and station in life. After all, it was lobster. Or had she used the wrong caviar? Perhaps it was too expensive and not meant to be served like that.

And yet, she was on a yacht worth millions.

Why did Marina feel like a little girl summoned to the principal's office? She had stepped up from home hobby cook to professional cook. Even if Marina hadn't had Ginger's encouragement, she knew her food was good enough to compete.

Over the years, she'd also learned about food safety, nutrition, presentation, and food cost calculations as she worked in cafes before Stan died. Marina realized she probably knew more than she gave herself credit for.

Swallowing her sense of trepidation, Marina pulled back her shoulders and marched from the galley.

As she walked onto the deck, touching chairs for balance, Anne waved to her to join them.

Marina glanced at their dinner guests, some of whom stared after her. Even in the cool breeze off the water, her face still felt warm. Thankfully, Jack wasn't at the table.

Charles introduced her. "Here is the woman responsible for the menu and dinner this evening."

Marina wasn't sure of the protocol, so she simply smiled and dipped her head in acknowledgment.

"When our resident chef was called away this morning, Marina agreed to come on board and cook for us." Charles smiled broadly. "Although our chef has never prepared anything remotely like this, I must say, we were all pleasantly surprised. Delighted, in fact. Kudos to the chef."

As the sound of applause filled the evening air, Anne leaned over. "Could you leave your lobster pizza recipe for Chef Jean-Luc?"

"It will be my pleasure," Marina said.

Smiling, Anne arched a brow and nodded. "Talented *and* smart." She glanced at Charles. "We'll have to let Marina and her sous-chef leave soon. We'll meet you in the galley shortly."

At the end of the evening, Marina was putting away supplies when she heard angry voices floating through a vent. She turned to Kai, who had also paused packing. The words sounded muffled, but they couldn't have understood them anyway because they weren't speaking English.

Kai raised her brow. "Is that Anne?" she asked in a hushed voice.

Len quickly looked away.

"It is, isn't it?"

"We're not supposed to talk about what happens on board," Len said, biting his lip.

Kai's lips parted as she listened. "That's definitely Charles and Anne."

"Do you think she's okay?" Marina asked.

"Seems to be holding her own." Kai tilted her head. "Are they speaking Russian?"

Len pressed a finger to his lips. "They don't know we can hear them in here," he said softly.

The conversation stopped as quickly as it had started, and Marina realized they had probably stepped away for a private chat.

"We're almost through here." Marina had a strange feeling. Many couples argued, but there was something odd about them switching to another language to do it. However, people in that financial stratosphere lived different lives, she figured. And it was none of their business.

A few minutes later, the couple appeared in the galley. Once again, Charles and Anne were smiling as if nothing had occurred. "Thank you for your efforts this evening," Charles said, handing her a thick envelope. "It's all there, with extra for the short notice. We appreciate your work tonight."

Anne nodded along with Charles. "And do remember, salads after the main course next time. That aids digestion, dear."

STILL THINKING about the odd way the evening ended with Charles and Anne, Marina eased her turquoise Mini Cooper into the Coral Cottage driveway. She shook off the thoughts as Kai counted the cash and squealed with delight.

"Fabulous new shoes, here I come," Kai said.

Marina glanced at an unfamiliar car parked beside them and turned off the ignition. "Wonder who is here?"

"No one I want to see me. I feel like I fell into a vat of lobster, but it was worth it." Kai slung her purse over her arm. "I'm calling first dibs on the tub."

"I'll use Ginger's shower." They were both exhausted after the dinner on board *Princess Anne*. But it was a happy exhaustion. Charles and Anne had paid them well and insisted they take several tins of beluga caviar, too, which Marina thought Ginger would like.

Marina had also passed out several cards among guests interested in catering and attending the Coral Cafe's grand opening. Building a restaurant clientele would take time, but as long as Marina could keep expenses down and quality and service high, she was confident she could make it.

Kai stepped from the car and regarded the late-model Mercedes next to them with some degree of envy. "Whoever it is sure has good taste."

"And the money to prove it." Still, Marina admired the sleek silver lines. "Must be a friend of Ginger's. They're probably sharing a glass of wine and a few laughs." Ginger had a wide group of friends.

"Shelly told me that actor, Rowan Zachary, tried to give Ivy an expensive sportscar for saving his life when he fell into the pool and almost drowned. She turned it down. Would you have done that?"

"I think Ivy made the right decision," Marina said thoughtfully. She looped the bag of caviar over her arm. "Gifts like that often have strings attached. I've always earned my way, so I have the luxury of saying *no thanks*."

Kai lingered by the car. "Sure is beautiful. But I won't need a car in New York. And I guess that won't be much longer. I tried to talk to Dmitri, but he now insists on keeping our original wedding date. Maybe he's right, and I'm just getting the jitters."

"That didn't sound like what you wanted earlier. And you still haven't worn his ring. Are you sure about this?"

Marina couldn't keep up with where her sister stood from day to day, and she wasn't sure that Kai could either. She knew the dilemma weighed on her sister. Dmitri might be a great guy who simply didn't want children. But they hadn't known each other very long. Marina thought that when a man moved too quickly, it was a red flag. Or it could simply be true love, but who was to know for sure?

When Kai didn't answer, Marina went on. "Axe heard you singing earlier. He was definitely impressed." Although she hadn't known Axe very long, their grandmother and others thought highly of him. When he built the deck for her, he'd shown her respect and never belittled her decisions.

Kai brightened. "Was he?" She gnawed her lip. "I'd love

to hear him sing. We talked a little about summer stock in Southern California. It's a shame there's no theater in Summer Beach."

As they strolled toward the front door, Marina thought about how much Kai loved Summer Beach. Whenever the musical theater tour went on break, Kai returned. Over the years, she'd spent far more time here than Marina had. "What if there was a theater here?"

Kai laughed. "Then Summer Beach would have almost everything I could want."

"Almost?"

Kai paused and gazed toward the ocean. In the moonlight, Marina would see the wistfulness in her sister's worried green eyes. "I've always thought that when I had a family, it would be great to be close to Ginger and Brooke to have a built-in support group." She swept some sand from the walkway with her deck shoe.

"If that's what you want, figure out a way to make it happen."

Kai turned back to Marina. "I've always dreamed about having a theater here. Do you think that's a crazy idea?"

"Why would I?"

"I don't know much about business or how to run a theater. I'm the talent."

"What did I know about running a cafe? As Ginger says, it's simple math. Figure out what you need and how much it will cost. And always sell more than you pay out."

"It's easy for you. You were always good at math."

"You're not as bad as you've imagined."

"You forget that I failed math."

"That was calculus."

"Twice. Even with Ginger's help. Let's face it; I have different genes than the rest of the family."

"But you passed on the third try. And believe it or not, I haven't had to calculate one single derivative to figure out my budget. Go figure." Marina tilted her head and grinned. "If that's what you wanted to do, I'll help you."

A flash of inspiration lit Kai's eyes. "I could still tour and manage the theater during summer breaks."

"Maybe Axe could help. I mean, he knows a lot of people around here."

"I could call him about that." She bounced on her toes. "Tomorrow."

Kai's face shimmered with fresh hope, and Marina realized how long it had been since she'd seen that expression on her sister's face. Kai began humming, and Marina recognized the tune from *Annie*, the popular Tony Award-winning musical.

Kai did a little dance step and took Marina's hand, twirling around, her skirt fluttering in the ocean breeze. She burst out in song. "Tomorrow, tomorrow—"

The front door to the cottage swung open, and a stocky, silver-haired man held his arms wide. Gold-and-diamond cufflinks on white shirtsleeves sparkled beneath a dark suit jacket that looked custom tailored.

"I'd recognize that voice anywhere," he said. "Surprise!"

Kai spun to a stop and pressed a hand to her chest. "Dmitri, oh my gosh." She squeezed Marina's hand and held it a little longer before letting go. "I didn't think you'd be able to come here."

"I missed you too much, babe." Dmitri swept Kai into his arms and kissed her deeply.

Standing right behind Kai, Marina glanced away to see Ginger standing in the doorway. She wore a jade-green silk caftan like an empress. Her grandmother crossed her arms and tilted her head at an imperious angle.

From Ginger's body language, Marina could tell she was not impressed, though she had always been tough on the girls' boyfriends. Stan had passed muster, but Brooke's husband Chip had to shape up. As Ginger arched an eyebrow, Marina could tell that Dmitri probably fell into the latter category.

After a few long moments, Ginger snapped on the porch light. Hastily, Kai pulled back. Her face was flushed—more out of embarrassment than excitement, Marina thought.

Kai quickly introduced Marina.

"You're Kai's sister?" Dmitri stared, inspecting her.

Sensing his disapproval of her appearance, Marina shifted under his scrutiny. She still wore her stained apron, and her hair was a hot mess. She might not look her best, but she'd had a successful evening, and she wasn't going to let this man dim her achievement. "One of them."

When Dmitri looked perplexed, Kai said, "I told you I have two sisters."

"No, you didn't. I would have remembered, darling."

Kai laughed. "Now you're just being silly. Or forgetful." She turned to Marina. "I talk about you and Brooke all the time. Dmitri just has a lot on his mind." She squeezed his hand as she spoke.

Marina noted the excuse and merely nodded.

Dmitri glanced at Kai's slender fingers. "Why aren't you wearing your ring?"

"I was helping Marina with a large dinner party. I was afraid it might slip off."

And a lie, Marina thought. Already she didn't like the way Kai was acting with this man. What sort of hold did he have over her?

"Mrs. Delavie mentioned that." He sniffed, held Kai's hands, and stepped back. "You were working in the kitchen?"

"Galley," Kai said brightly. "On the most magnificent yacht."

Dmitri held a finger up to Kai as if instructing her. "When we're married, you'll be a guest on yachts. Not the help."

Marina bristled and glared at him. "She was helping me. I'm starting a cafe."

"Kai must protect her voice," Dmitri said, disapproval evident in his manner. "The heat of a commercial kitchen could damage her vocal cords. We can't have that. And just look at you." He shook his head. "I've never seen you look this...disheveled." His lip curled as if the word itself was distasteful in his mouth.

"We call this beach casual, and helping Marina was just for fun," Kai said, throwing a look of apology toward Marina. "I was going inside for a bath."

"My beautiful lady will emerge like Venus from the sea." Dmitri nodded approvingly. "I'll unpack while you make yourself presentable."

From the doorway, Ginger's voice rang out. "You haven't even asked my permission."

Dmitri frowned as if he hadn't heard correctly—or Ginger had lost her mind. Neither of which Marina believed.

"To stay in my home," Ginger said.

Dmitri turned a patronizing smile toward Ginger. "Mrs. Delavie, may I stay with my lovely fiancée in your home?" He bowed and swept his hand across his chest in a theatrical gesture.

"That wouldn't be proper," Ginger said. "However, I can recommend an inn not far from here."

As Dmitri's face turned scarlet, Kai pressed a hand to his solid chest. "Dmitri, darling. It's her home, and it might be a little crowded. The Seabreeze Inn is quite nice, and we know the owners. You'll be more comfortable there, I promise."

"But my darling, it's been a long time. Don't you miss me?" He slid his hand down Kai's back.

Marina's lips parted. She couldn't believe what she was witnessing. Did he honestly think that Kai would persuade Ginger for him? This situation was worse than she'd imagined, and it showed her just how fragile Kai was at the moment.

"Of course, I do." Kai stepped back. "But my grandmother is right, and I'm awfully tired. Had I known you were coming…"

Clearly frustrated, Dmitri flexed the muscles in his jaw, containing his displeasure. Marina was sure that he was accustomed to having his way. Wealthy, powerful, confident—she could see why Kai had been attracted to him, but Dmitri certainly wasn't her type.

A conciliatory smile creased his strong face. "It won't be long before we're in New York." He pulled Kai toward him. "And then you'll be all mine, won't you?"

"Of course, but I have to finish my contract with the touring company first," Kai replied.

"Then you'll be glad to know I spoke to your boss. I persuaded him to let you out of your contract. He is already holding auditions for your replacement and sending you a release. Isn't that great?"

Kai's eyes blazed, and she took his arm. "It's late, and as you pointed out, I need a bath. Why don't I walk you to your car?"

From the measured sound of Kai's voice, Marina knew her sister was upset. Why didn't she say something? Marina felt like screaming, especially after the conversation they'd just had. *Come on, Kai*, she thought, willing her sister to find her backbone.

Dmitri nodded toward Ginger and Marina. As they disappeared around the corner, Kai's voice rose in the night.

Marina stepped onto the porch, and Ginger held the door open.

"Dmitri is a rascal," Ginger said, turning.

"That's too kind." As Marina followed her grandmother inside, she asked, "Did you have much time to talk?"

Ginger huffed. "Two minutes would have been enough. He's self-centered, egotistical, and views Kai as a pretty little possession he can brag about. A trophy wife. He seems eager to remove her from her family and friends so that they can associate with the right people in the business."

"How do you know that?"

Ginger's deep green eyes held her gaze. "That's what he told me." She swished her caftan around her. "Would you like a cup of tea or a glass of wine?"

"Definitely wine." With her dirty clothes, Marina didn't dare sit down on the canvas slipcovers that Ginger brought out every year, even if they were washable. She'd already had to wash them once after Scout had clambered onto the sofa with wet, sandy paws.

"Let's sit in the kitchen. I'm such a mess." The red Formica kitchen table and chairs were worn, but they were practically indestructible. Marina tucked the caviar into the refrigerator to save for a day when they had something to celebrate.

Ginger brought out a bottle of pinot noir and glasses from the wine alcove by the dining room. "I'm sure Kai will need one too, after that. But I haven't asked you how the dinner went. Successful, I hope?"

"Actually, I'm pretty proud of what we did. I couldn't have managed without Kai. And we had the sweetest deckhand helping us, too. I made lobster pizza with caviar, vegetable kebobs, Caesar salad, and crepes for dessert." Marina didn't mention that Jack was there.

"The pizza was an interesting choice," Ginger said, sounding intrigued.

Her grandmother's kitten heels tapped on the wooden floors of the old cottage and then onto the Saltillo tiles in the kitchen. She placed the glasses and wine on the kitchen table in front of a colorful hand-painted Talavera pot filled with chives and basil and tarragon for quick snips when they didn't want to walk to the garden.

The window above the kitchen sink was cracked open, and the sound of Kai and Dimitri arguing was quite clear. Marina was relieved that Kai was standing up for herself. Maybe she'd been too quick to judge. She gestured toward the window. "We really shouldn't—"

"Of course we should." Ginger held a finger to her lips.

Yet as they listened, Marina feared Kai was in more trouble than she had realized.

6

*J*ack started up the path to the mid-century home beach rental that John and Denise shared with Vanessa. Turquoise shutters—the color of the sea in the late afternoon—set off the white cottage. The cottage was close enough to the beach to get the fresh sea breeze, so all the windows were open.

Vanessa had asked him to come this morning, saying that she was better in the morning, especially with what they needed to discuss, so Jack had shifted his schedule. Generally, he liked to write and sketch early. If he were working with Ginger on a story, she preferred to start early as well—if she wasn't hiking to the ridge. She was an intriguing woman with a sharp mind, even at her age. Not that he'd asked or that it was important.

Her granddaughter was even more vexing. He and Marina had a coffee date scheduled for next week, and he found himself looking forward to it more than he should.

Since that dinner party on the yacht, something else had been running through his mind, too. Jack slowed his pace.

He couldn't explain it, but he'd sensed that something was amiss on *Princess Anne*. It wasn't the Russian captain and crew or the way Charles had sternly informed them that some areas were off-limits during the tour of the yacht. It was a feeling Jack sometimes had, like an extra sense that picked up on abnormalities and lies.

More than that, when he'd seen Carol and Hal in the village, he'd stopped to chat and asked how long they'd know Anne and Charles. To his surprise, the couples had met only last month in Los Angeles at a party. Yet from the way Anne and Charles spoke, they were old friends. Could Carol and Hal have forgotten? As celebrities, they met many people. Yet that wasn't likely, Jack decided.

He wondered why *Princess Anne* was docked in Summer Beach. People with grand yachts usually flocked together like rare birds. Anne and Charles were vague about where they were going next. Oddly, they seemed to be waiting.

For what?

Jack shook his head as he approached the steps. As Hank said, there weren't many stories to investigate in Summer Beach. Maybe he was reading more into the situation. Most likely, they were simply a well-to-do retired couple out for fun.

Yet Charles had been evasive about his line of work when Jack had asked him. *Investments.* That could mean anything. Jack had pressed him. *Stock market* came the answer. So Jack asked Charles about a high-profile merger and the broader implications.

Should be good for the market.

Jack had nearly gagged at that. All week, the news had reported that anti-trust enforcers were suing to stop the deal on the grounds that a merger would virtually eliminate competition and leave consumers with little choice and spiraling fees.

Why would Charles say that? And what did they have to hide?

Jack rocked on his heels. Maybe it wasn't any of his business anymore. Old habits were tough to change.

Jack ducked under purple wisteria that wound over the front porch and knocked on Vanessa's front door.

The door banged open. "Dad," Leo shouted, flinging his arms around Jack. He wore swim trunks, a superhero T-shirt, and flip flops.

"Hey, big guy." Jack tousled the boy's hair, which was the same shade his had been at that age. Leo had Vanessa's dark eyes, but he favored Jack in most other ways. Jack wondered how Vanessa felt about that. Still, she'd never wanted to marry or have a relationship. He only wished she'd told him about Leo sooner, but he understood why.

Jack hadn't been suitable husband or father material back then, always chasing stories around the world for the news. When Vanessa had contacted him to tell him about Leo, he'd offered to marry her, but Vanessa was too smart for that. She told him that when she discovered her pregnancy, she had known what she wanted—and what she didn't. But that decision had been years ago.

"I'm going to the beach with Samantha and her parents," Leo said. "Want to come with us?"

"I'd like to, but today I came to see your mom. Can I take a rain check on that?"

Leo looked perplexed. "The beach is better when the sun is out."

Jack laughed and hugged his son. "That's an old expression."

"It doesn't make any sense."

"It means you want to do something later."

"You could have just said that, right?"

Chuckling, Jack nodded. "That's what we call a cliché. You'll learn about that in school." Leo was going to keep him alert, for sure.

"Oh, yeah. Mom already told me about those," Leo said. "Come in. I'll get her." Leo took Jack's hand and then left him in the living room while he went to see his mother.

On a distressed, white-washed bookshelf, Jack noticed a group of photos that Vanessa must have brought with her. He picked up a picture of her with colleagues at a party and saw that he recognized several people in the photo. He and Vanessa had worked for rival newspapers; they had been professional acquaintances. And he had always respected Vanessa and her abilities.

Jack recalled the tough assignment they had covered. After one of their colleagues had been killed while reporting on the story, they'd sought comfort with each other late one night, not knowing if they would live through the dangerous situation.

She had never told him she was pregnant, even though he'd tried to keep up with her after they went on to other assignments. Eventually, she'd stopped returning his calls.

Only recently had Vanessa told him about Leo. She professed that she had not wanted to marry—Jack or anyone—even though she decided to have her baby.

Her parents had been thrilled to have a grandchild. They would have preferred to have a son-in-law in the deal, too. But Vanessa knew her parents. She had called them old-fashioned; they were descendants of aristocratic Spanish land-grant families in California, established long before statehood.

No, Jack wasn't their idea of good husband material. It wasn't until they had died and Vanessa had fallen ill that she had called Jack.

"I'm glad you came." Vanessa appeared in the doorway, looking weak but determined. A bright orange-and-fuchsia floral scarf was wrapped around her head where luxurious dark hair had once been, framing dark, expressive eyes that still held beauty and strength. "Let's work at the kitchen table."

Denise and John came into the room, their arms piled with towels and beach gear. Wearing a mermaid swimsuit and coverup, Samantha skipped behind them.

Jack helped Vanessa to the table and pulled out her chair. A basket of seashells rested on the rustic, hand-hewn table. On the back of a chair, he recognized a woven serape of red, blue, and green from her home in Santa Monica. Of course she would want her favorite things around her.

"Would you like some hot tea and crackers?" Jack asked. Vanessa seldom seemed hungry, and he could tell she'd lost more weight. Because her immunity was low, he kept his distance and didn't hug her.

"That sounds perfect, thank you."

Denise pointed toward a cabinet in the kitchen. "If you're looking for crackers, they're in that cupboard by the refrigerator, and tea is by the coffeemaker." She turned to Vanessa and rubbed her shoulders. "You'll call us if you need anything?" she asked with concern in her voice.

"I'll be fine," Vanessa replied, touching Denise's hand the way old friends do. "Jack is here, and I'll take a nap later."

Leo flung his arms around Jack again before they left. "Will you be here when we get back? You could have supper with us. Can he, Mom?"

"Jack might have other plans," Vanessa said, kissing the top of her son's head. "But we'll talk about it. Have fun, *mijo.*"

After the door shut, Vanessa gazed after them. "I want to spend every moment with him, but it's imperative that you two get to know each other, too." She gave a wan smile. "Leo and Samantha enjoyed having supper with you on the yacht. He couldn't sleep last night until he'd told me all about it."

"They're good kids." Jack touched her hand. "How did your doctor visit go?" He ached to ask if there was any good news, but he knew better.

"Same," Vanessa replied. She accepted this.

At a loss for words, Jack nodded. It wasn't fair that such a beautiful, talented, gifted woman and loving mother should have her life cut short because of a rare condition. Vanessa had called it an orphan disorder—so rare it was hardly worth studying.

At least it wouldn't make an orphan of her son. Jack would take care of him. With each sunrise, Leo was his first thought, and he fell asleep thinking about him, planning for him.

He was a father now. It was time to do the right thing. Turning down that offer from his colleague Hank had made him realize that he'd had his run, and it was time to build a new life.

Here in Summer Beach.

"There is a leather folder in the bedroom on my desk," Vanessa said. "Would you get it for me?"

Jack brought the stylish, gray leather folder to her. While she sorted through papers, he prepared green tea with mint and placed thin seeded crackers on a plate. He brought these to the table. It was meager fare but a feast for her.

Vanessa slid a packet of documents across the table to his side. "I asked you here to review plans for Leo's future."

"Can't that wait? I don't want to trouble you."

"We have to do this for Leo. Now, before—" She stopped abruptly and blinked.

"Whatever you want." Jack picked up the legal documents. The first thing he noticed was the name at the top. *Leonardo Rodriguez Ventana.* He raised his brow in surprise.

"Leo should have your last name now. It will make things easier for both of you. School, sports, doctor visits. Otherwise, they'll call you Mr. Rodriguez." She smiled. "My attorney prepared a Voluntary Declaration of Parentage if you would like to sign it now."

"Of course." Jack solemnly signed the document on the top. With a stroke of his pen, he was Leo's legal father.

Vanessa took the paper. "You'll be added to Leo's birth certificate."

"I am deeply honored," Jack said, pressing a hand to his chest. He meant it with every fiber of his being.

"John has agreed to act as executor of my estate." Vanessa spoke in a straightforward manner. Her voice gained strength —as if she had stored up energy to draw on for this critical task. "And that is the trust I've set up for Leo. His education and living expenses will be provided."

"Vanessa, I appreciate that, but I can support my son. I'm looking for a house I can rent, so Leo will have a room ready. Everything you leave him will go toward his education and his future."

"I thought you'd say that. But just in case you become unemployed or suffer an accident or illness, the trust will provide for Leo. And you, too." Vanessa smiled.

Jack shook his head. "I'll manage. I have a fair amount tucked away. I've had no mortgage or expensive cars or habits. I've worked so much that I didn't have time to spend what I made."

Vanessa sipped her tea thoughtfully. "My parents and their grandparents were quite comfortable. Well to do, you might say. Leo's trust is not inconsequential, and it will require management. Once my estate is closed, you'll become the trustee. I have a financial adviser I have worked with for years, and I'll introduce you to her. She'll manage the portfolio, but you'll make the final decisions."

"As you wish, Vanessa." Jack ran a hand across the back of his neck, trying to relieve the tightness drawing up his muscles. This conversation wasn't one he wanted to have. Yet even as he prayed for a miracle for Vanessa, he had to listen and accept the responsibility. For Vanessa and Leo.

"Now, as for my house in Santa Monica, the paintings, and all my personal effects, Denise has agreed to sort and settle everything. We've known each other so long, and she knows which family items I want Leo to have."

Vanessa's parents had collected high-end Mexican art.

Although they'd donated works by Frida Kahlo, Diego Rivera, and Rufino Tamayo to a museum in Los Angeles, Vanessa had kept paintings that had special meaning to her.

His heart aching, Jack gulped his tea. His throat felt constricted, and the warm, fragrant tea helped. "You've been thorough, and I appreciate it. I know how difficult this is for you."

"Actually, I feel better that my affairs are settled. I want you to feel like you can spend a lot of time with Leo and not have to work as much. He will need a lot of counseling, patience, and hugs. Scout is good for him, too." Vanessa hesitated. "Jack, I'm going to say something, and I don't want you to take it the wrong way. I know how you are about certain things."

"You can say anything to me." Jack put his hand over hers.

"Leo talks a lot about Marina. He and Samantha say that the two of you are boyfriend and girlfriend."

Jack laughed softly. "They ask a lot of questions. But I'm afraid that's wishful thinking on their part. Under the circumstances, that's a difficult call."

Vanessa twirled the end of her scarf as she studied him. "I want you to know that I like Marina. She's kind, and I've watched her with Leo. He likes her a lot."

"A lot of people like Leo, and he's an outgoing kid. You raised him so well that I won't have much to do."

Vanessa laughed. "I hope you don't really believe that. But I want you to know what I think about Marina. Should you ever want to get—"

"Hold it right there," Jack said, holding up a hand. "Leo is my top priority. I don't need a wife or even a relationship. Don't even go there." Just listening to Vanessa, his heart was already wounded enough for one day. He stood abruptly. "More tea?"

A slow smile gathered on Vanessa's face. "We're finished here. I'm so glad we had a chance to put things in order."

She glanced through an open door. "Let's have more tea on the patio by the fountain, and I'll tell you about what I've learned about the schools in Summer Beach. And if you're hungry, Denise brought home a loaf of Marina's rosemary bread from the farmers market. She says it's delicious with cheese and *pâté*. She left grapes and apples in the refrigerator, too. Please help yourself. And will you return for supper? Leo would like that."

"Sure," Jack said. He didn't want to disappoint Leo.

After their conversation, Jack didn't have much of an appetite, but he gathered bread and cheese and fruit on a plate, hoping that Vanessa might pick at it. As he guided her outside, he couldn't help thinking about what she'd said about Marina.

AFTER JACK LEFT Vanessa's cottage, he needed to clear his mind before meeting with Ginger about the children's book they were working on together. He stopped to pick up Scout, who'd been in Jack's room at the Seabreeze Inn. Ivy and Shelly had been kind to let Scout stay there, but it wasn't a place for an active dog.

As he walked through the yard, he could hear shrill barks from the old beach house, where the tall doors usually stood open to the cool sea breezes. *Sounds like Pixie*, he thought, a Chihuahua that had a reputation for being a kleptomaniac.

Suddenly, a stocky, silver-haired man barged through a rear door. A woman with short, spiky pink hair raced to grab Pixie, who seemed intent on chasing the man from the house. Jack waved to Gilda, a long-term Seabreeze Inn guest. She scooped up Pixie and rolled her eyes.

Jack wondered what that was all about. He opened the door to his room and whistled. "Come on, boy. Let's go to the beach."

Scout leapt at the word *beach*, his tongue flopping from the side of his mouth, which stretched into what everyone swore was a grin. Jack liked to think that, too. He knelt and rubbed his hands around the silky golden ruff of Scout's neck and scratched him behind the ears.

"We're going to have to get a bigger place, old boy. With enough room for you and Leo. Bet you'll like that."

Scout cocked his head as if he were taking this in.

Jack snapped a leash onto the dog's collar and led him from the room. Outside, the stocky man that Pixie had banished brushed past him on the walkway, causing him to nearly trample Shelly's freshly planted, yellow hibiscus.

"Watch it there, bud," Jack said, pulling up Scout.

"Keep your mutt on a leash," the man muttered. "Too many dogs around here."

"Welcome to Summer Beach," Jack shot back with sarcasm. "Should've checked your attitude before landing here."

The man stalked away. And went into the room next to Jack's.

"What a jerk. Had to be right next to us." The investigative reporter side of Jack went on high alert. Something about the guy was disturbing, and he didn't seem to fit in at the beach. He looked and acted more like a slick mobster from Chicago or New York. It wasn't any of Jack's business, but he'd still keep an eye on the guy.

Glancing up at the apartment above the garage, he saw the balcony doors to Bennett's unit standing open. Swept on the ocean breeze, the sound of Bennett's guitar and his soft song reached him. Jack enjoyed listening to him.

"Might as well get started," Jack said to Scout. The dog dipped its head as if nodding in agreement. Jack tented his hand against the sun and called out. "Hey, is the mayor in?"

Bennett appeared with his guitar in hand and leaned against the balcony. "Depends on who's asking."

"Your new real estate client. I need a place to live."

"What's wrong with here?"

"Scout needs a yard. Want to take a walk on the beach, and I'll tell you what I have in mind?"

"Hang on. I'll be right down."

Jack counted Bennett as a good friend now. He'd met the mayor when he'd first arrived in Summer Beach, but they'd spent more time together since Jack had returned to the inn after the tornado. They often saw each other on the beach in the mornings and shared breakfast in the dining room later. Sometimes after supper, they relaxed by the pool or the firepit, talking while Bennett waited for Ivy to tend to guests.

As Jack reflected on Bennett and Ivy, he thought they seemed like a good match. Bennett was about the same age as Jack, and they'd once talked about how difficult it was to find the right partner at their age.

Jack had quit smoking, so it had taken him time to get his breath back, but he'd finally started running with Bennett. Of course, Jack tired first and let Bennett continue, but that was an enormous improvement over a few weeks ago.

Bennett came down the stairs, and the two men started for the beach.

"What kind of property are you interested in?" Bennett asked as they walked near the water's edge. Shorebirds raced along the surf, pecking at the sand and dodging the waves. Scout was entranced.

Jack ran a hand across his stubbled chin. "I'd like a small cottage or bungalow. Something with enough room for Leo and a yard for Scout."

"Do you want to rent or buy?"

"Renting for now. I might need it sooner than I'd thought." Jack felt his throat catch. He hoped Vanessa still had time, but the practical side of him knew he had to be ready.

Stopping, Bennett turned to him. "I'm sorry to hear that."

Jack had told him about Vanessa's condition. "I need to be ready to take care of Leo."

"What about Denise and John? They have the beach house through the summer."

"I couldn't stay there, not if... You know what I mean."

Bennett nodded. "I'll see what I can find. Want to be on the ridgetop or near the village and the beach? Great views from the ridge, but the beach would be fun for Leo."

"Yeah, he'd like that. So would Scout, wouldn't you, old boy?"

Scout tried to race into a wave, but Jack pulled him back. He didn't have time to clean up Scout before he met Ginger. In the distance, dark rain clouds gathered above *Princess Anne*. An involuntary shiver coursed through him. "Come on, Scout. Stay with us."

"I'll have a look around for you," Bennett said. "You probably want to be close to the school for Leo. A lot of kids walk or ride bikes to school."

"Sure, that's good. And if there's a spot in the house where I can write—or even a good patio—that would be super."

"I'll see what I can find. How is next weekend to see some places?"

"That works."

The two men bumped fists in agreement. As they strolled and talked, Jack realized his life was about to change in ways he had never imagined.

Before he walked into his room, Jack took another look back at the yacht in the distance. Something wasn't quite right; he could almost feel it.

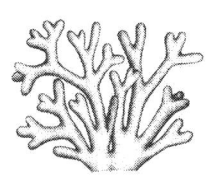

7

*S*purred on by the success of last night's dinner, Marina had risen with the sun, started a pot of coffee, and sat down at the dining room table with her laptop and a pad of paper. She had a lot of planning to do for the cafe and her Taste of Summer Beach project. Both were important.

Ginger had gone for a morning hike to the ridgetop, where she liked to meditate and look out over the ocean. Marina and Kai went with her sometimes. It was a bracing hike and an excellent way to start the day, but this morning, Marina had a lot on her mind, and Kai was sleeping late. Or maybe she was avoiding Dmitri.

Marina sure hoped so.

She put on soft music, opened the windows, and turned her attention to the menu for the cafe. What a pleasant way to work, she thought.

After listing items people often ordered—Caesar salad, house salad, hamburgers, sandwiches, and fries—she thought about dishes that would differentiate the cafe from other restaurants.

Last night, everyone had liked the lobster pizza, but the

ingredients were expensive. She could create a similar shrimp and pesto pizza with a lower food cost and save the lobster-and-caviar pizza for catering and special dinners. She jotted that down and few other ideas.

Most important, summer crowds were now arriving in Summer Beach, and she had to be ready to open as soon as Axe finished. His crew worked fast. They'd built the deck in record time.

While Marina was working, a flower delivery van arrived. If Dmitri had any class, he should send flowers to Ginger as an apology. A couple of minutes later, the doorbell rang. Through the screened door, a young male voice called, "Delivery for Kai Moore."

Clearly, Dmitri only cared about what he wanted.

Marina crossed the room. When she opened the door, the intoxicating scent of an enormous bouquet of roses and white lilies wafted inside.

"Are you Kai Moore?" the young man asked.

"I'm her sister, but I can take these for her."

"I can put these down somewhere for you," the young man said.

"On the coffee table by the couch is fine." After the scathing argument she and Ginger had overheard between Kai and Dmitri last night, the flowers must be from him. "Thanks very much," Marina said.

"I have more in the van," the delivery man said.

"I'll prop the door open. You can put them on the coffee table beside the other arrangement."

"They won't all fit there."

Marina peered over his shoulder. Through the windows, the van looked full. "Just how many are there?"

The young man's eyes widened. "A lot."

"Overdoing it, aren't we?" She rolled her eyes. "You can put the rest on the table." Marina moved the paperwork she had spread out to make room for Dmitri's overindulgence.

In came calla and stargazer lilies, a basket of yellow and white daisies, and a tropical Hawaiian arrangement with red ginger flowers and fragrant white pikake blossoms. Roses of every color bloomed in the living room—pink, yellow, white, lavender, coral, and red.

"Did he buy out the shop?"

The delivery driver grinned. "The owner is pretty happy."

Marina signed for the delivery and returned to her laptop and pad, which were now almost hidden beneath a heady blaze of flowers. No sense in waking Kai for this until she was ready to face Dmitri.

Behind her, the kitchen door slammed.

Dressed in a yellow windbreaker, Ginger appeared in the doorway, her lips pressed in a thin line. "Good heavens. I would ask who died, but last I checked, we're all still alive and kicking. So this must have to do with the disastrous Mr. D."

"He clearly wants to show he cares."

Ginger sniffed. "A bit extravagant. If he'd simply apologized for his boorish behavior, he could have saved a fortune."

With a heavy sigh, Marina closed her laptop. Kai would be up soon, and she wouldn't get any work done for a while. "I don't like the way he treats Kai. What do you think she sees in him?"

"He was probably charming and lavished attention and gifts on her in the beginning. When he feels her slipping from his grip, or when he doesn't get his way, that's when his bad temper emerges. I've witnessed this sort of behavior so many times. Perhaps Kai didn't know the signs."

"Better to learn that now."

Behind them, they heard Kai scuffling in. "What a pounding headache I have."

Marina shot a warning glance at Ginger.

Suddenly, Kai exclaimed, "Oh, how beautiful! What a fairyland of flowers." She flitted through the living room and dining room in her fluttery pink nightgown, exclaiming as she went. She clutched voluptuous blossoms, inhaling the scent of roses and lilies. "Aren't they exquisite!"

Marina watched her sister with dismay. "Can you guess who might have sent them?"

Kai opened one card speared into a vase and then another. A smile bloomed on her face. "They're all from Dmitri. He said that he was tired and didn't mean what he said last night. He'd had a long day of travel to reach Summer Beach."

Ginger arched a brow. "And you're accepting this excuse for his behavior?"

"Oh, it wasn't so bad." Kai's eyes glittered, and she pressed a hand to her mouth. "He has another surprise for me, too. He wants me to meet him at the inn."

"You will not," Ginger said. "He should come here to fetch you in his fancy car that he rented to impress you."

"What happened to your headache?" Marina asked.

Kai waved a hand. "He says he ordered a massage in the room, and it's better if I meet him there. I have to wear something nice. I don't think I've worn heels since I arrived."

Marina traded looks with Ginger. "Kai, we overheard your argument last night. We're on your side. He had no right to tell your boss that you're leaving the troupe. Is that what you really want to do?"

Kai threw up her hands. "I just want to belong somewhere to someone. I've been traveling with the show for years now. It was fun at first, but I guess I am a little tired of it. I want a real life now. Like other people have."

"And you think that going to New York with Dmitri will give you that?" Marina asked.

Kai glanced away and bit her lip. "It's not like I have other offers. Dmitri isn't always as argumentative as what you saw last night."

Ginger lifted her chin. "It wasn't the arguing. Kai, he's full of himself. His ego can't help but diminish you."

Marina stood and reached out to Kai. "He expects you to follow his orders, doesn't he?"

Kai stepped back. "Why can't you be happy for me? Look at all this." She waved a hand. "Isn't this proof of his love and adoration?"

"Kai, I don't understand you," Marina said. "Before you knew Dmitri was here, you were excited about bringing theater to Summer Beach. And calling Axe to help. What happened to that?"

Kai lowered her eyes. "Do you know how hard it is for me to date? A new city every week, and few men keep their promise once you're on to the next venue. Dmitri might not be perfect, but he's determined to make us work."

"What about Axe?"

With frustration etched on her face, Kai flung out her hands. "What about him? He hasn't asked me out, so what am I to think? Dmitri is here, committed to our relationship. You two are the ones who always told me that good marriages require compromise. Or have you forgotten that?"

Ginger stepped forward and put her arm around her granddaughter. "Compromise means that each of you gives a bit for the better good. When one person is always giving for the benefit of the other, that's unbalanced. That's not compromise; that's one person taking advantage of another."

"But just look at how generous he is."

"I don't mean items of fleeting monetary value," Ginger said.

Kai rested her head on her grandmother's shoulder. "I'm so tired of waiting for the rest of my life to begin. All my friends are married, and I feel like a big loser. Dmitri does a lot for me. Maybe it's not too much to give him what he wants in return."

"That's called a transactional relationship," Marina said. "Not a marriage."

Kai glared at Marina. "After Grady, you don't have much room to talk."

"Ouch," Marina said. "But well deserved. So, I speak from experience."

"Ever since we were kids, you've acted like you know better," Kai shot back. "But this is my life. Maybe I want different things than you do; maybe I'm not cut out to have a family after all. But not everyone gets to feel the lights of Broadway either. Dmitri is behind me; he believes in my talent and my ability to succeed doing what I love."

Ginger placed her palm against Kai's cheek, turning her granddaughter toward her. "Maybe that's so. If you follow the truth in your heart, you will never be wrong. The key is to listen to that small voice within you. Can you do that?"

"Of course," Kai said, jerking away. "I have to get dressed. And don't worry, I won't subject either of you to Dmitri again. And Marina, you can take care of the farmers market by yourself from now on. I'll probably leave with Dmitri when he returns to New York." She scooped a vase of red roses into her arms and flounced to her room.

Marina crossed her arms. "That didn't go so well."

Ginger stared after Kai. "She's a smart young woman. Kai will come to her senses one day. I only hope it's soon."

"But why the sudden change of heart? Yesterday she was excited about building a future here, and then she succumbed to Dmitri the instant he arrived."

Ginger tapped her chin in thought. "Do you remember that you and Brooke and Kai often took issue with each other's boyfriends? Infatuation can be blinding because you so desperately want to believe in the happily-ever-after. But when you love someone—a sister or a friend—you're looking out for each other. You see the flaws they don't. Now, I'm not saying the perfect man exists—they don't. But when we attacked Dmitri, she jumped to his defense."

"Just like we used to," Marina recalled. "Maybe we shouldn't have let on how much we disliked him."

"It's his treatment of her we dislike. Maybe Kai is trying too hard and letting him take advantage of her. Perhaps they find this dramatic game exciting."

Marina nodded. "Kai sure loves drama."

"It makes the heart race," Ginger said. "The heightened reality is fun—for a little while. But in the end, it's exhausting."

The fine hairs on the back of Marina's neck stood up. "How do you know so much about that?"

Ginger sat at the dining table and laced her hands. "I've never told you this, but Bertrand and I separated for a while. Early in our marriage."

Marina frowned. She'd believed her grandparents had an exemplary, loving relationship. "What happened?"

"We were both too full of ourselves and our selfish desires. Bertrand had his work, which was often critical. Countries and lives can depend on diplomacy, so it was never a question of whose work meant more. But when I showed an aptitude for math and deciphering codes—oh, it was simply fun and intriguing at first—he became jealous of the time I spent away from him. He began acting out. And so did I. Societal expectations of women's roles were quite different back then."

Marina took this in. "You've always said your work as a math teacher and statistician was important to you."

"And now you know more of my story. My finest work was as a code breaker." Ginger smiled with pride. "I'm sorry I couldn't tell you the truth about that before. National security prohibited me from doing so, and it was to protect you as well. I needed that intellectual stimulation in my life, as well as recognition of a job well done. The constancy was important, too. I had become lonely. We moved often, and it wasn't as easy to keep up with people as it is today with the internet and social media."

"I remember how it was with Stan in the military." Marina treaded softly with Ginger's memories, though she was curious. "How long were you separated?"

"A little more than a year." A sad smile crossed Ginger's face. "We almost lost each other. In the end, we had to adjust how we related to each other."

Marina reflected on this. Her grandmother probably had more secrets to share. "Do you think that Kai and Dmitri could do that?"

"If they're truly committed and care about each other's well-being. However, they're both much older than we were then. People really do become set in their ways. And Dmitri is an extreme personality."

"Kai has her moments, too." Marina traced a lazy figure-eight on the table with a finger as she thought. "Should we stage an intervention?"

Ginger rose from the table. "I don't think we'll need to."

AFTER KAI LEFT in a blaze of scarlet silk and a cloud of perfume, Marina took her work outside on the new patio. While the aroma of flowers inside the house was lovely, they reminded her too much of Dmitri and the trouble she felt Kai was in. She breathed in the fresh sea air and sat at a table under the warm morning sun.

Kai would do as she pleased, and Marina had work to do for the cafe. She missed having her sister's input on the food selection and the Coral Cafe menu design, but she couldn't wait.

Ginger said that Dmitri was planning to spend a week in Summer Beach. The less time Marina had to interact with him, the better. She would support Kai, but she couldn't in good conscience encourage this relationship. If Kai valued immediate gratification and adoration in exchange for anger and belittlement, there was nothing she could do.

Marina was disappointed in Kai, but as her sister had pointed out, it was her life. Still, she would be there for Kai when she needed her. And she wouldn't tell her sister that she and Ginger had warned her.

Marina shook her head, returning her focus to the work she needed to finish. She rested her chin in her hand and gazed at the endless ocean, thinking about what her clientele would like.

"Let's see… Sliced strawberry, baby spinach, and feta cheese salad with sweet honey-roasted walnuts and poppyseed dressing." She moved that under *salads* on the menu. The vegetable kebobs had been a hit, so she created a *sides* section. Or that could be a vegetarian option. She had a category for that, too. As she added her best dishes and client favorites from the pop-up dinners she'd been hosting, she could almost smell and taste each one.

People would return for favorite dishes they couldn't find anywhere else. She had to put unique twists on recipes that would delight people. And make old favorites so well that they would return.

She thought about a children's menu. So many restaurants served chicken nuggets and macaroni and cheese that she'd wanted to scream whenever she took her twins out for dinner when they were young. They were accustomed to more exciting food at home. Still, children could be picky unless they'd had a variety of food when they were young. *Familiar, yet different. Things children would try.* She drummed her fingers on the table.

"Farfalle with a sauce of Roma tomatoes and a touch of cream. Better than macaroni and cheese. I'll call it Pink Bowties." *It's all in the marketing*, Kai often said. Marina bit her lip. She would miss Kai so much.

The early tomatoes they'd planted in the garden would be coming in soon. After training Scout not to roll or dig in the garden, Marina had tended to the young plants. Jack had helped too. They had often talked as they weeded.

Marina looked out over the garden. She missed that.

Soon it would be time to harvest fresh tomatoes and zucchini squash, along with basil, oregano, and parsley. Marina could conjure quite a few Italian dishes with those ingredients.

Ginger had an orchard on the property behind the guest cottage that yielded more fruit than she could ever use. From her citrus trees came mandarin and blood-red oranges, Mexican and Persian limes, and Eureka and sweet Meyer lemons, descendants of the Italian *Lunario* lemon. They would have plenty of juice and fruit for summer salads. An old Haas avocado tree was still prolific and promised a lot of guacamole for appetizers.

Tomorrow, Axe and his team would begin work on the guest cottage's interior, which he said would go quickly. Marina needed to find appliances soon, too. Within the month, she would have her cafe. The thought sent chills of excitement through her.

The Coral Cafe would be open for business.

A car honked, and Marina looked up.

"Heather!"

Her daughter was waving from the window of her brother Ethan's car. Excited, Marina raced to meet her children. She hadn't seen Heather since spring break. Ethan had dropped out at Duke University and had just started a new job at a private golf club in San Diego, but Heather had persevered through finals. She'd stayed with a friend a little longer so she could finish a final community art project for children.

"Mom!" Heather called out. She leapt from the car and into Marina's arms.

Marina rocked her daughter in her arms. "I'm so glad you're back, sweetheart. I've missed you so much."

Ethan stepped from the car. "Heather wanted to surprise you, Mom."

"I'm thrilled to see you both," Marina said, beaming. "Welcome to Summer Beach, but I didn't expect you for another week."

"We finished early," Heather said, pushing her dark, golden blond hair over her shoulder. "It's so cool that I get to spend the entire summer here. Though I still can't believe the apartment in San Francisco is gone."

"I saw no reason to keep it," Marina said. "We have a lot of good memories, and we'll make many more here. I brought a lot of your things here and stored the rest, so it's all there when you need it."

"It's okay, Mom." Heather smiled. "Most of that was high school stuff anyway."

The twins shared the same dark, golden blond hair and misty, blue-gray eyes that their father had. Ethan was tall and gregarious like Stan, too.

Heather was quieter, a studious young woman who'd had difficulty making friends at Duke—partly because Ethan didn't like her friends and partly because she'd spent so much time helping Ethan overcome his dyslexia to maintain his grades for his golf scholarship.

Ethan pulled his sister's bags from the second-hand car he'd bought. He'd saved money from what he'd earned by working on a golf course at a country club during the school year. Marina hadn't even known he was working. Ethan was quickly forging a path for himself toward his goal of turning pro.

Her son had stayed a few days at the cottage when he'd arrived, but now he shared an apartment with a friend in San Diego. It's what she had done as a young adult, so it didn't surprise her. Marina was proud of Ethan, and even though she would have preferred that he finish college, she understood. On the golf course, he excelled with natural talent.

"Take her bags in Brooke's old room." Marina put her arm around Heather. "How about some lemonade? Are you hungry?"

Heather laughed as she lifted her backpack onto her shoulder. "You're always trying to feed us. I'm glad you decided to open a cafe so you can feed other people for a change."

"That's the idea."

"Ethan wanted to grab a burger on the way here, so I ate with him. But I've seen pictures of your dishes on social media. Aunt Kai has been posting a lot."

Ethan picked up his sister's suitcase. "If you have any more of that lobster pizza from last night, I'll take a couple of slices."

"Sorry, no leftovers. But I'm working on a pesto-shrimp pizza for the menu. You can be my official taster for that."

"Are Aunt Kai and Ginger here?" Heather asked.

"Ginger is." Marina raised her brow. "Kai is out with her boyfriend for lunch."

"Fiancé, you mean," Heather said. "She posted pictures of a thousand flowers on social media. I just saw it on the way here. And that ring he gave her—wow! But he seems kind of old for Aunt Kai. Have you met him?"

"Oh, yes." Marina pressed her lips together.

Ethan grinned. "And you'll get to meet Jack. The guy Mom is dating."

Marina put her hands on her hips. "Ethan William Moore, Jack and I are not dating."

He grinned. "Sure looked that way last time I was here. After the tornado. Even loaned him my clothes."

Heather's eyes grew wide. "Please tell me he's nothing like Grady." She shot a look at Ethan. "We couldn't stand him. I know we were supposed to try, but he was creepy. Grady cheated at golf when Ethan was winning. And now he's with that singer who is only a couple of years older than I am. Eew."

"You were right in the end," Marina said. "Just the same, we're not dating."

"Jack's not so bad," Ethan said. "He turned out pretty cool, helping us rescue that couple from their house that was damaged in the twister. You should have seen Mom slither in there to find them, like a real hero. Jack and I hung out on the beach a couple of times, too. He's cool."

"I appreciate your calling me a heroine, so I forgive you." Neither Ethan nor Jack had mentioned that they'd talked. Nevertheless, she wouldn't see Jack any more—except as a friend. When they got together, she'd have coffee and be cordial.

After all, Summer Beach was a small town. Since Jack planned to stay here with Leo, she would have to get used to seeing him.

8

*M*arina was finishing the supper dishes and thinking about the new cafe when the rear kitchen door opened. She looked up, surprised to see her sister Brooke, who had a large bag thrown over her shoulder. Her eyes were rimmed with red, and her braided hair was in disarray. Her usually centered younger sister looked like she was having a crisis.

"Hey, Brooke. I didn't know you were coming over. Has something happened?"

"I just can't…not anymore…" Brooke pressed her hands over her face. "I didn't know where else to go. The boys and Chip…they're driving me crazy."

Marina left the dishes and hurried to Brooke. "Let me take that bag." Marina placed it on the floor and hugged Brooke. When she did, her sister broke down, unable to contain her pent-up anguish.

"Oh, Marina, I just couldn't take it for another minute. I'm so angry at my husband."

"Relax, you're here, and you're safe. Sit with me. I want to hear everything." She guided Brooke into the living room. Her sister shuffled beside her in her Birkenstock sandals.

After they sank onto the canvas slip-covered sofa, Marina held Brooke as she sobbed against her shoulder. When she let up a little, Marina went to get her a glass of water.

Returning, Marina took stock of Brooke. Her nose was puffy and swollen as if she'd been crying for a long time. Her nails—which she always kept short and trimmed for gardening—were now bitten to the quick.

Brooke took the water and gulped it down. Catching her breath, she said, "I shouldn't have come here. With you and Kai here already, it's too much for Ginger."

"You're no trouble. We're all helping Ginger, and she's as lively as ever." Marina would move Heather onto the fold-out Murphy bed in the den. She had just left with Ethan and other friends to hang out on the beach.

"I don't see her often enough, and I'm less than two hours away." Brooke's voice was full of guilt. She brought her hand to her mouth and chewed a fingernail.

"Ginger is always busy. Don't worry about her."

"Is she here?"

"She went to a movie with friends." Marina asked gently, "Did something just happen?"

"It's been going on for a long time." Brooke pressed her hands on her head as if trying to keep it from bursting. "The boys are out of hand, always fighting. Chip works long hours, and I appreciate all that he does. I really do. But no one appreciates me. Not one of that uncouth bunch picks up their laundry, no one bothers to wash dishes, and they all expect three meals a day."

"I remember what it was like with the twins. It's not easy." Marina had thought Chip would be more helpful, but she wasn't surprised that he wasn't.

"Except for Oakley, all those man-boys are towering over me now," Brooke said, her eyes flashing with anger. "They're not babies, but they sure act like it. Heaven knows I have tried to teach them manners and responsibility, but they're like a wild pack of dogs."

"They'll grow out it soon," Marina said, trying to calm her sister.

"And Chip encourages them," Brooke continued. "Since he grew up with three brothers, he doesn't see any problem. By tonight, I was done." She sliced her hands apart. "Finished. They just lost their maid. They can fend for themselves for all I care. Too much testosterone in that house for me."

Chip certainly didn't sound very supportive. "What happened tonight?"

"Chip started wrestling with Alder and Ronnie—that's what Rowan wants to be called now—in the house, and Oakley jumped in. Brawling right there by my indoor herb garden. I was screaming for them to be careful and stop, but you can imagine what happened."

"Was it demolished?"

"They knocked over the entire baker's rack. Every. Single. Plant." Brooke punctuated each word with a jab of her finger. "Dirt and pottery and mangled plants flew everywhere. But did that stop them? Oh, no. They punched through my new wooden shutters, broke one of Mom's lamps, and fell right through the sliding glass door."

Marina pressed a hand to her mouth. "Were they hurt?"

"Thankfully, no. They landed in a heap, laughing their fool heads off. I was so angry. Instead of making the boys help clean up, Chip let Ronnie leave to spend the night with a friend. Then I heard a car honk, and Alder ran out the door to meet his friend. Chip had a poker game to go to, so he left me with a broom, saying, 'Give me a hand here. A man's got to relax after a long week. I'll make it up to you.' Of course, he never does. When do I ever get to relax?"

Marina could just imagine. Chip was a large man, captain of a local fire department, and often called a *man's man*. "I'm so sorry, Brooke."

Her sister fidgeted with the edge of her stained T-shirt. "So, that left me with Oakley. He felt awful, but he was just joining in with his older brothers and father. I couldn't make him clean up by himself. Chip set the example, as he always does."

"So what did you do?"

Brooke paused to draw in a ragged breath. "I dropped off Oakley at my neighbors. Then I called Chip and told him that he could be a real father and pick up his son when he was through with poker night. And here I am. Can you believe that Chip yelled at me for not cleaning up and deserting *them*?"

Marina slid her arm around Brooke. She had sensed that something was wrong the last time Brooke and her family had been here. Her sister had gone for a walk with Ginger, but she had still looked distracted. It seemed that Brooke's only refuge was her garden.

"They will come around. You'll probably hear from Chip in the morning with an apology."

Brooke shook her head. "No. They can take care of themselves. I'm tired of begging for help. Maybe I'll go work on an organic farm and finally have some peace."

"You don't mean that."

"Watch me," Brooke said, setting her jaw.

Marina understood her frustration. This pressure cooker of a situation had been building for a long time. Brooke was an earth-mother type who cared for everyone, who gave and gave and gave. For her sister to take this step, the situation had to be beyond her control.

Brooke needed someone to care for her.

Marina stood. "I'm going to draw a warm bubble bath for you and turn your bed down. It will help if you have a good night's rest. Are you hungry, or is there anything else I can do?"

Now that Brooke had let out her grievances, her anger

dissipated, and she seemed suddenly forlorn. "The only problem is that I don't know who I am without them anymore."

"You're an amazing gardener who can grow anything." For as long as Marina could remember, Brooke had an affinity for plants. She studied and cared for her vegetables as if they were the children she could count on to behave.

Marina held out her hands to Brooke. "Come with me."

WHEN GINGER RETURNED from the movie, Marina met her outside. After tucking Brooke into a warm bath, lowering the lights, and turning on soft music, Marina returned to work on the patio in the balmy evening air.

Marina waved at the friends who had given Ginger a ride home. When she stepped from the car, Marina said, "We have another guest in residence."

Ginger shifted her purse. "Who?"

"Brooke. She's had some trouble at home." Marina glanced at Ginger from the corner of her eye, wondering how much she knew.

Pausing to face the ocean breeze, Ginger shook her short hair back. "I had hoped it wouldn't come to this."

"So you knew how bad it was?"

"I saw the signs," Ginger replied. "Poor Brooke has been overworked for a long time. The boys need to help with chores, and Chip has to make his wife feel like a woman again."

"That sums it up," Marina said, putting her hands on her hips.

Ginger nodded thoughtfully. "I'm glad Brooke decided to come here. Might shock some sense into that family. Chip works hard, but so does Brooke. There must be mutual consideration."

"This is just like when we were kids," Marina said. "All of

us here together, and each of us with some sort of drama. I'm sorry we didn't grow out of it."

As Ginger went into the house, she chuckled. "Wouldn't be a family without some sort of drama. Brooke can tend the garden while she's here."

"And join us at the farmers market," Marina offered.

Marina followed Ginger inside. She had always liked Chip, but she was firmly in Brooke's corner. Her sister had put her family first for so long that they'd forgotten to look out for her. "Chip needs a wake-up call."

A sly smile crept onto Ginger's face. "I have a feeling he's answering that call right now."

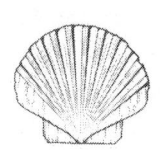

9

*O*ver the next week, Marina worked hard to test and finalize the menu for the cafe. She needed recipes that she could make over and over, the same each time. When she could afford to hire help in the kitchen, these instructions would be critical to have. Sure enough, Ethan had joined them the day she was testing variations on the pesto-shrimp pizza. He and Heather announced a winner, and they'd been correct. Her children had good taste.

Dmitri was still staying at the Seabreeze Inn, so Kai had been returning late, sleeping until noon, and then rushing out as soon as she dressed. She'd taken many of the flowers Dmitri had sent to her room, but she couldn't fit them all.

Marina was worried about her. Kai seemed to have changed overnight. Was she that smitten or obsessed with all that Dmitri represented—the wealth, the power, the connections? However, with that also came control.

While Axe and his crew worked to transform the kitchen and dining area into a single professional kitchen, Marina engaged Brooke to help her clean and paint the bedroom to turn it into a private dining room for small private parties and honeymooners. Doors opened to a beautiful view of the beach and sunset, and Marina imagined that they would stand open most of the time.

Today, Heather was helping her decorate the room. Ivy had given Marina a seascape painting with a vivid blue ocean and a blazing coral sunset. It was perfect for the private dining room.

This was also the day Marina was to meet Jack for coffee. She'd only agreed to do this for Ginger's sake. They would clear the air, agree to disagree, and get on with their lives. Earlier, Jack had called and asked if he could pick her up at the cottage.

"This won't take any more than half an hour, will it?" she had asked.

"Promise," Jack replied. "But you have to eat, right?"

"Jack. We agreed."

"Then we'll eat fast."

"We're meeting for coffee."

"Okay, sure. But I hope you don't mind if I have something. I'll pick you up."

This wasn't what she had intended, and she didn't want to have to keep up her guard for an entire lunch. "Jack, on second thought, I don't have time for this."

"Sorry, you just cut out. If you can still hear me, I'll see you at noon."

She had hung up, frustrated that he was trying to take advantage of her concern for her grandmother. She was only doing this for Ginger.

"Hey, how's this?" Heather asked, holding the painting to the wall. "Didn't you hear me?"

"Sorry, sweetheart. Had something on my mind. Okay, a little to the left. And a bit higher." Marina pulled a pencil from behind her ear. "That's perfect. Hold it still so I can mark it." She made a tiny dot on the wall.

Marina blinked as she stepped back. She had to get Jack

out of her mind, so she'd settle things with him today. That would be the end of these unwelcome feelings.

Heather put the painting down and picked up the hammer. Axe's crew was banging away in the kitchen, and Heather quickly added to the din.

Working together, Marina and her daughter hung the painting. They stepped back to admire it.

"It looks great in here, Mom."

"We're not finished yet." Marina had bought two trellises and painted them white. "We're going to mount these on that wall and trim them with fairy lights. It will be so pretty at night with the lights dimmed."

"Sounds magical. I'll hold while you measure."

Marina was glad to have Heather's help. As they worked on tacking the trellises to the wall, Marina paused and asked, "Are you sure you don't want to return to Duke in the fall? It's such a good school, and I would like you to continue if you want. We could get loans for your tuition. I also have money earmarked for your living expenses."

Marina had funds from the settlement with the television station she could use, although it wasn't much and wouldn't last long. But she wanted to support Heather's dream as long as she could.

"I don't want to graduate in debt or leave you on the hook for loans," Heather said, shaking her head. "A couple of my friends from high school are going to UCSD, and they love it. San Diego is not that far to drive."

"That's a good university, but are you sure? I don't want you to transfer just because I lost my job."

"Mom, even if you were still working there, I would want to return to California. Duke was great, but I belong in California. It's my home. I only went there because of Ethan and his golf scholarship."

"If you're sure…"

"I am," Heather said, giving Marina a quick kiss on the check. "I'd like to get a summer job, too."

After securing the painted trellises, Heather stretched out a strand of tiny white lights, and Marina picked up a staple gun to affix the lights to the trellis.

As she was stapling the tiny lights, taking care not to punch through the electrical cords, Brooke stepped inside the open doors. In her arms, she carried fruits and vegetables she had picked in the garden.

"This is looking so pretty," Brooke said wistfully. "I wish I could keep my house this nice."

Heather glanced over her shoulder. "Ethan and I should talk to the boys. They shouldn't be treating you like that, Aunt Brooke."

Marina knew that Brooke had been talking to Chip and the boys every day. They were grumbling because she wasn't there to wash clothes or make meals.

"You're welcome to speak to your cousins, but it's their father who is the problem. All he does is complain because the laundry is piling up. You'd think it would occur to him to put it in the washing machine and turn it on. Do I really have to say that?"

"Maybe you do," Marina said gently. "Chip could create a chores list for the boys, too."

"Ethan and I weren't crazy about that," Heather said. "But at least we knew how to do laundry when we got to school. A lot of kids were clueless. And having rewards, like going to the zoo or having lunch at the pier, was a good way to motivate us. I even use that on myself now."

"I wish my children sounded like that," Brooke said. "I hope we'll get there. You have no idea how many chores lists I have drawn up. Everyone ignores them."

"Maybe if Chip took the lead and sat down with the kids to get them to volunteer for chores, it would get them to commit."

"If only," Brooke said. "But Chip did agree to counseling. I'll bring up that idea. I've already told him I wouldn't return until he helps straighten up this mess. He's been an enabler by letting them get away with not doing what I ask. I told him those boys won't respect me until he does."

Marina had been through a challenging period with Ethan when he was a teenager, except she didn't have a husband to help—or undermine her efforts. "It's essential that your boys learn to respect you. Otherwise, they'll treat their wives the same way someday."

"I hadn't thought of that." Brooke shuddered. "I have to go wash these vegetables. I'd also like to talk to Leilani at the Hidden Garden. Maybe I could work there on the weekends. I'd be happy to volunteer."

Marina rested the staple gun on her knee. "How about working with me at the farmers market this week? I could use the help."

"I'd like that," Brooke said. "I need to be around adults for a change." She turned up a corner of her mouth in the closest thing Marina had seen to a smile since she'd arrived.

After Brooke left to wash the produce, Marina turned back to Heather.

"You're welcome to help out at the market, too." She rubbed her daughter's shoulder. "If you can stand having Mom tell you what to do. It's a lot of fun to see what everyone is selling. At the cafe, too. Without Kai, I'm going to need some help."

Marina had talked to Ivy about what it was like to have her daughter Sunny working part-time at the inn when she wasn't busy with school. Ivy had told her it wasn't always easy but that Sunny was developing important workplace skills and learning to budget her money.

"I'd like that, Mom." Heather grinned. "I promise I won't freak out on you like I did during final exams. I was so angry at Ethan for skipping out on finals and leaving me there."

"I'm glad you two made up." But then, the twins were never angry at each other for long. Heather was more mature than Ethan, but they were both determined about what they wanted.

Heather held up another strand while Marina stapled it to the trellis. "It will be fun to work near the beach and watch how you run a business. I might want to do that sometime. Not necessarily a cafe, but I like the idea of being my own boss."

"It's going to be a lot of work in the beginning." Marina planned to open for lunch and dinner and close in the mid-afternoon. But on the tourist-heavy weekends, the cafe would be open all day. "You can help me prep food and wait tables. I'll pay you, and the tips are all yours."

Heather's eyes brightened. "I'll do that. I need a car for school in the fall."

In San Francisco, Heather and Ethan had used cable cars and the rail system to get around, and they didn't have cars at Duke. But Heather would need one now, and Marina had been thinking about that. "I appreciate your pitching in, sweetheart."

Axe's large frame filled the doorway. "I've got the dimmer switch for this room."

Marina handed the staple gun to Heather and went to talk to Axe. "That will help set the mood in here. Could you also install an art light to illuminate the painting?"

"I've got just the thing in the truck leftover from another job. I've been meaning to take it out, but it must have been meant for you." Holding the dimmer switch, Axe hesitated. "Haven't seen much of Kai around here lately."

"Her boyfriend is in town from New York..." Marina caught herself shaking her head.

"I heard that they're engaged." Seeming self-conscious, Axe shifted from one foot to another. "I'm not one to gossip, but nothing is a secret once it hits Java Beach. Is she really moving to New York?"

Marina held out her hand and let it drop. "I'm not sure what she wants."

"That's a shame. Summer Beach is going to miss out."

"What do you mean by that?"

Axe's face lit up. "There's a piece of land I bought a couple of years ago. It's on a gentle slope and surrounded by the ridgetop hill. When I saw it, I thought it looked like a natural outdoor amphitheater. Wouldn't take much to create a stage and light it. People could bring blankets and picnics. If it's popular, I can expand it. It could be a smaller version of the Hollywood Bowl in Los Angeles."

"That would really add to the community—and bring in visitors."

"It's just been a dream, but I mentioned it to the mayor, and Bennett put me in touch with Carol Reston. He thought she might be interested in this—as a nonprofit—and she is. Now that I have some funding, I could get a production going as soon as this summer. Kai had asked me about summer stock in the area. With her help, we could pull it together and have a lot of fun. I've been hoping to see her here and tell her about it."

Marina's heart fell. "Kai would have loved that."

Axe stared at the dimmer switch in his hand as if it were a foreign object. "So she's really moving to New York?"

She heard a trace of sadness in Axe's voice. "I think you should call her. Tell her about the theater. Maybe she'll have time to do it. Dmitri is leaving soon." Maybe this would give Kai a reason to stay. Marina hoped she wouldn't leave right away with Dmitri.

"So you'd still have a shot with Aunt Kai," Heather interjected.

Axe chuckled.

"For the theater production," Marina quickly added and

then smiled. "Or whatever."

Heather had quickly learned that Ginger and her mother were not impressed with Dmitri. Maybe this could be the excuse Kai needed. "Try to catch her before she leaves in the morning. You'll probably hear her singing in the shower like we did the other day." Kai usually tore out of the house without speaking to anyone.

Axe shook his head. "I haven't heard her sing lately."

That said a lot to Marina. She hadn't noticed, but then she'd been busy with Heather and Brooke. Kai almost always sang in the shower or tub, belting out the show tunes against the hard-tiled acoustics, trying new inflections and phrasing. Kai was often humming or singing throughout the day. Marina had to help her, or at least throw her a lifeline.

"Then call her," Marina said, crossing her fingers that Axe would agree. "You could meet on the patio and tell her about your idea. I'll provide the coffee."

A corner of Axe's mouth turned up as he considered this. "I'll do that." He tossed the dimmer switch in his hand. The sound of hammering and sawing had stopped in the kitchen. "I'll put this in right away. Want to see the progress on the kitchen today? The guys have taken a break."

"Sure." Marina and Heather followed him into the other room. Without the old dividing wall between the kitchen and the dining area, the space seemed much larger. She turned around, taking it all in. "This is even better than I'd imagined it would be."

"Your large refrigerated unit will go there."

Marina had bought a used commercial refrigerator from a restaurant supply store that dealt in resales and got a good deal on it, along with a professional cooktop and ovens.

She put her arm around Heather. "We're going to have a lot of good times here. I can feel it."

Footsteps sounded on the patio outside the door, and Jack's voice rang out. "Hello, are you open for business yet?"

arina sucked in a little breath. Jack had arrived, and she hadn't even had time to change or brush her hair. Not that things like that mattered between people who were just friends. "Come in. You're early."

Jack stepped inside the guest cottage and greeted Axe. "Right on time, actually. The day has a way of getting away from me, too."

Marina remembered that while Jack knew Ethan, he hadn't met Heather. She introduced them, and Marina noticed that her daughter was smiling.

"Heather, I think we're finished here for now. Jack and I are going out for a coffee. Would you let Ginger know?"

"Sure, Mom." Heather looked like she would burst with this information. Whereas Ethan was more protective of his mother, Heather had encouraged Marina to date.

When Marina hurried inside to get her purse, she looked in the mirror beside the front door, where for years she'd watched Ginger pause to put on lipstick before going out. Her heart seemed to thud in her chest, and she blew out a breath. She quickly smoothed her hair and added a swipe of lip gloss, just as she would anytime she was going out in public, she told herself. Her jeans and faded blue T-shirt that read *Life is Better in Summer Beach* would have to do.

"Jack is the one who should be nervous," she said to her reflection.

Perhaps that wasn't entirely fair, she realized, because he'd never really called her before. They had seen each other around Ginger's property or on the beach. Maybe she had read more into their chats and walks, but she certainly wasn't going to discount the kiss they'd shared or how he'd wrapped his arms around her in the pool. Had that merely been a reaction of relief after the waterspout had morphed into a tornado?

Whatever had happened, she had agreed to listen to his side of the story, so that's what she would try to do.

For Ginger. Since he and her grandmother were collaborating on children's books, he might be in Ginger's life for a while. Marina would not make her uncomfortable.

They were all adults, right?

With that, Marina snapped her purse shut and walked out.

Jack was pacing the ground beside his old VW van. When he saw her, he hurried to open the door for her. The rear door was open, too, and she could see Scout panting on a bench seat in the camper area. Scout jumped up and wagged his tail.

Marina laughed. "Well, look who's here." She rubbed Scout's head before easing into the van.

Jack closed her door and the back before getting in on the other side. "I thought he'd like to get out and run today. Wouldn't you, old boy?"

Scout grinned and woofed his approval.

"He's excited." Marina laughed. "What did you have in mind?"

Drumming his fingers on the steering wheel, he said, "There's a quiet beach a few minutes from here. I took Leo and Samantha there last week for snorkeling. It's a sweet little cove."

"I know the one," Marina said, watching Jack. He seemed a little nervous, too. "The locals call it the children's beach. Many of us learned to swim there."

"No kidding?" Jack turned the ignition, and the old van roared to life. "I brought a picnic if you don't mind."

"I thought this was coffee."

"I have that, too, but I'm famished." Jack grinned as he pulled from the driveway and set off. "We can do this in half an hour if you like."

Marina sighed. "Why do I feel like I'm being kidnapped?"

"I'm sorry. I don't mean for you to feel intimidated."

"I'm not. Besides, Ginger put all of us in self-defense classes when we were young, so you should see my moves. I could be lethal."

"I'll be on my best behavior."

She nodded ahead on the road that lined the ocean. "If you keep going past the children's beach, there's a spot with some shady palm trees and picnic benches. We can stop there."

"Sounds good."

Marina glanced around the van, which was decorated with retro blue-and-white-striped seats and a checkerboard floor. A small unit held a mini-refrigerator, tiny sink, and a hot plate. Old license plates from across the country hung on the cabin walls. A road trip in this would be fun. Not that she would think of doing that with Jack.

Marina turned around. "I haven't been in one of these old VWs in years."

"It's vintage but completely renovated. The seat slides into a bed, and a table folds up for a workspace. I bought it to drive cross county."

"How did that work out for you?"

"It was great. In rural areas, I'd pull off the road and sleep. In the morning, I'd catch breakfast and a shower at a truck stop."

She arched a brow at him. "Really? Mr. Pulitzer Prize at a truck stop?" She couldn't resist teasing him, even though her parents had stopped at plenty of truck stops on family vacations.

"Hey, there are some very nice truck stops. Good food, shopping, showers, laundry facilities. And more. I always stop at Buc-ee's in Texas to get gifts for my nieces and nephews in Dallas."

"I stand corrected. It's been a long time since I've been on a road trip."

"This is my Rocinante," Jack said, patting the dashboard. "During John Steinbeck's cross-country trip while writing *Travels with Charley*, he named his pick-up camper that after Don Quixote's horse." He chuckled at the reference. "See, we're all a little past our prime but still forging on. This sweet ride took me from New York to Los Angeles and didn't break down once. I'd planned on selling it when my sabbatical was over, but now I'm going to hang onto it. Leo likes it."

Marina smiled. She enjoyed listening to Jack's stories. *As a friend*, she reminded herself. "I remember reading that book. Charley was a standard poodle that Steinbeck brought with him, so I imagine Scout must be your Charley."

"Almost named him that, too. Instead, he got *To Kill a Mockingbird*. Despite his limp, I saw courage in his soul. And he was determined to go home with me."

Marina eyed Jack. He seemed relaxed as he talked about Scout and traveling. "Are you planning more long road trips?"

"I'd like to take Leo on a trip. I think it would be good for him. Later, of course…"

Jack let the rest of the sentence hang in the air, but Marina knew what he meant, and it tore at her heart.

They rode in silence after that, and a few minutes later, Marina pointed out the spot. "Turn here. Scout can be off-leash here, too."

After Jack stopped the van, Scout leapt out and raced

toward the beach with his brave, odd little gait to chase shore-birds. Jack brought out a backpack.

Marina looked up. "Thought you had a picnic planned."

He patted the backpack. "It's a picnic basket in disguise. Want to eat outside or in the van? I can open all the windows."

"The van would be fun." Outside, palm trees rustled in the mid-day breeze. The gray marine layer that locals called June gloom had burned off, and the sun was high overhead. Scout was playing keep-away with waves lapping the beach.

Jack held out his hand, and Marina stepped into the rear area and slid onto the bench seat. Jack lifted the hinged tabletop and unfolded the leg support. "*Voilà, Madame. Charmant, non?*"

Marina laughed. "Does that impress many women?"

"None that I would want." He withdrew a thermos. "I hope you like cappuccino."

"Smells delicious."

He brought out a sandwich and unwrapped it. "Turkey, provolone, avocado, romaine, and sweet yellow peppers with lemon-garlic aioli on a croissant. Courtesy of Java Beach. I'll eat quickly. If you want one, I brought two." His bright blue eyes sparkled with amusement.

"Oh, all right. You're incorrigible. Maybe I can spare a little more time." She unwrapped the sandwich and took a bite. "Mitch makes a good sandwich. I'll have to raise my standards."

"I'm sure you will."

After taking a few bites and sipping a bottle of lemonade Jack had fetched from the mini-fridge, Marina gathered her courage. "This is nice, but we still need to talk."

"We're having such a good time that I almost forgot you were upset with me."

"No, you didn't." She hesitated. "This is a small town, Jack."

He nodded thoughtfully, finished his sandwich, and drank down his soda. "I'm ready for a cappuccino now."

"Jack."

He sighed. "I'm a jerk. That night we went for a swim has a permanent place in my mind. I've thought about it every day, Marina. I've thought about you."

"Please, don't. Not if you don't mean it." As her heart clenched, Marina put down her sandwich and leaned back. She wished she could banish the feelings she had for him.

Jack drew a hand over his face, and he looked out to sea. "But this is really about Leo. I'm a father now."

"Yes, you are."

"You raised twins by yourself while working full time. From where I sit now, you look like you have Superwoman powers."

"You do what you have to," she said softly. "You'll be fine."

"Two months ago, I had no idea. I thought I'd drive this van to the west coast on sabbatical, hang out in Summer Beach while I wrote an impressive book that would make every editor drool, and then wind my way back across the States to New York. I'd return to work, sell my manuscript, and go on the bookselling circuit. Maybe get a movie deal." He chuckled. "I had big dreams."

"And now?"

"My entire life has changed. It's not about what I want so much as what Leo needs. He's going to lose his mother, and it will take him a long time to heal, even with therapy. Leo likes you a lot. I feared if you and I began to see each other…" He stopped and pressed a fist to his mouth, searching for the right words.

Resisting the urge to speak, Marina waited for him to go on.

"…as I had hoped," Jack finished. "If our relationship didn't work out—because of me, not you—then that would devastate Leo, just when he was the most vulnerable. I would imagine that he would look to you as a mother figure. Losing his mother at that age is the saddest thing I can think of. But to lose you as well might destroy him. Vanessa said he's quite sensitive, although he doesn't show it much."

Jack hesitated as if ashamed of a secret. "Plus, my romantic track record hasn't been stellar. I've left women to chase stories and forgotten birthdays when I was on deadline. Essentially, I've been a self-centered jerk."

"And that's why you didn't try to get in touch?"

"Maybe I overthought it. But I figured the odds of you breaking off the relationship in a few months were fairly high, and that would be when Leo would be the most vulnerable." He clasped his hands. "First and foremost, I'm trying to be a responsible parent. For once in my life, my needs have to come second. I've missed Leo's first ten years. I have a lot to make up for now."

Contemplating what Jack had said, Marina ran her fingertip around the rim of her coffee cup. His thought process made a lot of sense. "That's plausible, and I understand the pressure you're under."

Jack's knitted brow relaxed. "I have turned over this dilemma in my mind for weeks now. I never meant to hurt you. But the longer I thought about it, the more I realized that my actions could hurt a vulnerable little boy. And, perhaps, a good woman who deserves better."

Jack seemed genuinely remorseful, and his earnestness and desire to be a good father to Leo was touching. Marina had learned that when a man told her he wasn't good husband material, she should believe him. As much as it might hurt.

"Thank you for explaining what happened," Marina said. "I do appreciate your concern for Leo." She allowed a little smile. "And for me. Maybe you're not as much of a jerk as you think you are."

He stretched his hand across the small table. "Friends again?"

Marina swallowed hard. "Friends. With both you and Leo." She shook his hand in agreement, though the warmth and sureness of his grip made her wonder if she could actually be Jack's friend.

If she focused on what was best for Leo, perhaps she could. She was accustomed to putting her children before herself. Now that they were young adults making decisions about their lives, she had a chance to think of herself, and this summer was her first step in following her dream.

Marina thought about how much Heather and Ethan had missed having a father when they were growing up. To make up for it, she filled in at Ethan's ball games and even escorted Heather to a father-daughter dance in a rented tuxedo. Yet their father was gone before they were born. Losing a mother at Leo's age would be especially difficult. Compounding that was the fact that the boy had only just met his father.

Releasing Jack's hand, Marina said, "Thank you for your honesty. I only wish it had come a little sooner."

"Duly and embarrassingly noted."

Marina bit her lip as the events ahead sprang to mind. "Vanessa seems like such a lovely, kind woman."

Jack blinked, his eyes rimmed with red. "She is one of the most intelligent, compassionate women I have ever known. Before she became ill, she was an extraordinary-looking woman, too. A natural beauty. Vanessa deserves a long life; she deserves to reap the love she has unselfishly sown."

"What a lovely thing to say." Marina recognized a depth of feeling in Jack that she hadn't seen before. Vanessa had touched his heart. Had he been more in love with her than he would admit?

What if Vanessa were well…? In her heart, Marina thought she knew that answer. She closed her eyes and thought about the dilemma each of them faced. Yet, the most vulnerable among them was Leo, a little boy who would love nothing more than to have both his parents with him.

Marina didn't know why certain people were brought together in the world, especially when it seemed that destiny was working against them. A lump grew in her throat. Maybe this wasn't her story after all.

Marina asked, "Has Vanessa exhausted all avenues of treatment?"

"She says she has. It's an extraordinarily rare condition. I'm sure she has conducted thorough research into all available options. That's what Vanessa always excelled at."

Marina nodded, but still, she wondered if there were any treatment or experimental drugs that might help Vanessa. However, she was sure that everyone had an opinion, and Vanessa might think it an invasion of her privacy. Marina would not disturb the poor woman or minimize her dignity. She only hoped that they would have the summer for him to remember.

As Jack whistled for Scout to return, Marina thought about what she and Kai and Brooke had often laughed about and discussed.

Ginger seemed to know all the right people.

11

"*T*his is a rather charming character sketch," Ginger said as she inspected one of Jack's drawings for their children's book.

Seated across from Jack on the terrace at the Seabreeze Inn, Ginger Delavie peered through rhinestone reading glasses and adjusted her broad-brimmed straw hat against the afternoon sun. She considered each of Jack's sketches spread out on the table before her in turn.

"From what you've told me, that's how I imagined the youngest girl," Jack said, pointing to one.

Ginger lifted her brow. "Why, yes. That's quite good."

"I've often wondered, where did you get your inspiration for the stories?" Jack suspected he knew. He enjoyed hearing Ginger speak. Her fascinating experiences were seemingly boundless, with one story inevitably spilling into another.

Ginger removed her glasses, and her emerald-green eyes glittered as she reminisced. "The first stories were about a little girl—my daughter, as you might imagine. Bertrand was stationed overseas, so we joined him wherever he was. London, Paris, Madrid, Stockholm. We traveled a great deal and returned to the cottage for holidays. The original stories were meant to engage her in history, science, and the unknown cultures in which she found herself. Early on, I discovered that she loved solving mysteries and puzzles, so these elements became integral to the tales. A smart one, she was."

Ginger blinked and lowered her eyes. "I miss her and that lovely husband of hers every day. But they left me with the greatest gift—three lovely granddaughters."

"Is that how your main character list expanded to three children?" Jack sorted through his preliminary character sketches.

"Exactly." As Ginger rested her chin on her hand, her colorful bangle bracelets clinked against each other. "The girls loved hearing about characters similar to themselves, although I always denied that inspiration. It kept them guessing, you see. They would give me ideas based on what they said they would do in such situations. Of course, when they were older, they figured it out."

"You have some fascinating storylines."

Ginger acknowledged that with a nod. "These stories are meant to intrigue children, especially young girls, about science, mathematics, and history."

"And will there be a mystery in each book?" Jack jotted a few notes as she spoke.

"Yes, but not always the way one thinks of mysteries." She fussed with the folded sleeves of her crisp white shirt as she spoke. "My girls loved adventure stories and following clues. In each story, the siblings solve mysteries using clues, ciphers, and codes. I immersed them in stories where they would encounter ancient hieroglyphics, secret messages, and mazes to teach them how to approach and unravel vexing problems. Sometimes they had to time travel through history to solve old riddles. Oh, the fun we had."

"And did you weave in some of your work?"

"I suppose I did. The girls became quite proficient in the

Caesar shift cipher—so named because Julius Caesar used it to encode military messages. Much to the consternation of their teachers, I might add." She chuckled. "However, the Alberti cipher disk was more vexing—a coding device fashioned out of two concentric rings. In the story, the children made a similar device out of cardboard to solve a mystery."

"Those are quite advanced subjects for children." Jack sipped a juice cooler that Shelly had brought out to them.

"I believe that children can grasp more than we often imagine. All the children in my family were quite advanced." Ginger sniffed. "Now, if those young women would only pair common sense with their intelligence. That goes for all of them, mind you."

"I'm sure they will." Jack smothered a laugh. He had no intention of stepping into a disagreement between members of the Delavie-Moore tribe. Fortunately, he and Marina had left their picnic on a friendly basis. Though he still had feelings for her, he couldn't risk the potential complications of a relationship with her for Leo. At least they had cleared the air of their disagreement.

"Back to the sketches," Jack said, steering her attention. "I have several variations of the other characters. Are any of these close to what you had in mind?"

Ginger slipped on her reading glasses again to peruse each sketch. "This one captures the wide-eyed look of the youngest child. An impish girl, I might add. But quite artistically talented. And this one is quite right with her look of curiosity and determination. She's the natural leader of the group." She tapped another sketch. "And this one is the voice of practicality. The caregiver of the trio."

From Ginger's earlier descriptions, Jack had sketched the characters with subtle physical traits or expressions he'd observed from Marina, Brooke, and Kai, suspecting she had modeled the stories on the girls.

Ginger slid an old manila envelope across the table to him. "Here is the rest of the first story for you to work on, too."

"It looks old. I hope this isn't the original." Jack had already transcribed part of the story, editing it as he went. Another editor experienced in children's stories would have another go at it after they submitted the manuscript. He was, after all, trained as an investigative journalist. But he was learning the landscape of children's books.

"I made copies long ago."

With Ginger describing how she saw the characters in her mind and their talents and interests, they continued talking. Jack erased and sketched as she spoke. Narrowing a face, shortening a nose, adding freckles. To him, this was pure play.

After a while, Ginger leaned back and removed her glasses. She snapped them into her purse. "Before I go, I trust that you and Marina have put whatever disagreement you had to rest. Not that she has confided in me, mind you."

"Yes, ma'am." Jack drew his eyebrows together in question, but she simply nodded her approval.

"Now, if only we could steer Kai and Brooke in the proper directions," she said pointedly. "But never mind that. What did you think of the menu that Marina prepared on the yacht? I heard you attended with Leo and Samantha."

Jack swept a hand over his chin. Not much went on in Summer Beach that Ginger didn't know about. "Her food is delicious. The lobster pizza was a huge hit." Jack's gaze trailed to the yacht still docked at the far end of the marina.

"What's wrong?"

Jack's mind had wandered. "Sorry, what?"

"You're frowning. Did something happen?"

"Not exactly, but something doesn't seem quite right about that vessel."

Ginger leaned forward with interest. "I'd love to hear all about it."

. . .

AFTER GINGER LEFT, Jack ran a hand through his hair. For all her little quirks, he admired her. Ginger was a woman who had been far ahead of her time and still relished matching wits with anyone. She had keen insights and a wealth of experience.

He was glad he'd shared his thoughts about Charles and Anne with her. *You're right to trust your instincts*, she'd told him. Those professional instincts had carried him quite far in his career.

Jack left the terrace to check on Scout, who was stretched out in the guest room under a warm ray of sun shining through the window. "Out we go, boy," Jack said, clicking his tongue. "We have a dinner date with Leo tonight."

As they stepped outside, Jack thought about the twists of fate that had brought him here and how much his life had changed.

AFTER HAVING supper with Leo and Vanessa at the beach house, Jack returned to the inn. Denise and John had been asking him to come for dinner more frequently—on Vanessa's request. She had looked better this evening and was more talkative than usual—more like she had once been. Later, she told him it was because she had wrapped up all her affairs, so she no longer had to worry about that. Although he understood, it was a bittersweet evening.

After Jack put Scout in the room, he decided to stroll around the property and unwind. Overhead, the moon cast a shimmering glow on the inky ocean. Onshore breezes cooled the balmy evening. He wandered a little way along the beach and circled back before easing into a chair on the veranda in a darkened section. Tipping his head back, he gazed at the canopy of stars twinkling in the clear night sky.

Car lights flashed in the car court, and a couple parked and got out. The man flicked a lighter, and the tip of his cigarette glowed in the night. Jack counted the days since he'd smoked. His stamina was returning. He was feeling better and able to run short distances with Bennett in the mornings. As smoke drifted toward him, he chewed his lip and fought the desire. Reaching into his pocket, he brought out a peppermint breath mint and popped it into his mouth.

That helped.

The couple made their way to a pair of chairs. He could hear them talking and recognized the woman from her silhouette against the moon.

It was Kai. She wore a white, fluttery dress illuminated by moonlight and high heels.

Jack also recognized the man with her. He had the room next to his, and he'd been there about a week. He was a large, imposing man who favored gold chains, cufflinks, and rings. Jack had heard him flirting with another guest—a young woman. The guy was smooth, but he was quick to insult the woman when she told him she wasn't interested.

What was Kai doing with him?

Then, a realization hit him with a jolt. That was Kai's fiancé.

The conversation floated to him on the ocean breeze.

"Come with me back to New York, babe."

Kai shook her head. "I want to stay at the cottage another couple of weeks. This is my summer vacation, Dmitri. And I probably won't see my family again for a while."

Jack leaned forward, elbows on his knees. He didn't mean to eavesdrop, but he'd been here first.

"You don't belong here anymore. That sister of yours and your granny—they don't like me much."

"They will when they get to know you."

"You know I'm not much of a family man." He clutched her hand. "Come to New York."

"I'll have to start auditioning as soon as I arrive."

"Why don't you relax for a while? No need to go rushing back into another show."

Kai swatted him playfully. "You're the one who told me I needed to aim higher."

"I've been thinking about that. If you land a part, you'll be stuck in New York performing most nights. Travel with me for a while. Sure gets lonely without you."

"Aw, that's sweet," Kai said. She kissed him on the nose. "But what would I do? Sit in a hotel room and wait for you to finish your business every day?"

"You could get massages, shop, do lunch. What all women like to do. Stay with me, Kai. You don't need to be on Broadway. I'll take care of you."

Kai pulled back. "You don't want me to audition, do you?"

"You don't need to be on stage anymore. You've got me. All those men leering at you when I'm not around to protect you. See what I mean? Better that you come with me."

A small silence hung between them. From what Jack knew of Kai, this probably wasn't going to resonate the way Dmitri had intended. He waited.

Dmitri's cigarette glowed as he took a long drag and blew out smoke.

Kai folded her arms. "I need to work, Dmitri. For me. Whether it's working on Broadway, a traveling troupe, or summer stock, I love what I do. I don't want to give it up to follow you around. I can't believe you'd even think that. I'm an actress."

"You've had your fun. Take a couple of years off. You'll need to decorate the condo."

"You can hire a decorator. I'm going to auditions when I get to New York."

"Now, Kai, I want you to think carefully about what you're saying," Dmitri said, his voice measured and controlled. "You're not considering how I feel."

"How *you* feel?" Kai's voice raised a notch. "I don't appreciate you telling my boss that I wasn't going back on tour. I wanted to make that decision. And I wanted to start a family, but I was willing to go along with your wishes."

"We've been over this. I'm not supporting any more kids."

"If I'm not going to be a mother, I want to continue working. I'd be bored out of my mind if I did nothing but follow you around like a jeweled pet. When did you change your mind?"

Dmitri ground his cigarette butt out on the tile and leaned in to kiss her. "Let's leave tomorrow, drive to Vegas, and get Elvis to marry us. We'll have a honeymoon while we're there, then I'll leave the rental car, and we'll fly to New York and start our new life."

"When I get married, I want my family there."

"When *you* get married?" Dmitri stood, towering above Kai. He clamped a hand around her arm. "First you push back the wedding, and now this. You'll do as I say, Kai. I'm not putting up with one of your little tantrums. Go home, pack your bags, and take a ride-share back here. I've had enough of Summer Beach. We're leaving tonight."

Kai shook her head. "I don't want to do this anymore."

Dmitri closed in on her and gripped her wrist. "What did you say?"

Jack's senses went on high alert. He pushed out of his chair.

"This isn't going to work for me," Kai said, beginning to cry. "Let me go."

"Why, you little—"

"Hey, you heard the lady," Jack yelled, closing the space between them in a few long strides. "Let her go."

Dmitri glowered at Jack. "And just who do you think you are?"

"A friend of the family." Jack held out his hand to Kai,

who tore herself from Dmitri and raced behind Jack. He turned back to her. "Are you okay?"

"Watch out," Kai screamed.

As Kai ducked, Jack quickly stepped aside, narrowly avoiding the big man's punch. Dmitri lost his balance and cursed. He turned on Jack again, and once more, Jack dodged his throw. Jack didn't want to fight, but he would if he had to.

Instead of going after Jack again, Dmitri lunged for Kai and flung his arms around her. "You're staying with me, and we're leaving now."

"I don't think so." Gritting her teeth, Kai grabbed Dmitri's hand clutching her shoulder, brought her other arm around him, then ducked back and under, pushing him forward off balance. Despite his protests, she kicked the back of his knee, and he collapsed on the ground, clutching his legs and wailing about his shoulder.

"Wow, what moves." Jack was impressed. He hovered over Dmitri, though it seemed Kai could take care of herself.

Dmitri's face turned bright red. "Why, you little—"

"You need to leave for Vegas right now," Kai said. "I never want to see you again."

"Where's my ring?" Dmitri yelled, holding his leg.

"With pleasure." Kai jerked a showy diamond ring off her finger and lobbed it into the pool. "Go get it."

"Let's get out of here," Jack said as Dmitri bellowed after her. "There's my van."

He and Kai sprinted toward it and jumped inside. Jack could hear Scout barking through an open window.

"I'm parked in front," she panted.

"I'll follow you home." Wheeling out of the car court, he glanced at her. "Pretty impressive moves."

"Thanks to Ginger." She pushed her hair from her face and blew out a breath. "Did you hear any of that?"

"Enough."

"I'm so embarrassed that I ever fell for him."

"I'm sure you're not the first one he tried to dazzle and then possess."

"Why, that's exactly what he was doing. I started seeing warning signs, but I couldn't believe it was actually happening to me. I should have known better, but he had seemed so infatuated and adoring when we met that I thought I'd hit the boyfriend lottery. How did you know?"

"I'm a guy. And I know how guys like that operate." He stopped the van beside her car. "Hurry and get in."

Kai did, and he followed her to Ginger's cottage. He pulled to a stop beside her.

"Please come in with me," Kai pleaded. "Just in case he comes back."

"Sure," Jack said. "But he's probably diving for diamonds right now."

"He can drown for all I care." Kai swung open the door.

In the light of the living room, Jack saw that Kai's white dress had been ripped in the scuffle. Ginger and Marina and Brooke rose with alarm on their faces. It looked like they had been sharing a bottle of wine and having a conversation.

Kai fell into Ginger's arms. "I'm so, so sorry for what I said. You were right about Dmitri. Both of you."

Marina embraced Kai, and Jack stood to one side, waiting. He shut the door and locked it behind him.

"Did he try to hurt you?" Ginger asked.

Growing flushed, Kai looked away in embarrassment, but she told her the entire story.

Ginger turned to Jack. "I'm glad you were there."

He held up his hands. "I didn't do anything but intervene. Your granddaughter took care of herself. She left him in a heap on the ground screaming about his knees and shoulder. Kai has some swift moves."

Ginger wrapped her arm around Kai. "Glad I made you go to those classes now?"

"I sure am," Kai replied. "Why didn't you send us to how-to-spot-a-jerk classes, too?"

Ginger shook her head. "Some lessons you have to learn on your own."

Marina took out her phone. "I should call Ivy and let her know what happened."

"He probably woke up the entire inn," Kai said.

Marina called her friend and quickly explained what had happened. She listened for a couple of minutes. After she hung up, she turned back to Kai.

"Sounds like Dmitri made such a commotion that Bennett and another guest had to restrain him. He had jumped into the pool fully clothed and was trying to brawl with both of them. Ivy called the police, and Chief Clarkson arrested Dmitri for assault. He was screaming about needing to get a ring out of the pool."

Kai drew her hands over her face. "This is all my fault."

"Oh, no," Marina said, pointing at Kai. "You will not take the blame for his actions."

"It was all Dmitri," Jack added. "I was sitting on the veranda when they came out. I didn't mean to listen in, but Dmitri overstepped the boundaries." He shifted on his feet, feeling a little awkward in front of Marina. Although they'd parted on good terms, his attraction to her hadn't waned.

"I should go," Jack said.

"I'll walk you out." Marina tucked her golden-brown hair behind her ears and gave him a small smile.

They walked to the van in silence. Jack hesitated by the door.

"I'm glad you were there." Marina flung her arms around him. "We've been so worried about Kai. And thank you for making sure she got home okay." She pulled back.

Jack held her hands for a moment, gazing into her eyes and wishing that everything was different. He cleared his throat. "Kai's going to be okay."

He only wished he could say the same about his heart.

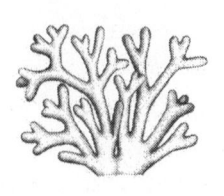

12

"Watch your step," Marina said to Kai.

She pushed aside plastic sheeting and stepped into the newly expanded kitchen in the guest house. Axe's construction team was almost finished. The last step was to sand the drywall and paint. Marina had chosen cheerful beach shades of sandy yellow for the walls with accents of coral and turquoise.

In the interest of time, she'd decided to let Axe and his crew handle the painting so that she could open a week earlier than planned. Marina needed to spend time preparing the menu dishes and making sure the kitchen was stocked with food, cutlery, and serving dishes. She was amazed at the thousands of details she had to address. The county would have to inspect and approve the premises, too.

Kai followed her through the plastic sheeting guarding against sheetrock dust and overspray. Paper lined the floors.

"Wow, what a transformation in just a week," Kai said, looking around.

"We're about to open for business." Marina smiled as she ran her hand over the newly installed cooktop. Although it was used, it was scrubbed clean and new to her. The appliance still had years of service left in it, and she'd bought it at a great price. Looking around the expanded workspace, she knew she could do so much more here in the expanded kitchen. She had warming drawers and more refrigeration.

"Are you going to throw a big party?" Kai asked.

Marina checked the new oven. "I talked about that with Ginger, Heather, and Brooke."

Kai had been occupied with Dmitri and had missed a lot, but thankfully, that chapter was closed. Dmitri had been released and left town, although he'd have to return for a court date. Kai seemed relieved.

"I'd like to have family and friends over," Marina said. "Nothing fancy, just good food. I'm going to need a marketing person soon."

"Heather said she's going to work with you."

"She will seat guests and wait tables. Maybe help in the kitchen if needed. I sure could use someone to help me set up a website."

"I could probably do that," Kai said, grinning.

"I know you have to find work again."

Kai twisted her lips to one side. "Thanks to Dmitri. I talked to my old boss, and they offered my position to another actress. Still, they're going to see about offering me a smaller role until something else opens up. Dmitri was such a jerk."

"He was a dangerous man."

"I'm angry at Dmitri, but also at myself for falling for him."

"Don't beat yourself up over that," Marina said. "We all make mistakes. Look at me. Maybe Dmitri was a good actor. Or maybe you wanted to believe that your dream life was finally coming true." She took Kai's hand. "I'm not saying insta-love never happens, but it's rare. A wedding is exciting, but building a marriage—a true partnership—takes time. He was moving fast to capture you before you had too much time to think. And you found out why."

Kai nodded glumly. "All he wanted was someone to make *his* life more pleasurable. He didn't care about my family or friends, and he refused to consider what I wanted or needed."

"And do you know what that is?"

"I still want to have a family. Maybe I won't, and I'll have to face that, but I have nieces and nephews that I adore. Maybe I'll look into fostering children. As for my professional life, I want to put my talents to use doing what I love. Acting, singing, and dancing. Spreading joy, making people happy."

Marina inclined her head. "You're very good at that. I heard you singing in the shower this morning. It's nice to hear you again." Hearing Kai belt out songs from *Dreamgirls* had made her smile. Only, Kai had changed the lyrics. Instead of singing about *never letting him go*, she'd been belting out *never letting him in again* with the same gusto.

"It's good to feel the joy of singing again," Kai said, lifting her gaze. Her eyes were now twin pools of steely determination. "Dmitri trashed my career for his selfish purposes, but I swear I will rise again, doing what I want even better than before."

Marina slung an arm around Kai and hugged her. "Welcome to the club."

The plastic sheeting rustled, and Axe stepped through the entrance. He greeted both of them, though Marina noticed that his warm brown eyes lingered on Kai a little longer. Turning back to Marina, he asked. "Are you happy with the progress?"

"Delighted. Once I receive final approval, I'll be open for business."

"And we'll get the party started," Kai said, flipping her hair over her shoulder.

"Give us two more days," Axe said. "We'll clean before we leave, so you can focus on what you need to do."

"I appreciate that," Marina said.

Axe clasped his hands. "If there isn't anything else, I

thought Kai and I could talk on the patio now. I want to tell her about an idea I have for a theater here in Summer Beach."

"Thanks for calling and thinking of me, Axe." Kai beamed. "It's such an exciting idea."

"I can't wait to hear all about it," Marina said. "I'm going inside to put on a fresh pot of coffee. I'll bring some out if you'd like."

"That would nice of you," Axe said. His lips twitched into a grin, and he nodded to her. "I sure appreciate everything you do."

"My pleasure," Marina said, ducking through the plastic sheeting outside before she broke out laughing. *Good for Axe*, she thought. And Kai needed a distraction to occupy her mind. What better than a new amphitheater? It didn't hurt that a kind, handsome man of good character was behind it.

Marina hurried into the kitchen. Brooke was there, watching Kai and Axe through the window over the sink.

"Look how courteous Axe is," Brooke said. "Chip needs to see how a man treats a woman." She pulled her phone from her pocket and began to film.

Watching Kai over Brooke's shoulder, Marina began to measure out coffee beans to grind. Axe pulled out her chair for her. *That's good.* And he didn't make a big deal out of it like Dmitri would have done. This man had natural manners. He'd been brought up well.

"Who are you two spying on?"

Marina whirled around, accidentally flinging coffee beans around the kitchen. "Oh, you scared me," she cried.

Brooke paused her video. "I'm trying to film this for Chip. Like an instructional video."

Ginger chuckled. Peering over her shoulder, she smiled. "Finally got the two of them together?"

"Axe wanted to talk to her about helping him with his new theater," Marina said.

"I've heard about that," Ginger said thoughtfully. "Quite the development Axe has in mind. He has formed a company as a nonprofit, and Carol Reston has already made a sizeable donation to cover the cost of the stage."

Marina wagged her head. "Is there anything you don't know in Summer Beach?"

"If you live here long enough, there's not a lot that goes on without your knowledge." Ginger paused. "Look at their body language. Both are leaning forward. That's a good sign. I thought she might be quite defensive after Dmitri."

Brooke restarted her video. "I need this, too."

"Kai is in a very determined place now," Marina said.

"And that's a good place to be." Ginger peered past her granddaughters. "Look, he has her laughing about something, and she—"

"What are you all staring at?" Heather stood in the doorway with her hands on her hips. "And why are there coffee beans all over the place?"

Marina turned around. "Shh, it's Kai and Axe."

Heather peeked past Marina and Brooke and Ginger. "Can't they see us in here? It's not like this is a one-way mirror."

Just then, Kai glanced back toward the kitchen. The four of them ducked away from the window, laughing in hysterics as they slid onto the floor.

"Way to be discreet, Mom." Heather shook her head. "Remind me not to bring guys here."

"In a family with this many women, it's to be expected," Ginger said, chuckling.

Between gasps, Marina said, "Kai's probably wondering what happened to the coffee."

"Don't be in too much of a hurry." Ginger threw her arms around her brood. "I haven't laughed like this in a long time. Sure is fine to have all my girls back in the fold."

Brooke's lower lip drooped at that comment.

Ginger hugged her close. "I daresay you won't be here much longer. But you're not leaving until Chip and the boys have some training."

Marina rose. "We should clean up all these coffee beans. Heather, could you do that for me? I promised Axe some coffee." She measured out more beans into the coffee grinder while Heather and Brooke swept the floor and wiped the counters.

All the while, Marina couldn't help sneaking glances outside.

At last, the guest cottage was completely transformed. Marina and Ginger stood by the door to the new patio. Beyond them, the ocean roared onto the shore and rushed out again, and palm trees swayed overhead. A few tourists and locals strolled along the beach.

Marina and Ginger were taking a final inventory of supplies and inspecting everything, from kitchen equipment and supplies to table decorations, lights, and artwork.

"This new cafe is all I've ever dreamed of," Marina said, pressing her clipboard to her chest.

Ginger waved a hand across the patio. "This is your dream. Your vision come to life."

"Without your help and encouragement, it never would have come to pass." Her grandmother had always been her most ardent supporter.

"Perhaps, but you did what you had to do."

Marina laughed. "In a strange way, I have Grady to thank for this. Had I not made a complete fool of myself over him on the air, I wouldn't be opening a new cafe next week."

"Do not thank or excuse that man for his actions," Ginger said, standing tall. "Not even as a joke."

"You're right. I believe I said something similar to Kai."

"See? You have wisdom within you, too." Ginger put her

arm around her. "Have you decided on the menu for the opening?"

Marina slipped a list out from under her sheaf of papers on the clipboard. "Here it is. Kai and Heather are going to create little table placards with details about every dish. I'll have an assortment of everything on the regular menu. I'm adding dishes that I can't quite decide on to see what people like the most."

"Smart choice. Who is on your guest list?"

Marina ticked off guests on her fingers. "Ivy and Shelly and Poppy and the Bay family, Denise and John and Samantha, Axe, Bennett, and Mitch, Cookie O'Toole, Leilani and Roy, and Gilda and Pixie. Boz from City Hall, Rosa from the taco stand, and Imani from the flower kiosk. Ivy is bringing Jen from Nailed It. Kai has the full list; I know I'm leaving out a lot of people." *Including Jack.* But she had casually invited Jack and Leo.

"You've been hard at work."

"Actually, Kai is in charge of invitations."

Ginger nodded her approval. "You can't do it all. Delegating well is the mark of a leader."

They strolled around the perimeter of the new patio, and Marina made notes to buy various supplies.

"Kai and Heather are in charge of decorations," Marina said. "They have some ideas, but they won't tell me what they're doing."

"I think you'll be delighted." Ginger arched an eyebrow. "Do you need a sous-chef to help you prepare for the event?"

"I thought you'd never ask. You already know many of the dishes on the menu. But I've made a few changes to the recipes." She'd lightened up some of them, making healthier versions and adding seasonal Southern California ingredients.

"As we often do." Ginger nodded. "I'm glad those recipes are being put to good use. My old friend Julia would be proud. Of course, I prefer my versions." She chuckled. "I miss arguing with her about that. She was a true original. In a world where one can be anything, sometimes the hardest thing to be is yourself."

Marina thought about that. There was a lot of truth in what Ginger said. For years, Marina did what she had to do for her children, and she took pride in her ability to provide for them. But now, it was her turn. "And the greatest luxury and privilege is to do your soul's work. Cooking is pure pleasure to me."

"Remind yourself of that when the going gets tough." Ginger patted her arm. "Running a restaurant is hard work. You'll have your share of challenging customers." She winked at Marina. "But, oh, the fun we'll have."

"I'm thinking of this as a soft opening party. And a test-run for the Taste of Summer Beach event."

As they made their way inside through the private dining room, Ginger asked, "And how is that going?"

"I have a date picked out, and I've been contacting restaurant owners in town. We all need to work together on this. I'm planning one evening to invite several over to discuss it. My greatest fear is that the chain restaurants will drive the entrepreneurs out of business and take over their places."

"Then you must be proactive. We've talked about this, and you're still welcome to have it here." Ginger checked the closet where the old safe was stored and jiggled the knob.

Marina had made sure it remained locked.

"We might need a larger place. In the future, anyway." Marina thought if all the local restaurant owners banded together, they could make Summer Beach a destination for foodies. But first, she had to make sure the Coral Cafe was off to a successful beginning.

They threaded their way into the kitchen.

"Did you see what arrived this morning?" Marina motioned toward a rustic, hand-hewn table with benches that she'd found at a Mexican furniture importer.

She had positioned the furniture on the Saltillo tile floor near the raised adobe fireplace. The hearth ran along the side, giving more room for people to sit and visit while she cooked. Bright coral and turquoise floral cushions enlivened the dark wood.

"What a perfect chef's table," Ginger said. "Why, when I was at dear Alain's restaurant—that's Alain Ducasse, of course—at Le Meurice in Paris, you can hardly imagine the fare that sprang forth from the chef's hand as if by magic. Bertrand and I had one of the most enchanting evenings. But nothing was ever as special as our evenings in Boston spent learning at Julia's side in the kitchen, with Bertrand and Paul creating new cocktails for us and pouring the finest wines." With a fond look, she pressed a hand to her heart at the memories.

"We're not quite that fancy," Marina said, smiling at her grandmother. Ginger glided from one story to another with ease. To spend an evening with her over a bottle of wine was to embark on a world tour of fashionable places and memorable people—most of all, Ginger and Bertrand.

"You don't have to be a virtuoso, or even very sophisticated—just serve wonderful food, provide a comfortable ambiance, and let guests enjoy their time with you. That's all there is to it, my dear. Relax." Ginger made a grand gesture. "A new world awaits you."

Marina could hardly wait. She was growing so excited that she could scarcely sleep at night. Her mind was so full of ideas, new dishes, and an endless to-do list. But within a few days, whether she was ready or not, the Coral Cafe would be open for business. She was anxious for this debut to turn out better than her disastrous one at the Seabreeze Inn. But she would be among family and friends—old and new.

Ginger looked around in approval. "It's too bad that Jack couldn't stay here longer, but he tells me that Bennett will have some cottages for him to look at soon. Isn't it nice that he's staying in Summer Beach? He'll soon be one of us."

"And he has his hands full."

Ginger huffed. "I can't imagine that my little books require that much of his time. Although his sketches are quite remarkable."

Marina twisted her lips to one side. She knew what Ginger was trying to do. "It's not going to happen."

"What?"

"Whatever you're trying to set up. We might have more luck with Kai, though." And then, as Marina thought about Jack's situation, she remembered what he'd said about Vanessa and Leo. As the widow of a career diplomat, Ginger knew people all over the world. "However, there is something I'd like to ask you. An important favor, but not for me."

"Always happy to help your friends if I can."

"I do hope so," Marina said. A sliver of chance might be just enough.

13

*M*arina loved the new kitchen in the guest cottage. With the windows open to the ocean breezes and upbeat jazz playing in the background, Marina worked deftly preparing dishes from the menu for the open-house guests, anxious for everything to be perfect tonight for the new opening.

Ginger was working beside her, slicing avocados for Marina to use on a molded seafood tower.

Marina alternated sweet yellow peppers with mango, avocado, and seared red tuna that she'd tossed with a light ginger vinaigrette in narrow cylindrical molds. They would remove the molds just before serving. With the combination of flavors, colors, and textures—plus crunchy Asian noodles on top and wasabi on the side—the presentation would be lovely.

Marina blew out a nervous breath and brushed her hands. "Once we finish these, we'll move on to the street tacos. I have three versions, one with mahi-mahi fish, one with Korean barbecued beef, and one vegetarian version with black beans and mango salsa." She pressed a hand to her head. They didn't have much more time, and she was afraid she forgot something. "I made salsa, but I'm worried we'll need more."

"I'll prepare that," Ginger said quickly.

Marina flipped open the book of recipes that she had prepared and tested. Each page was encased in a plastic sleeve for easy reference in the kitchen. She read off the ingredients to Ginger, who gathered everything she would need on the counter.

What else might she have forgotten? Marina's heart raced. Everything needed to be perfect today.

She thought about how much she had invested in the cafe, perhaps money that should have gone to Heather's private university education, though the cost was so high that it would have only paid for a semester or two. What then? She'd be in the same place, with little means of support. The jobs her agent had been talking about in lesser markets weren't bad, but they didn't pay enough to support a Duke education for Heather. Unfortunately, Ethan's golf skills had been valued more for a scholarship than Heather's stellar grades.

The cafe *had* to be successful. Yet Marina knew the survival rate for new restaurants was dismal. She pressed a hand against her heart.

Ginger cast a worried glance at Marina. "Are you okay?"

"I'm probably overthinking everything."

"That's opening night nerves." Ginger touched her hand. "You're extremely well prepared. Go get a breath of fresh air." When Marina didn't move right away, Ginger gave her a little pat on the back. "Go."

"Okay. Be right back." Marina did as her grandmother instructed.

Stepping onto the old front porch of the cottage, she gazed out to the ocean. She had felt this anxiety on the ship. The sudden self-doubt. *Why?* Some people called it an imposter syndrome. She had triple-checked her supplies, feeling like she had to be prepared for anything.

Still, she knew she was capable of running a cafe. She had

worked in many restaurants, and she had been cooking for as long as she could remember.

Closing her eyes, she breathed in to calm her nerves and began to repeat the words she'd often said after Stan had died —the words that Ginger had once shared and had seen her through each day with two young lives under her sole care.

I will welcome this day with optimism and excitement. I will approach this day with the intelligence, wisdom, and talent that I know I possess, even when doubt creeps into my mind. I will seize this day with all the energy I have within me, and I will radiate enthusiasm to light the path of those who follow me.

Marina opened her eyes and took another deep breath, feeling the sea breeze cool her hot face. Immediately, she felt much calmer. She stepped into the kitchen.

Not everything had to be perfect. There weren't any restaurant reviewers or food bloggers who could trash her work just to drive reviews to their publication or website, as she knew some did. They could damage a restaurant's chances before it built a following.

Her food was good; what mattered would be the welcoming, relaxing ambiance. People wanted to have fun and connect with friends on the beach. That's what the Coral Cafe would be about.

Good food, good friends, great memories.

Ginger nodded to her. "You're looking much better. Tonight, and this cafe, is going to be successful. You have a great team behind you."

"Thank you," Marina said. "How'd you know I needed a little mental health moment?"

"You'd gone a bit pale." Ginger hugged her. "Stress can do that to you, sweetheart. But we're going to have a fabulous evening."

Marina checked on the beef kalbi marinating for sliders. What was a beach cafe without a good burger? Or her version of it. She would also prepare a vegetarian patty with the same flavorful marinade she'd prepared and serve them on the seeded buns she'd developed.

Kai, Brooke, and Heather walked in through the open door.

"Would you like to see the decorations on the patio?" Kai asked, her eyes sparkling with excitement.

"You came in at just the right time," Marina said. "Let's all take a break. We don't have much more to do."

They made their way outside, and Marina exclaimed, "Fabulous! Exactly what I had in mind. Even better, actually."

Marina gazed around a profusion of white orchids, bird of paradise flowers, and red ginger flowers on serving tables and guest tables. The patio looked like a tropical paradise. Overhead, Kai and Heather had strung strands of lights to match the adjoining patio. After the sun set, the lights would cast a magical glow over the area.

"I asked Shelly for help," Kai said. "In New York, she was a floral designer, and she helped decorate a lot of fancy parties. I saw some of her photos, which were spectacular. Shelly gave me a few great ideas, and Imani sent these flowers."

"And Leilani and Roy sent the plants," Heather added.

"They always have the healthiest plants," Ginger said. "These are similar to the ones Jack bought for the other patio."

Marina recalled that lovely surprise after she'd had the first patio built. She wondered if he would be here today.

Kai gestured toward the surrounding trees. "Shelly and Brooke and I placed lights to illuminate some of our palm, lemon, and orange trees, as Shelly does at the Seabreeze Inn. The effect will be stunning."

"I love it," Marina said, pressing her hands together.

"People should begin arriving at six o'clock," Brooke said. "That will give us all time to get ready."

Marina wondered if Brooke had invited Chip and the boys. She had left that up to her sister.

"Even though I'll be in the kitchen most of the time, I have to circulate and welcome people," Marina said. "I haven't thought about what to wear." She looked down at the stained apron tied over an old T-shirt.

"But first..." Heather bounced on her toes with excitement. "We wanted to make today extra special, so we have a few surprises." She glanced toward the driveway and signaled for Ethan to join them.

"Being here and doing all the decorating is enough," Marina said.

Ethan got out of the car and brought a large, brown-wrapped package with a big coral bow with him to the patio.

"Happy grand opening, Mom," Ethan said as he hugged her. "Heather and I thought you might need this. Open it."

"What on earth could it be?" Marina tore off the paper. "A sign," she exclaimed, running her hand over the lettering. *The Coral Cafe.* The hand-painted driftwood sign reminded her of the sign in front of the cottage that Heather and Ethan had painted years ago. That was a replacement for the one that Marina and her sisters had created so many years ago.

"I love it," Marina said, gathering her children in an embrace.

"We will illuminate it, too," Ethan said. "I'll set it up now. I have a stake and support for it."

Marina had been so busy she hadn't given much thought to signage. Everyone coming tonight knew where the Coral Cottage was, but new guests wouldn't.

"And there's more." Kai brought out a large gift bag from behind a skirted serving table. "Surprise!"

Marina opened the bag and smiled broadly. "Just what I needed." She brought out a Hawaiian floral print chef's jacket with *Coral Cafe* embroidered on one line, and beneath that, her name. She held up the jacket. "Perfect fit, I think."

"Remember when we were talking about chef jackets and aprons?" Kai asked. "While your apron is fine for the farmers market, we thought a chef's jacket would be better in the kitchen for extreme cooking. When we were on board the ship, I saw how the food was flying."

Even though that had only been a few weeks ago, Marina thought about how much she had learned since then.

Every day she'd been researching recipes, creating new ones, and learning to run a professional kitchen. She had also found plenty of chefs' blogs and instructional sites. Everything she had learned from working in cafes twenty years ago and all the cooking shows she had watched was coming back to her as well.

Marina ran her hand over the jacket. "I love this fabric; the pattern will hide stains. And it's very bright and on-brand for the cafe."

"We thought so." Ginger brought out another bag. "That's why we bought several for you. Along with a pair of cute, sturdy clogs that cooks rave about. And pants to go with all the tops. Your new cafe wardrobe."

"Oh, I love it all." Marina blinked back tears. "I don't know how I would have managed all this without you."

"We're having fun, too," Kai said. "Thanks for including us. I know I wasn't much fun to be around when he-who-shall-remain-nameless-forevermore was here. I'm so glad to be back in the family now."

"We reserved your space," Ginger said, her eyes twinkling.

"Thank goodness, because I'm the one who brings the fun around here." Kai burst into song and spun Marina around in an impromptu dance.

Laughing, Marina twirled. "We're going to have as much fun as our guests do tonight."

"No opening night stress?" Heather asked.

"Not anymore." Marina felt prepared and confident. She

spread her hands wide. "I've dreamed of this for years. I want tonight to be a happy occasion."

Marina joined hands with Ginger and Heather, and Brooke and Kai and Ethan joined in the circle. "The tone and mood we set for our guests will ensure that they have a great time. Word will spread, and the cafe will be successful." She breathed in, filling her lungs with the fresh sea air that always energized her. "We will handle whatever problems might arise tonight with grace and good humor."

"Hear, hear," Ginger said.

Kai grinned. "I don't see any waterspouts on the horizon, so we should be good to go."

Marina let go and clapped her hands. "Let's go," she cheered, and everyone joined in.

She and Ginger returned to the kitchen to finalize the dishes that remained. Marina had created a schedule for the food. Appetizers, salads, main courses, and desserts. Heather and Ethan would circulate through the crowd with platters and place other dishes on tables.

Kai would be in charge of drinks. Ginger and Marina would be in the kitchen, although they had already prepared many of the dishes ahead of time, or as much as they could. The warm appetizers and entrees would require time to cook, but Marina had worked that into the schedule.

Marina and Ginger would take turns circulating to greet guests, which Marina knew would be important, and she didn't want to overwork Ginger. She'd asked Brooke or Kai to step in as needed. Heather and Ethan would also pitch in wherever needed.

"Where did you perfect your scheduling skills?" Ginger asked. "On the air?"

As Marina thought about it, she laughed. "That too, but I had to be highly organized with the twins." When Heather and Ethan were young, she'd had a neighbor's college-age daughter take them to school in the morning, and Marina would pick them up in the afternoon. When they were older, they walked to school together.

Marina went on. "Between the outfits, homework, and lunches that had to be prepared, and my work and clothing, I had to pay attention to details and timing. Those were stressful years but being organized sure helped me keep my sanity."

While Ginger made the salsa, Marina readied the first hot appetizer. She seasoned tofu and checked on the marinating chicken for the lemongrass kebob appetizers. The Thai peanut dip was ready to go.

The chef's table was also set and ready for guests. She imagined that Brooke might stay close there as she was still feeling out of sorts over Chip. Mitch had said he would stop by to see how she and Ginger were doing. After all, Ginger had taught him how to make many of the popular items on his Java Beach menu, such as his croissants and muffins.

Kai appeared at the doorway. "We're going to get ready, but everything is all set. I also have a table reserved for Vanessa where she can be comfortable."

"That was a good idea, thanks. I hope she's up to coming."

After Kai left, Marina finalized preparations while Ginger wiped down the counters. "I think we're ready to go. Let's clean up and change clothes. And now I have a brand new outfit."

Ginger hooked her arm into Marina's, and they set off for the main house. "About that request you had about Vanessa's condition. I've reached out to a few specialists and researchers I know."

Marina's heart quickened. "And?"

"They will check around. Their network spreads around the world. But I wouldn't hold out hope. As you know, her condition is extremely rare. Still, it's thoughtful of you to ask."

"Thank you for taking the time."

"It's no bother at all. Young Leo needs all the help we can

give him. Preparing the young minds and hearts of the next generation is imperative work."

Marina held the kitchen door for Ginger. As tough and tenacious as her grandmother could be, she also had a soft spot, especially for children. Although Ginger had loved globetrotting with Bertrand over the years, she once said that her time spent teaching was the most personally fulfilling and gratifying work she'd done. That from a woman whose work in codebreaking had probably saved countless lives as well.

Ginger never ceased to amaze and inspire her.

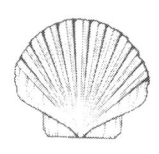

14

"This platter is ready to go," Marina called out. "Red tuna, avocado, and mango towers."

With just ten minutes until the party began, Ethan and Heather were carrying out the cold appetizers. Kai was orchestrating placement while keeping watch for early arrivals.

"Save some for us, Mom." Ethan lifted the platter with ease and swung out of the kitchen.

"We have plenty," Marina said to Heather. "Take some for you and Ethan. Can't have you going hungry."

"Are you kidding? You've had us tasting all day. I'm stuffed, and I have no idea how Ethan can eat so much."

"He's golfing and working out every day."

Heather paused. "He's much happier here than he was in Durham. I feel guilty for giving him such a hard time."

Marina brought out a large iced bowl of shrimp with several sauces, including her special cilantro and avocado sauce. "I'm sure he's forgiven and forgotten, darling." Ever since they'd been young, Heather and Ethan had been bickering, yet they always settled their differences.

"Thanks, Mom." Heather picked up the shrimp bowl and followed her brother out.

Everyone had worn Hawaiian-inspired clothing for the evening, even Ginger, who had layers of shell necklaces tucked under one of the new chef's jackets. When she'd protested, Marina had insisted.

"Look who's here," Kai called out.

Their friends Ivy and Shelly from the Seabreeze Inn stepped inside, and they all greeted one another. Marina was happy they'd come early so they could talk before it got too crowded.

"You've done an amazing job with the guest cottage," Ivy said. "I can hardly believe the transformation from the last time you brought me over to see it. Just look at this kitchen. It's so professional."

Marina was proud of what they'd accomplished. "Axe was wonderful. He and his crew set it up just as I wanted. I miss the old O'Keefe and Merritt stove in Ginger's kitchen, but this is more practical. And we can still use that for overflow." Which they had in prepping for opening night.

Ginger gave Ivy and Shelly two of the red tuna tower appetizers. "Try these. Beware the hot wasabi masquerading as avocado."

"Great presentation," Shelly said before she tasted it. "Hmm, delicious. Is that a ginger dressing?"

"Ginger and sesame seeds," Marina said. "Very light. Is it enough?"

"It's perfect," Ivy said, nodding.

"Everything we're serving tonight is what will be on the menu," Marina said. "With a few extras that are under consideration." Those depended on how busy they might be. A wide menu meant she had to have more ingredients on hand, and until they were busy, it could also mean potential food waste—though instead of wasting it, she planned to give her excess to the local food bank.

Still, Marina had a critical window to reach profitability. Ivy had told her that while the summer was busy, the winter trade was mostly local people. The two sisters had run special weeks and weekends during the slow winter months to bring in guests. Ivy promised to send diners to the cafe.

"So this is where the party is," Bennett said, kissing Ivy on the cheek.

Marina laughed. "It usually ends up in the kitchen." She gestured toward the chef's table. "That's what the new table is for. Make yourselves comfortable."

Axe had also installed double doors that they could leave open to the patio, so Marina could see guests on the patio while she worked in the kitchen. The open doors created an open kitchen plan that worked even in a small space. During the colder months, Marina planned to use heat lamps outside. With the weather in Summer Beach, there weren't many days that people couldn't sit outside and enjoy the ocean view.

Ivy glanced outside. "More people are arriving. Can you spare a few minutes to greet guests?"

"That's the plan," Marina said. "We're starting with the cold appetizers. After a little while, I'll return to the kitchen, and we'll start sending out the hot appetizers and entrees."

"Sounds very well organized," Ivy said.

"Marina is the best," Kai said. "Let's all go out onto the patio."

Ginger angled her head. "Go on. You're the star this evening. Everyone wants to congratulate you."

"I'll come back as soon as I can," Marina said as she cleaned up.

Ginger tapped the plan for the evening posted above the work area. "Don't worry. I have it all here in case you're delayed." She pressed her cheek to Marina's. "I want you to know how proud I am of you for recreating your life. And I think my old friend Julia would be impressed with what you've done here, too. Especially with her *coq au vin*."

Marina put her arm around Ginger. "This is as much your

night as mine. You inspired my love for cooking. Come with me, and let's greet everyone."

"As you wish, my dear." Ginger took off her jacket with a flourish and hooked arms with Marina.

Kai grinned. "It's showtime." Humming a tune, she followed them onto the patio, where more people were arriving, and then took up her station to dispense icy Italian sodas, sparkling water, and other libations.

The party was underway.

"Welcome, everyone," Marina called out, and her friends and family broke out in applause. She greeted Poppy, who was Ivy and Shelly's niece, and some of their long term local guests from the inn. Imani Jones ran the local floral stand, and with her was Clark Clarkson, the tall, barrel-chested police chief.

Marina recognized him at once. She had encountered Chief Clarkson the first night she arrived unannounced in Summer Beach and was trying to get into her grandmother's cottage.

Gilda, who wrote magazine articles, arrived with her shivering Chihuahua, Pixie, tucked into a backpack fashioned for her.

People were exclaiming over the new cafe concept and lining up to sample the food. Leilani and Roy, proprietors of the Hidden Garden, arrived with Jen and George, a couple who ran the hardware shop, Nailed It. Marina chatted with Celia and Tyler, a young retired tech couple from the Bay area who supported the local schools' music programs.

"This is so delicious," Celia said, referring to the macadamia nut hummus with sliced vegetables and home-made seeded bread rounds. "I've never had hummus prepared like this."

"I'm so glad you like it," Marina said, feeling relieved. She'd fused it with a touch of powdered coconut for a Polynesian accent. "I love combining the fresh produce of Southern

California with Hawaiian and Asian flavors, along with Mexican, Spanish, Italian, and French accents."

"That's what sets California cuisine apart," Celia agreed. "We have so many people from different cultures who built this state. My great-great-great grandmother's family moved from China in the 1850s. Since we moved to Summer Beach, we've missed the fusion of flavors we enjoyed at restaurants in San Francisco. Tyler and I are so glad you've opened this cafe. We'll spend a lot of time here."

Marina valued the feedback. "You're always welcome."

Heather had crafted signage that sat beside each dish, and as she and Ethan circulated with platters, they explained each dish to guests.

Watching her children filled Marina with pride. They had always been good, hard-working kids eager to help. Like many, they'd had their share of teenaged angst, but they were both discovering what they loved now.

"If I had to be evicted, I'm glad it was for a good cause."

Marina turned around. "Jack, you made it." Her heart quickened, but she corralled her feelings.

"How could I miss your grand opening?" He grinned at her chef's jacket. "That's a nice touch. You look great."

"Ginger and Kai surprised me with several of these. They're wonderful to cook in. Would you like to see how the guest cottage looks now?"

Jack took a moment to respond. "I'd like that very much."

"Come this way," she said, guiding him to the open doors of the private dining room she and Heather had made out of the old bedroom. "It's less crowded if we go in through the back." People had gathered in front of the open kitchen area.

As they stepped inside, Jack's face lit. "Wow," he said, gazing around. "What a jewel box of a place. You did all this?"

"Heather and Brooke helped." Besides Ivy's painting and the white latticework illuminated with fairy lights, Marina had also asked Axe to hang an antique chandelier made of hand-blown crystal shells she'd found at an antique shop in the village, Antique Times. One of the owners, Nan, whom Marina had met at City Hall, had cleaned it up for her. The light fixture had been retrieved from an old beach cottage the new owners were renovating. Marina loved it. With the lights dimmed, the chandelier created such a romantic ambiance. In the corners, parlor palms rustled in the gentle breeze. She'd also found a set of chairs that she'd white-washed and reupholstered with deep coral velvet using a staple gun.

"This is our private dining area for parties or honeymooners."

"Quite a change from the old bedroom. Is the old safe still in the closet?"

She laughed. "That beast isn't going anywhere. It would take a forklift to move it. Now, wait until you see the new kitchen." Out of habit, she held out her hand before she could stop herself.

Jack caught it.

As their fingers touched, Marina felt a surge of energy so strong pass between them that she sucked in a breath and stared at him.

Jack met her gaze. "We're still friends."

Numbly, she nodded and led him toward the kitchen.

Ginger turned around, and Marina saw her gaze dip slightly to their hands. Quickly, Marina slipped her fingers from his. He yielded, although something deep inside of her immediately registered the loss.

"Jack wants to see the kitchen," she said, perhaps a shade too brightly. "We expanded the kitchen into the old dining area and added a chef's table in the living room. Axe opened up that wall with new doors to the patios, and then there are the new appliances, and—"

"Maybe Jack would like something to eat," Ginger cut in, saving Marina from babbling on about the obvious.

Jack grinned. "I've been looking forward to this."

Marina felt her face warm as Ginger prepared a plate for him. "Have a seat."

Ginger tapped the schedule. "I'm caramelizing Maui onions."

That was Marina's cue. Turning to the refrigerator, she pulled out a pre-prepared tray of savory palmiers. She'd used puff pastry dough, or *pâte feuilletée*, curling it into the palmier shape. The tray went into an oven, and while that baked, she mixed softened brie and caraway in one bowl and set it aside.

Next, Marina fired a burner, and in a skillet, she swirled olive oil and added mushrooms and spices. While that simmered, she brought out the tray of palmiers and slid half of them onto a serving platter.

She scooped a mixture of softened brie with caraway into the two ovals and topped it with Ginger's steaming caramelized onions. She reserved a few for Jack, Heather, and Ethan.

"Shall I drain the mushrooms?" Ginger asked.

"Thanks," Marina replied. Using the rest of the warm palmiers, she filled the hollows with the savory mushrooms and caramelized onions. Stepping back, she rang a shiny bell that hung overhead—the signal for a ready order.

Heather rushed into the kitchen. "These look yummy, Mom."

"Thanks, sweetie. Mushrooms on the left, brie on the right." Marina put a pair of palmiers on Jack's plate. "And here you are. *Bon appétit.*"

"My compliments to the chef," he said.

Laughing, Marina said, "You're supposed to say that after you taste the food."

"Depends on what he's complimenting you about," Ginger said. "Am I right?"

Jack chuckled. "Exactly."

"Stop that, you two." Marina fanned her face as she felt

herself blush. "Oh, it's getting hot in here." She pushed an open window a little wider.

Next, Marina broiled vegetable kebobs that Ginger prepared similar to those for the yacht dinner. After that, Ginger suggested they circulate for a few minutes.

"You have time on the schedule," Ginger said. "I see a lot of new faces here."

"If you'll excuse us," Marina said to Jack. Bennett and Mitch had joined him at the table, so she didn't feel bad about leaving him alone.

Marina was eager to get away from him. Not because she didn't enjoy his company, but because she did. And that was going nowhere. Why was he suddenly acting like they were the best of friends? She shook her head. *Men.* He also made her a little nervous, and she would have to concentrate more on the upcoming entrees and sides.

As Ginger began to greet old friends she'd invited, Marina went to check on Kai. "How's it going?"

Kai beamed. "What a fabulous crowd. They love the Italian sodas you ordered, but I'll tell you what's been really popular." She had a mischievous twinkle in her eye.

"What else did we have?"

"Exactly," Kai said, holding up a finger. "Remember the fruit and yogurt I'd bought? Well, I thought, what if I whipped it up and made smoothies—because what's a beach cafe without smoothies? And then I ran out of yogurt, so I switched to ice cream."

Beside Kai sat a blender and small paper cups of smoothies. Marina couldn't help but laugh as she remembered the smoothie stand that Kai had set up in front of the cottage for a couple of summers to earn extra money.

"Seems all my old favorite recipes are still as good as they were." Kai handed her one. "Hope you don't mind."

"I think it's a great idea. We'll call them Kai's Coolers."

She sipped a frothy mixture that had a creamy scoop of ice cream in it. "You used the Italian soda and ice cream?"

"Sort of like a fancy root beer float. I think it would make a great dessert, too. You could add berries."

Marina's mind was whirring with new ideas. She wrapped an arm around her sister. "Have I told you lately how much I love you?"

"Aw, ditto, kiddo," Kai replied, using one of Marina's sayings when Kai was young.

Marina laughed. "So, have you seen Axe?"

Kai angled her chin to the right. "We chatted about the new theatre, and he introduced me to Carol Reston."

At the mention of the legendary, Grammy-award winning singer, Marina glanced around. "She's *here*?"

"Shh, don't sound so starstruck. She's talking to Ginger. Axe has done a lot of work at their estate on the ridgetop."

Carol Reston at my cafe. Marina shook her head in amazement.

"You haven't asked what Axe and I talked about," Kai said. She pursed her lips as if her secret would escape.

Marina nudged her. "You'd better tell me."

"After I met Carol, he told me that she really liked me. You won't believe it, but she saw one of my shows in Seattle last year, and…" Kai paused dramatically. "She actually remembered my performance!"

"Oh, Kai. I'm so happy for you." Marina knew how much that meant to Kai.

"That's not all. Axe wants to meet tomorrow. He and Carol are going to make an offer to me." Kai looked like she was about to explode with happiness.

"To perform at the theatre?"

"Well, probably, yes. But to help them organize, cast, and promote the new theater. Can you imagine? I'll be a co-producer." She flicked her hand. "Take that, Dmitri."

Marina hugged her. "You deserve it. Go get your dream, Kai."

"I think I might be," she said with a little smile. "Who knew it could be so close?"

While Marina didn't ask about Axe, she didn't have to.

"Guess who else arrived?" Kai lifted her chin toward the front, where Chip and the boys were standing awkwardly.

"I'll greet them," Marina said. Chip seemed to have made an effort to look nice. The boys' clothes looked slightly wrinkled, but this was a beach cafe.

"Wait. Brooke is going over there."

Marina and Kai watched as Brooke took Chip's hand, and the boys hugged her. This was the first time Brooke had seen them in almost two weeks. They all shed a few tears, and Brooke seemed happy.

"Brooke says they're starting marriage counseling this week," Kai said. "Do you think they'll work things out?"

"I hope so," Marina replied, concerned for their middle sister. "There's a lot of love there. It just got buried under the demands of their lives." Brooke had told her she wasn't in a hurry to return until Chip realized she was his partner, not his housekeeper.

A guest picked up a smoothie and asked a question, so Marina moved on. There were so many guests she wanted to greet before she returned to the kitchen.

"Everything is magnificent," Nan said as Marina approached. The City Hall receptionist and Antique Times partner had a plate full of Marina's cooking, and she was clearly relishing it. "I have a lot of people who are dying to meet you."

"I'd love that," Marina replied.

Nan stopped an attractive younger couple. "I'd like you to meet Megan and Josh Calloway. They just bought a home within walking distance of here. Megan is working on the documentary of Amelia Erickson, the former owner of the Seabreeze Inn, or Las Brisas del Mar, as it was known then."

"Ivy had told me all about that," Marina said, greeting them. They chatted a little while before Marina directed them to the vegetarian options on their request.

As the sun was setting, a rosy hue settled on the patio. Kai flicked on the string of lights overhead, immediately creating a cozy atmosphere. They'd chosen well, Marina thought, satisfied with the look.

Before returning to the kitchen, she stopped to say hello to Denise and John. Leo and Samantha were at Kai's station, sampling the Italian soda floats. Vanessa sat at the reserved table, sipping a broth that Marina had asked Heather to deliver to her. Leo brought one of Kai's creamy shakes to her, and she hugged him and kissed him on the cheek. Marina's heart ached for them.

On her way back to the kitchen, she greeted Jim Boz, the head of the Summer Beach planning department, who'd guided her in fulfilling the requirements needed to open.

"You've pulled this together in record time," Boz remarked. "Beautifully, too. Congratulations."

"I appreciate your help, even though I might have had a moment of exasperation at all the red tape. Although it wasn't that bad, and I understand the reason for it all."

Boz chuckled. "I get that a lot. This sure makes up for it."

Ginger gestured to her, and Marina joined her.

"Since you and Ivy are such good friends now, I'd like to introduce her parents, Carlotta and Sterling." Ginger made the introduction to an artistic-looking older couple. Ivy had told her that they were preparing to take a voyage around the world.

"What a pleasure," Marina said. "Are you enjoying everything?"

"The shrimp with cilantro and avocado dip is marvelous,"

Carlotta said, waving an arm full of hand-painted wooden bangles. "It reminds me of a sauce my mother used to make."

"I see you've met our parents," Ivy said as she joined the group with her sister Shelly.

Marina chatted for a while, and then Ginger said, "We have some special main courses that we're going to prepare next."

They excused themselves and made their way back to the kitchen. "You're a hit," Ginger whispered.

"With your help," Marina replied.

Jack was still at the chef's table. Marina couldn't very well run him out of the kitchen, especially when Leo joined him. Marina flexed her jaw. She didn't have time to think about Jack. Putting on her emotional blinders, she went back to work.

She and Ginger plated their *coq au vin*, and sent it out with a toast to Julia Child. Next, they moved on to Marina's shrimp and pesto pizza. Leo snagged the first piece, and Marina saw that it was just as popular as the lobster pizza had been. The lobster version would be a chef's special, Marina decided.

Marina rang the bell when the kalbi and vegetarian sliders were ready and then moved on to the baked lasagna that had been baking in the old O'Keefe & Merritt oven indoors. She'd covered all the bases: beef, chicken, seafood, pasta, and vegetarian options for entrees. She'd also thought about having a seafood grille evening once a week. Another restaurant specialized in steaks. Her niche would be beach fare for leisurely dining. She couldn't be everything to everyone, but she would serve light fare in the afternoon, with heartier entrees in the evening.

She was going to be very busy. At least, she hoped she would be.

"Final round," Marina said. "Ginger, why don't you sit this one out. Kai can help me with the rest."

"I'll take you up on that, my dear. I'll send Kai in."

Just then, the music grew louder. A few moments later, Kai swayed into the kitchen, snapping her fingers. "You called?"

"Help me with these desserts. I forgot the whipped cream."

"No problem."

"Add a couple of shakes of cinnamon, too." Marina stopped. "Are people dancing out there?"

"That's the idea. It is a party," Kai added with a wink.

Leo peeked over the counter. "What's for dessert?"

Marina laced her fingers and leaned across the counter. "Do you like ice cream?"

Leo's eyes brightened, and he nodded.

"Well, then, I think you'll be happy. I have homemade cookies 'n cream. With gooey chocolate brownies."

"Yum," Leo said. "I'll tell Samantha."

As he darted away, Jack laughed. "Remember when we used to get that excited over ice cream?"

Marina arched an eyebrow. "You haven't had my home-made ice cream."

"Sounds like a threat," Jack said, grinning.

Marina shook her head. She supposed she was going to have to get used to Jack being around. Good friends, that's all he wanted. Maybe he was just naturally flirtatious. After all, she hadn't known him that long.

Marina arranged the cheesecake and carrot cake squares onto another serving platter and then she brought out chilled fruit cups. She scooped a small amount of whipped cream over strawberries, blueberries, and raspberries. Not everyone in a bikini wanted a calorie-laden dessert.

"Party time," Kai said as she rang the bell.

On the patio, a lot of the young people were dancing. Marina recognized Ivy's daughter, Misty, along with Imani's son, Jamir. Marina was sure that Kai would be out there soon, along with the twins and their friends.

Heather and Ethan appeared for the desserts. "Hope you saved some for us," Ethan said.

"You know I did," Marina said, gesturing toward the kitchen. "It's in the refrigerator whenever you're ready."

"Thanks, Mom," Ethan said.

"At last." Marina stepped out of the kitchen and sank onto a bench at the long chef's table. Jack had lit a fire in the fireplace, and he poured a glass of red wine for her.

"Where did this come from?" she asked.

Jack nodded toward Ginger, who sat across from Jack. "Part of your grandmother's special reserve."

"It was one of Julia's favorites," Ginger said. "I thought this was the right time to bring it out."

Marina swirled the silky red wine and inhaled its dusky aroma. "This smells delicious."

"Tastes even better," Ginger said, touching her glass to Marina's.

"I couldn't have done this without you," Marina said. "Letting me convert the guest cottage, being my sous-chef, and the best grandmother in the world."

Ginger clasped her hand and kissed the back of it. "You've helped me realize one of my dreams, too."

Jack joined in. "Looks like you've found your place here in Summer Beach."

"I have." In many ways, Marina thought. Now the real work would begin. Filling the cafe every day might be challenging, especially with the increased competition from the neighboring community. But that was for another day. Tonight, she wanted to enjoy the moment.

She tapped Jack's glass. "To Summer Beach." Somehow, as much as he disturbed her, it seemed only right that he was here.

15

"Is that the house?" Jack asked Bennett as his friend pulled his SUV in front of an old beach house on a rise. "There's no sign."

"It's not officially on the market," Bennett replied.

Bennett had already shown him a few properties, but none of them were quite what Jack had in mind. He didn't need much space for himself, but he had to think about Leo and Scout now. A house within walking distance of Leo's school was important to Jack. He preferred to be close to the beach and the village, too. For that reason, he had ruled out properties on the ridgetop.

"Since you said you were good at repairs, I thought you might want to look at this one. Some might consider this a tear-down, but that would be incongruent in this neighborhood. And it's a historic district. But it had great bones, even if the décor is a little…unusual."

Jack laughed. "You sure know how to lower a client's expectations."

"Just giving it to you straight, buddy." Bennett jingled his keys.

"So what's the story on it?"

"It belongs to the father of one of my clients. This house has been his home for most of his life, but he is moving in with his son and his family. So they're willing to rent it until they figure out what to do with it. If you like it, you could probably make an offer to buy it later."

"Sounds like you left something out."

Bennett chuckled. "The owner was quite a well-known artist."

Jack wondered what Bennett meant by that. "Maybe I could do something with it."

"It's a good neighborhood," Bennett said. "My sister and her husband live right behind this house. Their son Logan will be in the same grade with Leo in the fall."

Another friend for Leo would be good, Jack thought. As they walked up the steps, he considered his need for urgency. Vanessa's condition could worsen at any time, so Jack had to be prepared to take Leo on short notice. Even if Vanessa's condition improved by some miracle, he would still need to provide a home for Leo. Scout needed a backyard, and Jack could put in a garden. He'd love a view of the ocean, too.

However, Jack had to put his son's needs first. His life had shifted quickly, but he was growing to like it. For the first time in his life, he had others to look out for. More than that, he wanted to.

Jack still couldn't get Marina out of his mind, and he hoped he hadn't made a fool of himself at her opening party. After he'd caught her hand as she was showing him the changes she'd made to the guest cottage, he'd regretted it. He shouldn't send her mixed messages, but it was hard to conceal his feeling for her.

Bennett opened the door and stepped inside. Immediately, Jack saw what Bennett meant. In the living room, a seascape mural covered one wall. A bank of windows opened out to a view of the ocean, and an open-beamed ceiling slanted up to the middle of the house, making it seem larger than it was.

"I like it," Jack said, walking around to view the painting. "It's well done, and it certainly has the beach vibe going."

Bennett laughed. "Indeed it does."

A fireplace made of smooth, natural white stones flanked one wall. The wooden floors were worn, but he could clean those or throw rugs over them. "It's got possibilities. Let's see the rest of it."

They made their way to the kitchen, where the owner had painted a palm tree on a wall where a table had probably stood. Large and old-fashioned, the kitchen had plenty of counter space, an old stove similar to the one in Ginger's kitchen, and a deep single-basin sink.

"You've got the original farmhouse sink that is so popular today," Bennett said. "The appliances are old, but they work fine." He motioned to the old stove. "Funny thing is, as old as this stove is, it looks like new. They didn't cook much."

Jack ran his hand over the dark blue enamel. "That's the way I lived in New York. Take-out was easy, and the kitchens were small."

"The owner went to the deli every day for a big breakfast and paid a neighbor woman to bring him a home-cooked meal in the evening. If she didn't cook, he went out. He always maintained that cooking interfered with his creativity. Everyone around here knows him."

Jack rocked on his heels as he gazed around. "This would do." Bennett was right. It had good bones.

They continued into a bedroom. On one wall, an underwater scene featured a scuba diver in vintage gear swimming with schools of colorful fish, while an octopus perched on a rock, and a lobster waved.

Jack smiled. "Leo might really like this."

"This was the son's bedroom. Today, he's an oceanographer."

"Let's see the master bedroom," Jack said. They walked through the hallway, their heels echoing as they went. Bennett opened the door.

The bedroom was larger than Jack expected. It had plenty of room for a large bed and included a sitting area with a second fireplace. "Quite nice," Jack said.

"You might notice this room doesn't have a mural," Bennett said.

"Why is that? "

"The owner said he was waiting for just the right inspiration. But he could never decide. So in this one, the decor is your choice."

Jack stepped through an adjoining doorway into a sunroom, which looked like it had been added onto the house.

"What great light," Jack said, running his hand over the old wavy glass panes. "I could do a lot with this room."

He envisioned setting up his workspace here. On one side, he could see clear out to the ocean. On the other side, he had a view of the backyard. He imagined Leo and Scout playing outside. He'd have to put protection around his garden, which could go in a sunny spot he spied.

Except for helping Marina replant Ginger's garden after Scout had torn it up, he hadn't had a garden—or any piece of land, for that matter—since he'd left his family's farm in Texas.

"This will be quite a change from my apartment in New York," Jack said. "A good change, but not one I saw coming."

They checked out the bathrooms, which were serviceable if a little dated. Jack didn't mind. The master bath had a large tub and a separate shower. Tiny black-and-white hexagonal tile covered the floor. Another similar bathroom in the hallway would work for Leo.

"There's another unit over the garage that the owner also used as a work and storage space. It's two rooms with a bath and kitchenette." They tromped up the stairs over the garage to look at the unit.

A bank of windows opened onto another expansive view of the ocean. In that room, paint splatters covered the wooden floors, and in the other room, an old desk still stood in one corner, and a kitchenette lined another wall.

"I probably won't use the space back here," Jack said.

"You could sublet this rear unit."

"It needs work."

Bennett shook his head. "Surfers don't care about paint on the floor."

They walked back to Bennett's SUV, and Jack looked at the front of the house again. "Are they ready to lease it now?"

"It could be yours by the weekend. Want me to draw up an offer?"

Jack blinked. This was really happening. He laughed to himself. He didn't even have any furniture. His apartment in New York was sublet to a colleague, though Jack didn't have much there in terms of personal effects. All these years, he'd traveled light. In his line of work, he was always ready to pack a bag and move on. Too much stuff only weighed him down.

"I'm not trying to rush you, but houses like this don't come up that often. When they do, they go fast. Especially when the price is right."

"It's a big step." Jack rocked back and forth on his heels.

"Take your time," Bennett said.

They stepped into the SUV. As Bennett pulled away, Jack stared after the house. Next door, he saw a girl and a boy about Jack's age. They waved at him, and Jack held up his hand in response.

"Do you know who lives next door?" Jack asked.

"A nice couple. They have a shop in town, and those are their children. They're close to Leo's age." Bennett waved at them, too.

Jack blew out a breath. "On second thought, it's perfect."

"Good. I've got the lease with me. How about lunch?"

"Your choice," Jack replied. They were talking about the house, so Jack wasn't paying attention to where they were going until Bennett pulled in front of the Coral Cafe.

"It's good to patronize the new businesses in town." Bennett glanced around at the sparsely filled patio. "I'm surprised there aren't more people here. I thought Marina had a great opening."

"She mentioned that the fast-food chains in the next community are pretty competitive."

"I know they're convenient," Bennett said, shaking his head. "I take some heat from some residents, but fast-food and chain restaurants would put a lot of our local restaurants out of business. Not only does that hurt those business owners, but it destroys the character of the community over time. Many local businesses in Summer Beach rely on tourist traffic. That's why we don't allow chains in Summer Beach. Being different and offering a unique experience is what brings people here. And our restaurants offer better food at a comparable value."

Jack thought of the places he often visited just because he liked certain restaurants. Bennett had a point, and he was glad the mayor was standing up for individuality and small businesses. "Better for people to own a restaurant than slinging hamburgers for a big chain, I suppose."

Bennett nodded. "And they source locally, rather than from some out-of-state or out-of-country corporation, which in turn keeps money in the community. We take the long view around here."

As they walked to the patio, Ginger greeted them. "Well, if it isn't two of my favorite men. Do have a seat, and I'll have Heather take care of you." She showed them to a table.

"Is Marina cooking?" Jack asked.

"She sure is. I'll tell her you're here and asking for her."

Jack held up his hand to tell her that wasn't necessary, but she'd already gone to tell Marina. "Ah, gee." He ran a hand over his face.

"Ginger's a real matchmaker," Bennett said, smiling. After pausing, he asked quietly, "Is there something going on between you and Marina?"

Torn between his head and his heart, Jack pondered that question for a moment. "We had a moment, but I messed up by not following up. I like her a lot, but the timing is all wrong. What with caring for Leo and Vanessa's fragile health, I just don't see how it's possible."

"Vanessa seems to care a lot for you, too," Bennett said.

Jack valued Bennett's friendship. There weren't many men that Jack could really talk to, even though he had a lot of acquaintances. Men didn't share personal problems as women did, but Jack wished they would. Many men were concerned about keeping up appearances and afraid to show any sign of weaknesses.

But Bennett had shared the experience of losing his young, pregnant wife a decade ago. Jack figured that gave him a different perspective than most. He was also seeing Ivy, Marina's old friend from her teenage years here in Summer Beach.

"Vanessa and I covered some of the same stories for different newspapers." Jack told him the story and the situation they'd found themselves in. "I'm not proud of that, but I'm committed to being a father now. I wish she'd told me earlier."

He'd vacillated between emotions—from doubt and fear to anger at Vanessa for failing to tell him he had a son. Yet, in her condition, his anger had been transmuted into compassion.

"Vanessa appears to have a strong will."

"She does. But she is also extremely realistic. Pragmatic. She cares about other people's feelings, which is why she kept her pregnancy from me. For her parent's sake."

"You don't seem to be such a bad guy," Bennett said with a trace of laughter. "Or maybe you changed."

Jack stroked his stubbled chin. "Changed, for sure."

"Don't we all."

Absently, Jack folded his napkin into triangles as he thought. "I probably got a little too personal with Marina at the opening party. Tried to hold her hand. I know, I know, that seems fairly innocuous—"

"Not to a woman."

"And I don't want to lead her on. It just happened so naturally, I wasn't even thinking about it, but when we touched…" Jack raked a hand through his hair. "It's Leo I'm thinking about. I don't hold onto relationships with women very well. If he transfers affection to Marina after Vanessa…you know…that would be pretty rough on the little guy."

"Is there anything I can do?"

Jack wagged his head. "Try not to let me make a fool of myself around Marina. I know that's hard."

Bennett glanced around. "I didn't realize all this. Maybe we should have gone somewhere else."

"No, this is fine. I want to give her business. I just don't want it to seem like I have any interest in her."

"Even though you do."

"Right." Jack grinned. "I knew you'd understand."

Bennett chuckled and bumped fists with Jack. "Actually, I do."

Someone that Bennett knew stopped by the table, and Bennett introduced them. While the two men were talking about city business, Jack gazed out toward the ocean. The cafe had a clear view of the marina. *Princess Anne* was still docked.

After the other man left, Jack lifted his chin toward the yacht. "Why do you suppose they're still here?"

"Couldn't say. Enjoying their time here, I suppose."

Jack lowered his voice, even though the cafe wasn't

crowded. "You haven't heard anything unusual about that couple? Charles and Anne?"

"Should we be concerned?"

Jack felt a little foolish. "I don't know. This seems like an unusual port for them to hang out at."

"They're friends with Carol and Hal, as I understand."

Jack shook his head. "They barely know them."

"Do you smell a story there?" Bennett asked.

"Or something," Jack replied. They spoke a little more, and then Heather approached the table.

"Welcome to the Coral Cafe. How about starting with one of our summer smoothies?" Heather handed each of them a menu. "This is our starter menu, and we'd love to have your feedback about what else you'd like to see on the menu—or if there's something you don't like. You can tell me, and I promise I won't tell my mom where it came from."

Jack arched an eyebrow. "Totally anonymous?"

"Totally." Heather nodded. "We want to give our customers what they want. Within reason, as Ginger and Mom say."

Bennett chuckled. "Spoken like a true entrepreneur."

"I'd like to start a business someday, too."

"Your mom is a real inspiration to you, isn't she?" Jack asked.

"You have no idea. She brought us up by herself. I didn't understand what all that meant until I went to college and had to do everything myself." She tapped her pencil on a pad of paper. "So, what kind of smoothie can I get started for you?"

Jack glanced at the list. "I think it's a peachy kind of day."

"Strawberry for me," Bennett said.

"Oh, and my mom said that the salads are good and pretty filling, but unless you're on a diet, which you're probably not —am I right?—then you'll also want to order something more substantial. A salad and something like the sliders would be good. Unless you're vegan. Oh, I forgot the vegan list, but I can get that for you. Some of my guy friends don't eat much salad, but my mom says it's really important for digestion. Sorry, what kind of shakes did you want? I meant smoothies."

Heather made a face; clearly, she was a little embarrassed. "Mom told me not to talk too much, but since I know Jack, I'm sure you don't mind. And Ginger says Bennett is the best-looking mayor Summer Beach has ever had, and she hopes you stay around a long time because you also know what you're doing at City Hall." She stopped and bit her lip. "I said too much, didn't I? This is my first day. I'm trying to do this right, but I've never waited tables before."

Jack laughed as Bennett's face grew pink, too. "Heather, you're doing great. Though you might want to keep some of that to yourself. You know, the part about the mayor. I hear he's kind of shy. And, that's peach and strawberry smoothies."

"Oh, right." She scribbled the order on her pad and then leaned in. "I hope you don't think I'm a total airhead. I'm just a little nervous."

"Your mom has been bragging about your grades," Jack said, assuring her.

Heather beamed. "Thanks, I'll be right back."

"Remember being that age?" Bennett asked.

"Sure do. She seems painfully honest. Reminds me of her mother." Jack could see Marina in the kitchen now, and he tried not to stare.

"About that lease," Bennett said. "We can also include an option to buy if you'd like." He brought out the documents he'd carried in with him, and the two men went to work on them. As Jack looked through papers and signed the application to rent, Bennett tapped his pen on the table.

"One thing I've learned about women—the right ones that you want to build a life with—is that you have to have patience."

"Are you talking about Ivy?"

Bennett grinned. "She's the one for me. Now, I don't know if Marina is the one for you, but you two have a lot in common, besides having worked in news media. Play the long game, my friend. You won't be sorry. And who knows? That house is big enough for a family. You'll have plenty of time to renovate it."

Jack thought about Bennet's advice. "Patience was never my strong suit. In my line of work, you had to trust your gut and go for the story when the opportunity was right. But patience and research always brought me my best stories."

"And a Pulitzer to prove it, I've heard."

Jack chuckled. "There won't be any more of those, but yeah. That's how I did it."

"You might not get any awards in this phase of your life, but it will be plenty rewarding."

"Do you ever miss not having kids?"

"You met my nephew Logan at the party. He's my boy as much as he belongs to my sister Kendra and her husband Dave. They just don't know it. But Logan and I are pretty close. He and Leo were getting along well at the opening party."

Jack watched Heather bring their order from the kitchen, where he could see Marina. She leaned out and waved to him, and Jack waved back.

Bennett had a lot of good advice for him to consider. *Patience.* Never one of his virtues, but maybe it was time to start practicing it.

When they finished lunch, Bennett dropped Jack off at the inn as he had other meetings at City Hall.

After taking Scout for a walk, Jack grabbed his phone and wireless earbuds and eased onto a chaise lounge on the terrace. He found some relaxing music and closed his eyes.

The sun was warm, and he'd been up early for a jog on the beach. A short nap in the sun, followed by a swim, was just what he needed to revive him before joining Leo for supper at the beach house with Vanessa and her friends.

He had a lot on his mind, but having a house would lessen a lot of his concerns. Soon, Leo would have a room and another place to call home. Bennett promised to let him know as soon as the owner accepted the lease offer.

At some point, Jack needed to contact his boss, who expected him back at work after his sabbatical in a few months. He could shift to freelancing in investigative journalism, which didn't include benefits, but that could help him ease the transition to his new life. The fact was that he enjoyed the intellectual stimulation. Sketching and assisting Ginger was pure pleasure. He would earn royalties, but those would fluctuate depending on book sales.

As Jack mulled over his future, he dozed off.

Muffled voices floated toward him on the ocean breeze. One of his headphones clicked off. He had forgotten to charge the battery. A few minutes later, the other ran out of juice, too. Sounds rose in the air.

Without opening his eyes, he shifted his hand.

"Shh, he moved."

"He can't hear us. Headphones."

"All the same…"

Jack stilled his hand. Immediately, his professional training kicked in. He was attuned to details. *A man. A woman. Older.* Probably embarrassed over some sort of domestic argument. He relaxed, but his interest was piqued. What didn't they want him to hear?

The couple began to talk again in low voices. In another language.

Russian.

The sea breeze carried those voices, whirled them under the eaves of the old house, and swept them toward him.

Jack had taken a few classes in college, hoping to gain assignments in Russia someday. He had, but his proficiency wasn't as high as it should have been. Listening, he picked out words.

When the couple got up to leave, Jack slit an eye. *Charles and Anne.* They probably hadn't seen him at first. And they weren't certainly weren't stopping to say hello.

16

*M*arina sat at the dining room table with her laptop computer, entering the first week's revenue and expense figures into a spreadsheet. She frowned and bit her lip. Revenue wasn't as high as she would have liked.

She thought about the levers she had to control costs. Reduce menu size, save on food costs. She would say personnel, but Heather was working for very little, and Ginger was donating her time. Marina had to attract more customers. Many locals were supporting her, and she was thankful for that.

The kitchen door slammed, and Ginger arrived home from her hike. "I would ask how you're doing, but your face is telling me everything."

Marina drew her hands over her face. "I'm not making any money yet."

"It's usually hard in the beginning. Anything I can do?"

"Wave a magic wand?"

Ginger eased into a chair beside her. "You'll figure it out. Tell me about your marketing plan."

"My ad budget is pretty slim, and I plan to keep plowing profits back in to build the business."

"When I say marketing, I mean other things. Your mailing list, social media. How is the Taste of Summer Beach going?"

"I found a clear calendar date at City Hall, and I've started contacting restaurant owners in town. But we need a lot of marketing outreach to make that successful, too. I just don't have time to do everything. Or the money to pay someone to do it."

"This event would benefit a lot of people. Didn't you think about this when you decided on the project?"

"I did. But I don't have time to do everything I'd thought about."

"So, barter with someone. Everyone has to eat."

Marina looked up from her spreadsheet. "Why didn't I think about that?"

"Because you're too close to the problem and a little over-whelmed."

"Brilliant. All I need is a hungry marketing pro. Literally." She thought about it for a moment. "And I know just who to call. Thanks for the advice, Ginger."

She rose from the table. "You would have figured it out. Sometimes we just need shortcuts. My students used to come to me with a math problem, and by the time they'd finished explaining it, they'd come up with the answer themselves."

Marina tapped a number on her phone. "Hi Poppy, it's Marina. We chatted at the opening party. I have an idea that I'd like to talk to you about."

AFTER THE SPARSE LUNCH RUN, Poppy arrived at the Coral Cafe, and Marina was ready to greet her.

"Hi Marina," Poppy said. "I'm so glad you called. And yes, I'm starving."

"Come into the kitchen. I can make whatever you want."

"That pesto-shrimp pizza you served at the party was delicious."

"Coming right up." Marina asked Heather to watch the front while she spoke to Poppy.

Poppy had a sunny personality, and her long blond hair was pulled back from her fresh-scrubbed face. She looked younger than her years, but Ivy had told her that she had graduated from the University of Southern California and had several private clients in Los Angeles in fashion and design. She was making a name for herself by handling their marketing and publicity. And Ivy told her that Poppy was extremely well-organized and proactive.

While Marina brought out ingredients for the pizza, she began. "As you know, I'm just getting started, so I don't have a lot of free cash available. I can pay you a little, but I can also give you a generous number of free meals here, or cater any event you might want to do. That goes for the Seabreeze Inn, too. Would bartering work for you?"

While watching Marina spread pesto sauce onto the pizza dough, Poppy brought out a notepad. "I can work with you on that. I'd like to have a place to bring clients or pick up dinner."

"I sure appreciate that," Marina said, relieved.

Poppy tapped her pen. "I have a list of bloggers and influencers that I've built up. I can write a press release, take pictures and videos of the cafe, and interview you. We could plan a media lunch and invite people to meet you and ask questions."

"That would be a tremendous help." Marina added her Italian cheese blend and shrimp to the pizza and eased the pizza into the oven. "I'm also putting together a Taste of Summer Beach event, and I have a lot of restaurants here on board. They might kick in something for a budget to promote that event, too. I'll have to ask."

"I can handle both jobs," Poppy said, making a note. "I'll work up a proposal for that, and I'll be kind. I have a couple of major fashion clients in L.A. who are super generous. They make up for passion projects like this."

"What do you think about having the event here?"

Poppy looked around. "Depending on how many restaurants participate, it might not be enough room. How about we host it at the inn? I'll ask Ivy and Shelly, but we have more room, and we had a great turnout for last year's art fair. I think part of the attraction is that people are curious about that old house. Everyone thought it was haunted."

"Is it?"

Poppy laughed. "Only by a friendly apparition, but Ivy will never admit to that."

Marina let out a breath she didn't realize she was holding. "I'd love that, and I think the other restaurant owners would, too."

"I'm on it," Poppy said, adding to her list.

Marina pulled out the pizza, and Poppy pushed aside her notepad. Marina joined her, and as they shared the pizza and a salad, they continued talking about potential participants, the schedule, and other details.

By the time Poppy left, Marina was relieved and excited. She made her way back into the cottage to tell Ginger about her successful meeting.

Tapping on her grandmother's bedroom door, Marina waited, respecting her privacy. While the rest of the cottage was casual beach décor created with rowdy grandchildren and great-grandchildren in mind, Ginger's room was different. It held the memories of a lifetime and reflected her refined taste. Her perfume lingered though, just as Bertrand's library still held the faint scent of his vanilla pipe tobacco.

"Do come in," Ginger said.

After slipping off her shoes, Marina walked over the soft, intricate silk rug that Ginger had bought on a trip from a top

Persian rug dealer. Everything in Ginger's room had a story behind it, usually associated with her travels and her life with Bertrand.

Marina loved the scent of roses that was ever-present in Ginger's room. Her grandmother cut fresh roses from the garden, and when her rosebushes were dormant, she bought others from Imani at the flower stand. A crystal chandelier sparkled overhead in the sunlight. This room had the best ocean view of the entire house.

Ginger's private suite was a window into the lives of Marina's grandparents. Framed photos of the attractive couple with diplomats and heads of state were positioned throughout the bedroom and adjoining sitting area. Needlepoint pillows that Ginger had made with coded phrases sat on a love seat. These had been Ginger's gifts to Bertrand. Some memorialized their love, while others had held a surprise, such as the trip to Capri Ginger had once planned for their anniversary.

Ginger was seated at an antique French desk writing a letter. Removing her half-glasses, she turned around. "From the revised expression on your face, it looks like you have good news."

"Poppy and I just had the best conversation. You were right. She agreed to help with marketing for the cafe and with the Taste of Summer Beach event. She has some marvelous ideas and many connections with travel bloggers."

"Sounds you have a symbiotic relationship with the Seabreeze Inn. You're catering to a similar audience." Ginger patted a chair next to her desk. "Have a seat. I have news for you as well."

Marina sank onto the chair. Ginger sounded serious, and it made her nervous. Her grandmother was a healthy, spirited woman, but she was no longer young. "What is it?"

"I've spoken to a doctor friend of mine."

Marina held her breath.

Ginger saw the expression on her granddaughter's face. "Relax. This isn't about me. I asked her to check around on Vanessa's condition."

A sense of relief filled her. "And?"

Ginger took her hand. "She discovered research is being conducted on Vanessa's very rare condition in Europe. It looks quite promising. And given Vanessa's relative youth, they will reach out to her medical team so that it can be made available to her. If she is a viable candidate, they would like for her to be part of their study. The treatment is still in the experimental stage, but thus far, results have been quite good. Miraculous, in fact."

Marina wrapped her arms around Ginger. "Thank you so much. I think Vanessa will be thrilled to hear this. And Leo…" Marina pressed her hand against her heart as she choked up.

Ginger smiled. "She might never know that you were the one who extended this kindness. Are you all right with that?"

"Of course. I don't need any recognition. I only want to see her live a longer life—for herself and the sake of her son. Even today, the twins miss the father they never knew."

Ginger placed a hand on Marina's knee. "If Vanessa recovers, you must understand that what you've put in motion will impact Jack. Are you prepared to accept those consequences?"

"I don't understand what you're getting at."

"Vanessa appears quite fond of Jack," Ginger mused. "With this new treatment, she may have a very good chance of survival." She chose her words carefully. "Knowing Jack, he might want to do the right thing as he sees it, which could be to reunite with Vanessa for Leo's sake. I know you care for him. Are you prepared for that?"

Marina sucked in a breath. "That will be Jack's decision. And if that is what he decides, then I'll give them my blessing." She blinked back hot tears that rimmed her lashes. "Maybe I'll be a little heartbroken, but I've learned that hearts heal. A wise woman once told me that scar tissue makes the heart tougher and stronger."

Ginger gripped Marina's hands. "I couldn't be prouder of you."

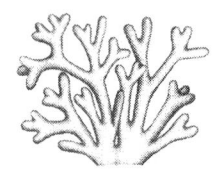

17

*M*arina busied herself with the details of running her business. She made changes to the menu, trimming some items and adding others based on what people were ordering. Beachgoers seemed to like pizzas, salads, burgers and sliders, and appetizers at lunch, while the dinner guests preferred full course meals. She added a list of pizza toppings that people could choose from, along with sweet potato fries with garlic aioli and curly fries. The popular standbys were easy—and easy for people to order. Marina focused on making them well.

To encourage local business, she printed flyers with a complimentary appetizer coupon. She walked from store to store in the village, introducing herself and inviting shop-keepers and employees to the Coral Cafe. Nan Ainsworth asked if she'd like to leave extra flyers for their customers, and Marina did. Others allowed her to do that, too.

She enjoyed meeting other shop owners, and they all promised to spread the word about the Taste of Summer Beach, too. If that brought people to the community, then it was good for everyone.

Business picked up steadily, but the numbers still weren't where she wanted them to be.

Carol Reston and her husband Hal came to lunch one day. Marina waited on the legendary singer. Heather was simply too nervous.

"It's so nice to see you again," Marina said, handing them menus. Carol was a petite redhead with a powerful voice. Marina and her sister had grown up listening to her belt out hit after hit. Her husband was an attractive man with silver hair. "Ginger should be back soon, and I'll tell her you're here."

"Ginger is one of my favorite people in the world," Carol said. "Why, the stories she has. She can carry on a conversation at a dinner table with anyone. I once sat her next to a brilliant, though rather reticent, scientist, and do you know that Ginger was familiar with his studies? Who would have thought it? The man left feeling like he'd been the toast of the party. Ginger is simply divine."

"We hear good things about the new event you're organizing," Hal said. "Taste of Summer Beach, right?"

"With more than thirty local restaurants," Marina said with pride. "It's going to be on the grounds of the Seabreeze Inn. We're hoping to draw people to Summer Beach to discover the cuisine. We can make this community a haven for foodies."

"We'd like that," Hal said.

Carol made a face. "I heard the chain restaurants are stealing your business."

"Everyone's, I'm afraid. I'll come back in a few minutes if you'd like to look at the menu."

Hal held up a hand. "We know what we want." He gave Marina their order.

Marina turned to get started in the kitchen, but Carol called her back.

"I just had an idea." Carol's eyes sparkled with excitement.

"You need an A-lister to draw people to the event—and I don't mean me, although I will be there. No, I mean someone in the foodie world. A top chef. Do you know any?"

Marina shook her head. "I know some in San Francisco, but I wouldn't call them top chefs."

Carol drummed her lacquered nails on the table. "Hal, darling, we should call Alain George. He's a dear friend of ours. He cooked for our daughter Victoria's wedding at the Seabreeze Inn after that dreadful fire. We had to move the entire wedding on such short notice. Ivy and Shelly provided a spectacular venue, and the acoustics in that old house are surprisingly good."

Hal looked doubtful. "Dearest, this is short notice for Alain."

"He could be a judge. He'd like that."

"There has to something in it for him."

Carol tapped faster. "I'll think of an angle."

"How about a throw-down like they do on those cooking shows on television?" The words were out of Marina's mouth before she realized the full implication of that. To cook in a competition against a world-class chef? She'd probably end up with another meme of colossal failure.

She bit her lip. Ginger would tell her to stop thinking like that. She lifted her chin. "Alain could choose a dish that he is famous for, and we could all compete. We could film it for social media." Poppy could find someone to take professional videos. They would find the money for that.

"I'll call him," Carol announced. "Alain owes us because I send him so many hungry customers. Besides, he loves to stay with us. It gives him a reason to escape his restaurants."

Marina returned to the kitchen, feeling a little overwhelmed. What had she put in motion? Cooking against a top chef was crazy. But if they could get Alain George to cook, the event could get the media and attendance they needed. It was a long shot, but one worth taking.

Marina was in the kitchen preparing lunch for Carol and Hal when Ginger strolled in. She looked up. "Carol and Hal are here. And you'll never guess who they want to bring to the event?"

"Knowing Carol, it must be an A-lister."

"Chef Alain George."

Ginger's green eyes flared with excitement. "What a marvelous idea."

"And then I suggested a throw-down."

"I'd better speak to them." Ginger hurried toward their table.

Heather sailed into the kitchen carrying a tray. "Mom, I just heard what you said. That would be amazing."

"Fingers crossed. It's pretty short notice."

"That would be so cool. Wait until Ethan hears about this." Heather motioned toward another table. "When you have a minute, your presence is being requested at table number four."

"Who is here?"

"Jack and Leo. And Leo's mom."

"Tell them I'll be there soon."

Marina finished the order for Carol and Hal and sent it out with Heather, who assured her that she could manage now. Marina composed herself and made her way toward table number four.

"It's so good to see you all here," Marina said. She ruffled Leo's hair, and he grinned up at her. Vanessa had more color in her face than Marina recalled, and Jack was beaming. They all looked like they had a secret of some sort.

Vanessa began. "The last time we were here for your party, I couldn't eat much, but it all looked so delicious." Vanessa reached across the table for Jack's hand. "So when I began feeling better, this was the first place I wanted to come."

"I'm so glad to hear that," Marina said. "I'll make anything you want, as long as I have the ingredients in the kitchen." She tried to keep her gaze from Vanessa and Jack's clasped hands.

"You see, we're celebrating," Jack said. "Vanessa's doctor called and told her they had a new experimental treatment that she could begin right away. And now look at her."

"I haven't had this much energy in ages." Vanessa put her arm around Leo. "I was so tired that I could hardly imagine starting a new treatment, but since Leo insisted, how could I not take a chance?" She kissed his forehead, and Leo beamed up at her. "My two men have been here for me."

"That's wonderful news." Marina thought about what Ginger had said and blinked back sudden tears. This was as it should be. Jack and Vanessa and Leo were a family. She swallowed a lump in her throat. "What can I make for you?"

Vanessa laughed softly. "I'm not quite ready for a feast. But if you could manage a chicken broth with tomatoes and avocado and cilantro—a lighter version of tortilla soup—I would love that with a little salsa. And I think I can manage a small mango smoothie. Those look yummy."

"I'm glad your appetite is returning," Marina said, and she meant it. To see Leo looking at his mother with such pure love in his eyes reminded her of Ethan and Heather at that age. Those were among her most precious memories. She had cherished her time with them, knowing all too well that it could be cut short as their father's time had been.

Marina thought of what Ginger had once said. *To live without fear is the bravest act of all.*

She took the rest of their order and hurried back to the kitchen. Thoughts of Jack clouded her mind as she worked, and she brushed errant tears from her cheeks. Ginger had predicted this.

Working more quickly than she probably should have been to keep her mind off Jack, she poured chicken stock into a pan. She brought out sliced tomatoes, an avocado that yielded perfectly to the touch, and a bunch of cilantro, which she placed on a cutting board. Blinking through misty eyes, she picked up her chef's knife and began chopping.

All at once, she bobbled the knife, and she cried out as it slipped from her hand.

Jerking her hand back, she jumped as the knife clattered to the floor. Blood seeped from a long slice along her finger.

Heather rushed into the kitchen. "What happened?"

Marina flipped on the water faucet and held her wounded finger under the warm water to clean it. Blood gushed, and her finger stung. "You know how I like sharp knives."

"Mom, you're crying." Heather rushed to her side.

"It's going to be okay. Just startled me, that's all." She glanced back at the half-finished order. Ginger was with Carol and Hal, and she didn't want to take her away from that discussion.

"Is there something I can do?"

Marina checked the wound. It was deeper than she'd realized. Instantly, she felt light-headed. She applied pressure to stem the rapid bleeding. "Heather, you have to finish this order."

"I'm not sure I know how…"

"I'll walk you through it. I have to clean my finger and keep pressure on it. First, get rid of that cutting board and knife. And all the food on the board. Get the disinfectant and make sure the area is clean. You'll have to start over."

Marina peeked at her finger again. She was fairly certain it would need stitches. But she wanted to make sure that Vanessa's wishes were met. This meal meant a lot to both of them.

Heather could do it.

Step by step, Marina coached Heather through the order. Her daughter had grown up watching her in the kitchen, pitching in on holidays, and making omelets and grilled cheese sandwiches as she grew older.

As Heather was placing the order on a tray, Ginger walked into the kitchen. "Good heavens! What's going on here?"

"Just a little cut, but I've been applying pressure. Heather's got this. Any more customers out there?"

"Don't worry about that—let me see your wound," Ginger commanded. When Marina showed her, Ginger said, "Heather, take your mother to the clinic on Main. She needs stitches right away. I'll look after the cafe." She looked at Heather's tray. "I'll take this out."

Marina wrapped a clean dishtowel around her hand while Heather got the keys to the Mini Cooper.

"Be sure they do a good job because you have an important appearance," Ginger said while they waited for Heather. "You and others from Summer Beach are going to be cooking against Alain George. It's all set. Carol called him and told him it's for charity. With a summer beach theme, the key is to use an ingredient associated with a tropical paradise. I'll explain later. Now go."

18

"Hold on, boy," Jack said to Scout as he turned the key in the door to his new house and stepped inside. *His new home.* It was more than a rental—he had an option to buy and put down roots for the first time in his adult life. He had once dismissed such thoughts of stability, but now, the idea appealed to him. No more chasing the next story or venturing into dangerous territories for the thrill of making it out alive.

He owed this change of heart to Leo and Vanessa.

Scout bounded inside and raced through the house, sniffing every corner. Jack's footsteps echoed in the empty living room. Reaching up, he unhooked a dusty drapery and let it fall to the wooden floor. Dust mites billowed around it.

Through weather-streaked panes, sunlight illuminated the room, and the house seemed to wallow in the welcome sunshine.

"That will warm your old bones," Jack said, running his hand over an old mantle. "Bennett was right. Good bones."

Jack opened the windows to let fresh sea breezes waft through the musty house. He deposited his backpack in the bedroom. When his sublet tenant's term was over at the end of Jack's original six-month sabbatical, he'd return to New York and clean out his place. He'd rented the apartment furnished, so he didn't have much to ship to Summer Beach except for clothes and books.

"Anyone home?" Vanessa and Leo were at the door.

"Hey, Dad," Leo said, slamming into Jack with his usual enthusiasm. "Can I see my new room?"

"Sure can. Come on, kiddo." Jack took Leo's hand.

Jack had planned to pick up Leo, but Vanessa said that she and Denise had booked a spa day for massages and facials. They would drop him off. Vanessa seemed to be improving every day. Although she still had a long way to go, her doctor and medical team were encouraging.

"Wow!" Leo cried. He stopped at the door of his room in amazement. "I can pretend I'm an underwater explorer."

Leo raced to the wall and ran his hands over the old undersea mural. Since the drapes had been closed, the marine-blue and turquoise-green ocean colors were still vibrant. Brightly colored fish appeared to dart between red coal. "It's like the day we went snorkeling. Can we go again, Dad?"

"You bet," Jack said, laughing. "But first, we need to buy a bed for you."

"After we do that, can we go then?"

"Why not?" Almost everything could wait. Jack figured he'd take a day to stroll around Main Street and buy whatever he needed, which wasn't much. A couple of beds, some pillows, sheets, and towels. A coffeepot, a set of dishes, cutlery, and pots, and he'd be good to go. A few bar stools for the tile counter in the kitchen to give them somewhere to sit would work for now.

Jack was more concerned about planting his garden because it was late in the season. He could probably still manage fast-growing tomatoes, peppers, and snap peas if he could buy healthy plants. Luckily, a row of citrus trees lined one side of the property—tangerine, lemon, grapefruit—and on the other side were apricot, plum, and peach trees. A sprawling avocado tree in one corner looked like it would yield all the avocados they could eat, along with leftovers for neighbors.

"We're off," Vanessa called out. "Have fun, you two."

"I'll drop him off after dinner."

"*Adios, mijo,*" Vanessa said, wrapping her arms around Leo. "You be good for Jack. For your father," she added, smiling at Jack.

Before she left, Vanessa hugged Jack. "Thanks for doing this. Leo is so excited to spend more time with you. I'll miss him, though."

Denise rested a hand on Vanessa's thin back. "I'll keep you busy. You have a lot to catch up on."

"Go relax and enjoy yourself," Jack said. He could hardly believe how responsive she'd been to the new drug treatment.

"Dad, can I go in the backyard with Scout?"

"I'll meet you there."

Jack walked Vanessa and Denise out to Denise's car. He opened the door for Vanessa, and after he made sure she was safely inside, he knelt beside her on the curb. "You're looking so good, Vanessa. You won't need any of those documents you had your attorney draw up anymore."

"We'll see, but I appreciate your saying that." Vanessa smiled. "This is the most hope I've had in a long, long time. I still can't believe my doctor discovered this experimental program. It's such a blessing. Especially for Leo."

"And for me. I don't want to lose you, Vanessa. You're the mother of my child. It seems weird to say that."

She laughed. "Did you ever think you would?"

He shook his head. "No way. But I couldn't be happier."

"I hope you are, Jack. I worry that you'll get the itch to take off and travel again."

Jack jerked a thumb toward his van. "That van sleeps four. Plenty of room for Leo and Scout."

"You know what I mean."

"I ducked my share of bullets out there. I'm not pressing my luck. Sitting on my sun porch sketching and helping Ginger bring her children's books to life is all the excitement I want. Except for maybe harvesting a killer tomato crop. I'm a farmer's son at heart, remember?"

A smile brightened her eyes. "I'll see you tonight. Don't let Leo gorge on sweets."

Jack promised, then shut the door and waved as they drove away. He was climbing the steps to the porch when he heard another car. He turned around to see a turquoise Mini-Cooper pull to the curb. His pulse quickened, and he walked to meet Marina.

In her arms, she carried a pizza box. "Thought I'd bring over the traditional moving-in fare."

"You have no idea how good that sounds. Leo is in the backyard with Scout. Come on in."

Marina stepped inside, and her reaction was just as his had been. "This is incredible. Ginger told me about the artist who lived here for years."

Jack detected a whisper of scent from her hair when she turned—like wildflowers. He was so close that he ached to touch her, bury his face in her hair—but he couldn't. He'd promised.

Jack cleared his throat. "Most rooms have murals, and the guest rooms above the garage make you feel like you're inside a Jackson Pollock painting. Paint splatters everywhere." He glanced down at her bandaged hand. "How is your finger? Ginger told me what happened."

"I had a few stitches," she replied, holding his gaze a little longer than necessary. Breaking it, she added, "Well, quite a few, but it should heal just fine. Cooks usually have an assortment of scars from cuts and burns." She turned over her other hand. "I have a small collection already, but this will be the showstopper."

"I hope it stays that way," he said, taking a step back. "Did the knife get away from you?"

Marina looked a little embarrassed. "I got distracted. Anyway, you and Leo should eat this while it's hot or put it in the oven. Which way is the kitchen?"

"This way," he replied, leading her into the kitchen. He patted the hulking oven that had reigned here for decades. "Look at this old relic, would you? I'm told it works, so I imagine it will be good for reheating pizza."

Marina laughed. "And a lot more. That's an old work-horse." She ran a hand over the smooth enamel. "It looks like it's hardly been used. You really lucked into a great kitchen. Someday I'll have to find a little cottage like this."

"You don't plan on staying at your grandmother's house?"

"She might like that, but I think we both need our privacy. It's a full house right now." Marina flipped her hair over her shoulder. "Sometimes I think she's having more fun with the cafe than I am. All the socialization and cooking when she wants, but none of the bookkeeping and ordering."

"She's an amazing woman." *Like her granddaughter,* Jack wanted to say, but he decided to back off. With Vanessa's health improving, a question he hadn't thought about loomed in his mind.

Jack took Marina on a quick tour of the house, and then they joined Leo and Scout in the backyard. They explored the rooms above the garage, which Jack didn't have much use for.

But Marina's eyes gleamed. "You could do so much with this space. Once your friends and family know you're living by the beach, you're going to have a lot of visitors."

"I hope they're okay with an air mattress," Jack said, only half-kidding.

Suddenly, another little boy called over the back fence. "Hey, Leo. My uncle said you were moving in."

"Is your uncle the mayor?" Jack asked as Leo tore toward the fence.

"Uncle Bennett."

The boy's parents came to the back fence. "You must be Jack," the woman said. "I saw you at the opening party for the Coral Cafe, but we didn't have a chance to talk. My brother was telling me about you. I'm Kendra, this is my husband Dave, and this is Logan. The boys met at the party, and I spoke to Vanessa."

Jack introduced them all. "Is it okay if Logan comes over for pizza? Marina brought it from the cafe."

When his parents agreed, Logan climbed over the back fence and dropped to the other side.

"You want to see my room?" Leo asked. "It's so cool." The two boys raced off, and Jack and Marina followed them inside.

"He has a friend already," Marina said, smiling. "You've landed well."

When Marina jingled her keys, Jack quickly asked, "Can you stay for pizza?"

"I can't. I'm on my way to meet Poppy at the Seabreeze Inn to talk about the venue for the event with Ivy and Shelly. I just wanted to drop off the pizza. Are you keeping your room at the inn until your furniture arrives?"

"I checked out this morning. I've got a bed in the van that will work just fine until I get beds in here."

"Camping in your driveway?"

"Sure." Uncertain whether to hug Marina or shake her hand, he shoved his hands into his pockets. Between Vanessa and Marina—and a sense of duty and persistent feelings for Marina—his mind was a jumble.

Marina smiled. "That works. I'll see myself out." She left quickly.

As Jack watched her go, he felt his heart constrict. He

recalled Bennett's words. *Patience.* But Vanessa's recovery might change everything.

LATER THAT EVENING after the boys had devoured the pizza and gone home, Jack made his way to his old VW van with Scout trotting behind. He rapped his knuckles on the side of the van. "Good evening, Rocinante, old friend. How are you holding up?"

He opened the door, and Scout climbed in, settling in a corner while Jack slid the bench into the bed position and tossed down a sleeping bag. *Simple.*

He'd only have a couple of nights here, he figured. Jack didn't mind; it had been his home base while traveling across the country. After drawing the curtain, he pulled out his laptop and accessed his company's research databases through his phone connection. Something had been nagging him.

His fingers flew over the keyboard. *Princess Anne yacht.* He hit the *enter* key, and began to scroll through material. He couldn't find much until he began to construct a series of Boolean searches with Charles and Anne and a few other keywords.

Jack raised his brow. Charles and Anne had quite a past, although that didn't mean they were guilty of anything now. He stroked his chin in thought. Still, that was an awfully expensive yacht. One of his early lessons in journalism had been, *follow the money.*

Jack wondered what Charles and Anne were up to.

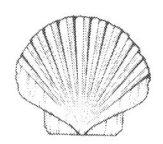

19

*M*arina and Kai strolled around the grounds of the Seabreeze Inn. Kai had arrived earlier, and Ginger was minding the cafe, which when Marina left meant she was regaling a table of gray-haired friends with her travel stories. They were ordering appetizers—tapas, Ginger preferred to call them—and she was pouring lemon spritzers. Marina suspected one guest had brought a bottle of limoncello. They were having a grand time when she left.

But they had been the only customers.

"And over there is where you can set up booths and tables," Poppy said, twisting her long blond hair to keep it from blowing in today's gusty ocean breezes. "We have electrical extension cords, which we make sure are covered."

"This is going to be so much fun," Kai said.

With her floral print sundress billowing around her calves, Marina paced off the space. "You're in charge of fun; I'm in charge of getting everything set up and cooking."

"Look at you, worrying again," Kai said with a good-natured bump of the shoulder. "I told you to relax. Because we all know that's how accidents happen."

192 | JAN MORAN

Marina had to agree. "I'll be sure to put fun on the menu."

If she hadn't been so upset, she wouldn't have nearly sliced off her finger. And now she had to compete in a throw-down against a world-class chef with a bum finger that she would have to shove into a glove somehow.

"It's usually not this windy out here," Poppy said, turning away from another gust.

"It's the beach," Marina said. She made a mental note to secure anything that could blow around at the cafe.

"I can coordinate the other vendors for you, too," Poppy said. "I did that for the art show, and I imagine you have other things to do."

"That would be wonderful," Marina said. "Getting the cafe off the ground, even with only a few customers, has been a lot more work than I thought it would be."

"So was turning this old place into an inn," Poppy said. "The first year is the hardest, but we're doing a lot better now. We have repeat customers from last year."

"Thank you for sending customers our way," Marina said. "That has really helped."

"I've been meaning to tell you something," Poppy said. "We had guests out for the morning walk yesterday, and I noticed that you can't see your sign from the beach because the bougainvillea obscures it. You should trim that plant or transplant it. And think about putting one where people would turn onto the lane, too. I bet the city will let you."

"That's a great suggestion," Kai said. "I can get Axe to make a couple of signs. Ethan and I can paint them. And I'm sure Axe will help put them up."

"Good ideas." Marina traded a grin with Poppy. "Kai started working with Axe on the new theater."

"I heard about that," Poppy said. "A theater is sure to bring more visitors to Summer Beach."

"It's super exciting," Kai said, her eyes glittering. "We're planning a special holiday performance. We haven't released that yet, but I can tell you it's going to be spectacular."

"And I hope you're in it."

Kai grinned and nodded.

Marina snapped her fingers. "The Coral Cafe could offer picnic basket meals and munchies to take to the show. And early seatings for those who are going." All she had to do was make sure the cafe could stay afloat until then. At the rate it was going, she was nervous. But that's one reason they were here today.

"All great ideas," Poppy said. "But back to the Taste of Summer Beach. Is there any chance Carol Reston will sing?"

"I think Ginger can convince her," Marina said.

"Imagine singing with Carol Reston," Kai said, her eyes lighting. "What a dream that would be."

"Then we can set up the stage we used," Poppy said. "It's stored on our lower level. I'll make sure it's set up. My job is to anticipate what could possibly go wrong."

"Like what?" Marina asked.

"I've learned you should just say no to Flaming Ginger-bread Martinis."

Kai burst out laughing. "I heard about that. At Christmas, right?"

Poppy nodded. "Could have burned down the place."

"We'll try our best not to do that," Marina said. "I'll order a few fire extinguishers." She'd certainly had her share of flaming disasters. She gazed across the lawn. "This is really going to happen, isn't it?"

Poppy laughed. "Of course it is. Come inside, and I'll go over the response we've had so far."

When Marina worked at the television station, she'd never had the chance to dream up an idea and see it come to fruition like this. She found this exciting, and it gave her a deep sense of accomplishment. More than that, she felt like she was becoming a part of Summer Beach now.

A gust of wind carried them inside, laughing as their hair blew around their faces. Ivy greeted them in the foyer of the grand old house. With its honeyed wooden floors, crystal chandeliers, and tall French doors open to the sea, the stately beach retreat was still beautiful and more than a hundred years old.

"How is the event planning going?" Ivy asked.

"Poppy is working wonders," Marina said.

They all followed Poppy to the library, where she shared the Taste of Summer Beach press release on her computer screen. "This effort is going swell. I've had a lot of responses. You're getting good coverage in local newspapers and online travel sites."

Marina leaned over and began to read. "Summer Beach: A New Destination for Foodies. Celebrity Chef Alain George to Host New 'Taste of Summer Beach' at the Seabreeze Inn Featuring Award-Winning Local Restaurants."

Ivy peered over Marina's shoulder. "It sure helps to have a celebrity chef headlining."

"That's thanks to Ginger and Carol." Marina knew where credit was due.

"You came up with a brilliant idea," Poppy said. "Especially the cook-off. Can you tell us what the competition will be about?"

Marina arched an eyebrow. "I wish I could, but all the entrants are sworn to secrecy. Chef Alain wants the unveiling to be a surprise. But I can say it's a popular food that will have a beach spin." When Chef Alain had suggested it, Marina had been surprised. But then she learned it was one of his favorite dishes.

Poppy shared more progress, and Marina was impressed with the job the younger woman was doing.

As the women walked toward the front door to leave, Ivy said to Marina, "You should join us for our morning beach walks again. Kai is in Shelly's yoga class so come together in the morning. You'd have a chance to meet new guests and invite them to the cafe."

"What a good idea," Marina said. "I'll bring my sister Brooke, too." Brooke was at a counseling session with Chip this afternoon. They were making progress, and Brooke was meeting him and the boys at restaurants for supper. She refused to cook again until they helped set the table and wash dishes. Marina didn't think that was too much to ask, but Chip had to get on board, too.

"That would give us a chance to chat more," Ivy said. "There's so much I've learned about Summer Beach since I moved here. I know Ginger has lived here for years, but I mean from a business perspective. We can all help each other."

"I'd like that a lot," Marina said. "Besides, I need some regular exercise." Tasting dishes was starting to add weight around her already pleasantly rounded middle, and she knew she had to be careful. She also needed to maintain her stamina to stand on her feet and work in the kitchen. As much as she loved what she was doing, running a restaurant was demanding work.

As Marina and Kai were walking to the car, Kai asked, "Would you like to see Axe's property and hear about the ideas we have for the theater?"

Marina checked her watch. "I think Ginger and Heather can handle things for a little longer." They got into Marina's car.

While Marina drove, Kai pointed out the vacant parcel, and Marina slowed the car. The theater property was within walking distance of the village. "I didn't realize it would be so close."

"It's about a ten-minute walk from the Coral Cafe, too," Kai said.

"That will be good for our business."

Marina pulled to the side of the road, and they got out. A

large sign with a painted rendering stood on the property. It read, *Future Home of the Summer Beach Performing Arts Theater.*

Kai whirled around with happiness. "We'll have to come up with a catchier name, don't you think? Like the Summer Beach Bowl or Theater on the Beach."

"You'll think of something. Wow, this is quite the setting." Marina gazed across the property, which was level in one section and sloped up a small hill on the other side.

"Axe explained that the terrain lends itself to a natural amphitheater," Kai said. "Carol donated the stage, so for the summer season, we're going to invite local troupes in to perform. That's one of my jobs. New productions also like to test performances in front of live audiences before they go on to Broadway or other important theaters. What better place than Summer Beach?"

"This is perfect for you, Kai." Marina was amazed at her sister's transformation post-Dmitri.

Kai's eyes sparkled with enthusiasm. "This fall, when there aren't as many tourists and as much construction work, Axe is putting a crew to work on building seating. I'll also help raise funds for that. Carol has given me some leads, and I have a few of my own. Besides Dmitri."

"This is quite the vision, too." Marina reached out to clasp Kai's hand and squeeze it. "Who knew there was so much we could do in Summer Beach?"

"As much as I liked to travel, it was time to get off the road," Kai said. "This is the perfect opportunity. I get to produce and perform. I can even start directing."

Although Kai had only been in her position a short time, Marina had detected a profound change in Kai. She suspected it wasn't just the work that Kai found exciting. "And how is Axe?"

Kai pressed her lips together as if she had a secret. "He's a gentle giant. And you should hear him sing. We went out for karaoke in the village. When he got up, the crowd applauded." She pressed her hands to her cheeks. "He has the most incredible baritone voice—he could go on Broadway, he's that good. He spent a year at Julliard before he had to return to the ranch to help his folks one year during a tough time."

"And he didn't return to Julliard?"

"He said that by then, he was older, and money was tight. He thought he could work construction until he got a break in Hollywood or with a band. That didn't work out, but his construction company did. It's funny how life works out, isn't it? And now, here we are, working on what could be the next Hollywood Bowl. A little smaller, but it can still be very successful."

"Life is sure funny sometimes." Marina was aware that Kai hadn't quite answered her question about Axe, but that was fine. Kai was still healing from Dmitri's treatment. For Kai to work with Axe and get to know him over time was a good idea.

Marina thought about how she'd landed here in Summer Beach. Despite the challenges, she truly loved what she was doing. Her children were finding their way now. Marina could also be close to Ginger as her grandmother grew older—though Marina suspected that Ginger would be an active centenarian, enrobed in her collection of silk caftans and stunning necklaces she'd collected from around the world.

Marina could see the entire vision stretching out before her. Ginger had once told her not to plan too far ahead so that she could take advantage of opportunities that she might have never even imagined. There was a lot of truth in that. She'd never thought that she'd be cooking with Chef Alain.

A year ago, she'd thought that her fiancé would be designing their new home and they'd be planning a wedding. As lovely as that sounded, it wasn't real. This was. She could be just fine without a man in her life. She lifted her chin in the brisk ocean breeze.

And that included Jack Ventana.

. . .

"THAT'S PERFECT." Marina stepped back to admire the Coral Café's new signage that Axe had driven into the ground.

Marina had appealed to Bennett and Boz at City Hall for signage on the road that led to the Coral Cafe. As an entrepreneur, Marina was learning the powerful lesson of asking for what she wanted. While she had learned to be assertive at the television station—she'd had to working for Hal—running a business was different. She had to think two steps ahead to be ready for the unexpected.

She had joined Ivy on morning beach walks with guests, which had helped bring people into the cafe. Slowly, tables were beginning to fill. The new signage would help as well. Everything added up, and people were telling their friends, so word-of-mouth referrals were building, too.

Returning to the cafe, she went into the kitchen to work on the pizza dough that she had been perfecting. In the spirit of summer—and in keeping with a new restaurant he was promoting—Chef Alain George had decided on the theme of pizza. Born Alain Giorgeschi in Naples, the chef planned to bring his version of Italian flatbreads and new pizza combinations.

Marina thought about the evolution of pizza on the west coast of the U.S. In Berkeley, California, chef and restaurateur Alice Waters pioneered gourmet pizzas with exotic ingredients at her restaurant, Chez Panisse, one of Marina's favorites.

Drawing on Waters' ideas, Chef Wolfgang Puck, along with former Prego chef, Ed LaDou, electrified restaurant patrons in Los Angeles when he opened Spago in West Hollywood, serving high-end pizzas to an affluent clientele in an airy, white-tableclothed, fine dining setting. Soon, Spago and its high-concept pizzas brought fame and licensing deals to Wolfgang Puck.

Alain George was following a popular trend, but Marina wondered what changes he might make.

She also thought about what she could do that would be different. Against Chef Alain, what she chose would have to be spectacular.

It was on.

"$\mathcal{W}$elcome to the first annual Taste of Summer Beach." Marina welcomed the first attendees onto the Seabreeze Inn lawn, which Poppy had transformed into a culinary extravaganza. Though the morning had been overcast and breezy, the sun was peeking through the chilly marine layer. People were already shedding jackets and warming to the sun's rays.

Marina wore one of her new Hawaiian-style floral chef jackets with *Coral Cottage* and her name embroidered. She and Heather were handing out guides to the booths.

At an area in the middle, Alain George was holding court with a team of assistants helping to create his most popular dishes. In the afternoon, Alain would invite other chefs to cook with him in a friendly competition. At least, Marina imagined it would be friendly.

Tantalizing aromas rose in the air, from Mitch's gourmet breakfast sandwiches with prosciutto, melted camembert, and eggs on homemade croissants to Rosa's authentic tacos with perfectly grilled salmon, roasted corn, avocado, and chipotle-orange sauce. Another new plant-based restaurant in town was serving vegan and vegetarian fare, with grilled jackfruit tacos, tofu scramble breakfast muffins, and buffalo cauliflower tapas.

"We were fascinated to hear about this on our favorite foodie podcast," one woman said as she stepped to the entrance. "We often brought our children to Summer Beach, but we never thought about this community as a hotbed of culinary activity. We usually ended up in the next community at a burger joint because they wanted those meals that come with toys."

"Wish we'd stayed in Summer Beach," her husband said. "Mmm, just smell that."

"You have to know where to look." Marina winked. "The locals decided they'd kept their best secrets long enough, so we're opening these insider restaurants up to everyone."

From her media training, Marina recalled how to put an exclusive spin on topics. The more exclusive or hard to find a restaurant was, the more people wanted to go. "Some have VIP events, so be sure to get on their list. And get their cards."

"I'm so glad you mentioned that," the woman said. "The best places are always the most crowded."

Her husband looked at the pamphlet Marina had given him. "And the entrance fees are benefitting local children's charities?"

"That's right. For scholarships in culinary arts studies and other arts." Marina waved a hand. "Chef Alain is very charitable, and we are pleased he selected Summer Beach."

Satisfied, he tapped the paper he held. "We'll have to visit Summer Beach more often."

"We'd like that. You'll find casual beach fare on the right and our higher-end restaurants on the left. *Bon appétit.*"

Marina saw another news crew make its way around the side entrance, and Poppy welcomed them. Marina had been surprised at the good media turnout, though Poppy had told her that interest had been high.

After Poppy showed them where to plug in equipment as

needed and the complimentary press table full of goodies, she made her way back to Marina.

"I'm surprised so much media is covering this," Marina said.

Poppy grinned. "All you need is one top celebrity with a large fan base. The way they can draw crowds is incredible. Now, Marina, I need to get you in as many photos as possible, too. Can Heather and Brooke manage the front? You need to be at your Coral Cafe booth, especially since you're going to be on the center stage cooking with Alain."

"Only if I make it into the finals," Marina said. Since there were so many restaurant owners and chefs who'd like to cook with Alain, his team had offered a cook-off. Those who would have the honor would have to compete for it.

"You go, Mom." Heather took the pamphlets from her. "Sunny and Jamir said they're going to join me in a few minutes. They're standing in line to get the seared poblano chili tacos with ricotta cheese and lime. I'm starving."

"Those are some of my favorites." Marina was already testing different gourmet tacos on her friends and family at the chef's table in the kitchen.

Heather looked across the early crowd and waved at her friends to hurry. "They're going to the university in San Diego, and they're going to tell me everything I need to register in the fall." She paused and smiled. "I feel really good about this decision now, Mom."

"I'm glad you do. Thanks, sweetie." Marina was pleased that Heather was making friends here.

Ivy had told her about the problems she'd had with Sunny, who'd been so spoiled by her father that it took her daughter some time after her father died to realize their lifestyle wasn't going to be the same. After making friends with a more down-to-earth group of young adults, Sunny was even talking about starting a business with a friend after college. Imani's son

Jamir was on the pre-med track, and Marina thought she couldn't find a better friend to show her around.

As Marina and Poppy made their way toward the Coral Cafe booth, they stopped along the way to welcome other restaurateurs and sample their dishes. Marina had been impressed with the friendliness of her colleagues in the food-service industry in Summer Beach. Most were welcoming and happy to help. And the ones that weren't had declined to join the event anyway. Wherever you went, there were always bound to be a few sour people, Marina decided.

Ginger was at the Coral Cafe booth, and next to them was the Starfish Cafe, a Victorian hillside home converted into a cafe. The owner served American and French cuisine, from savory and dessert crepes to popular Parisian grill dishes.

"Glad you came," Ginger said. "People have been asking for you. Word has gotten around about some of your dishes."

Ginger had set up a hot plate and plugged in a portable refrigerator. They'd decided on a few dishes that they could serve hot, and Ginger was showing Brooke how to prep.

Marina cleaned her hands and put on food safety gloves, which she had to stretch to ease over her finger, which was still bandaged. It slowed her down, but she was thankful she still had her finger. She would exercise more care with knives in the future. "If you want to go socialize, I can take this over, Ginger."

"This is right where I want to be, my dear." Ginger sniffed. "At my age, if people want to see me, they know where I am."

"Chip and the boys are coming today," Brooke said.

"How are your sessions going?" Marina asked.

A smile that had been missing for too long lit Brooke's face. "Chip and the boys sat down and worked out a chore schedule together—they have to reach a certain number of points to go out with friends. Chip agreed to help enforce it.

And he's repaired the door, the lamp, and my new shutters. The boys created a new kitchen garden for me."

"That's wonderful," Marina said, truly happy for his sister.

"And I learned so much by helping you at the farmers market that I'm going in with a friend to run a booth at our local market. With part of the money I earn, I'm going to hire a person to clean once a month. While the boys are improving, I still don't trust them to clean under their beds or behind the toilet."

"That sounds fantastic." Marina hugged Brooke while Ginger nodded with satisfaction.

"So, it looks like I won't be at the Coral Cottage much longer." Brooke turned to Heather. "You can have my old room back tomorrow. I'm leaving tomorrow. But I want to have a sister lunch once a month, a least."

They all agreed and then returned to work.

Marina and Ginger had prepared as many dishes as they could in advance. While Ginger handed out small bowls of the strawberry and spinach salad, Marina turned on the hotplate, poured olive oil into a skillet, and organized the dishes she needed to cycle through. They also had two large toaster ovens to heat the shrimp-and-pesto pizza slices they were handing out.

Two women stopped by to sample Marina's homemade bread and salad assortment. "Delicious," one woman said, while they stuffed money in the tip jar.

Ginger handed them a postcard that Kai had designed and printed. "The Coral Cafe is brand new and right on the beach with some of the best views in town. Where are you ladies from?"

"San Diego and Riverside. We decided to meet halfway between, so here we are. What a great idea. We love coming to Summer Beach."

"Come more often," Ginger said.

"I think we will." The women moved on to the Starfish Cafe booth next to them.

Next to them, the Starfish Cafe booth team was handing out miniature savory vegetable crepes drizzled with hollandaise and béarnaise sauce, as well as mixed berry dessert crepes topped with whipped cream. A woman in a bright, tie-dyed T-shirt leaned across the divide to hand them plates. "Welcome to Summer Beach. I've known Ginger a long time. My name is Colette."

Marina introduced herself and gave Colette an assortment of the dishes they had prepared. "And there's more to come."

"Thank you for coming up with this idea," Colette said. "This will be a real help to all of us who have restaurants in town. Many tourists don't know we exist."

Going back to cooking, Marina eased homemade spinach ravioli filled with pureed zucchini squash and mascarpone into a ginger-spiked coconut broth. In the skillet next to it, she quickly sautéed a side of spiralized sweet potatoes, giving them a crispy finish. She wanted to see people's reaction to this dish she was considering for the evening menu. Or on the appetizer and sides portion of the menu. The ravioli were fairly easy to make, and they had a unique flavor profile, different from traditional Italian-style ravioli.

"Keep the goodies coming," Ginger said. "I'm filling in with your salads."

"You're the best sous-chef ever, but you know you should be standing in my place."

"With all that responsibility? No, thank you." Ginger laughed. "I get to have all the fun and still live my dream."

Marina bumped her grandmother's shoulder. "What would I have done without you? You taught me almost everything I know about cooking—and life."

"Some of that you had to learn the hard way, and I'm sorry for that."

A deep voice rang out. "Sure smells good over here."

Marina looked up. "Jack." Immediately, she tamped down the tight feeling that always gathered in her chest whenever she saw him. She'd just have to get used to that.

"Would you like something?"

His gaze held hers, making her even more uncomfortable. "Anything you make is good."

Ginger stepped in and handed him a taster. "The ravioli is quite different. We call it Paradise Ravioli."

"Try the array of salads." Marina couldn't make any mistakes. She diverted her attention, quickly unwrapping the fresh fish she'd bought early that morning from a local fishing vessel that served many local restaurants—something she wouldn't have to slice. After dusting filets with panko and crushed pistachio, she placed them into the sizzling skillet. "Where's the lemon butter?" she asked Ginger.

"Right here." Ginger passed it to her. She went back to putting samples of the macadamia nut hummus and pita triangles out on a tray.

"The ravioli is excellent," Jack said, polishing it off. He dropped a few bills into the tip jar. Behind him, Denise was swaying to jazz music that filled the air. She waved across the crowd.

Marina looked up. Vanessa was making her way toward them with Leo in one hand and Samantha in the other.

"There you are," Vanessa said. She greeted Marina and Ginger.

The first thing Marina noticed was Vanessa's very short, curly hair. "I like your new style," Marina said.

Vanessa ran her hand across the short layer. "The patches are filling in. I had grown so tired of wearing scarves. When we went to the spa and salon, Denise coaxed me into having it trimmed." She ruffled her short hair. "It feels so good."

"You look lovely," Marina said. "Does anything here sound good to you?"

"Your tortilla soup was delicious. I never had a chance to

tell you that."

Marina held up her bandaged finger. "I had to rush out to take care of this."

"I'm so sorry."

"It will mend."

A small smile touched Vanessa's lips. "The human body has an amazing capacity to heal."

"I'm glad you're feeling better, Vanessa." Marina and Ginger had agreed not to tell her about their involvement lest she think they were meddling. The decision to pursue treatment, or not, was best made privately.

"Cool curly fries," Leo said, his eyes widening at the sweet potatoes.

"I think I'll try the hummus," Vanessa said.

As Marina handed them samples, Vanessa touched her shoulder. "Leo told me you brought pizza to the house. I want to thank you for being so kind to my son. And such a good friend to Jack."

Jack coughed. "I'm standing right here, ladies."

Marina only smiled. "It's good to see you all. Oh, have you ever tried the Starfish Cafe?"

"Hello," Colette called out.

After a lingering glance, Jack moved on with their little group.

A moment later, he returned. Jack leaned in toward Marina with a worried look on his face. "Have you seen Anne and Charles lately?"

"They were here earlier," Marina replied.

"If you see them, could you let me know?"

"Now you want me to call you?"

"Please. It's important."

Finally, Marina agreed. As he walked away, Marina sighed.

"What does that sigh mean?" Ginger asked.

"That you were right."

Ginger put an arm around her shoulder. "You'll be fine."

"Yes, I will be," Marina said with fresh vigor.

She was building the new life she wanted here in Summer Beach and making friends in the community. Most of all, she was making a difference in people's lives while she was supporting herself. Her revenue was climbing, perhaps slower than she would have liked, but it was trending in the right direction, and her expenses were low.

Her children were doing fine, too. Ethan was pursuing his dream, and Heather was shifting her choice of school. And they were all spending more time with Ginger than they had in a long time.

Marina tapped her head against Ginger's. "I'm so glad you're here."

"Wouldn't have it any other way." Ginger kissed Marina's forehead. "Do you know how proud your parents would be of you right now?"

"I wish they were still here. And Grandpa Bertrand."

"Life goes on, darling." Ginger patted her heart. "I carry them with me every day, so I'm never alone."

Marina loved her grandmother's outlook on life. She wondered if Ginger had ever doubted her abilities or if she had been born with such natural confidence. Either way, the woman she was now inspired all of them.

"Here's your friend," Ginger said.

Ivy cut through the gathering crowd. "How are you doing here?"

"We're giving out a lot of samples," Marina said, offering her some samples. "It's a much larger crowd than I'd thought we could draw."

"That's Poppy for you." Ivy took a bite of pizza. "Mmm, that's delicious. We've had a lot of people inquire about rooms, too. I'm so glad you decided to have this event here. We have to do this every year. Shelly and Mitch are having so much fun."

Ivy's sister was nearby at the Java Beach booth with Mitch, and they were in full beach mode. Shelly wore a sarong and a crown of flowers in her hair, and Mitch had an old straw beach hat tipped at a rakish angle.

A loudspeaker crackled above them. "And now, the list of finalists who will cook against Chef Alain." The announcer was Nan's husband Arthur—the other half of Antique Times —read off the list in his English accent.

Thirty restaurant owners had competed for just three spots in the beach pizza competition. These didn't have to be beach-inspired, just devour-on-the-beach good. Marina had submitted her Vegetarian Beach Supreme, with grilled mushrooms, zucchini, and artichokes, caramelized Maui onions, and marinated mozzarella balls piled high over a marinara sauce. She'd made it for Kai, and it was another favorite on the lunch menu.

Most other entrants had opted for traditional tomato sauces, meats, vegetables, and cheeses. In Marina's opinion, they all seemed exceptional. People were standing in line for what had been left over after the judges made their decisions. Marina had been aiming to stand out to get to the next level.

Arthur read the first two finalists, and applause filled the air. "For the third and final contestant, who will cook against Chef Alain, we give you the creator of the Vegetarian Beach Supreme, Marina Moore of the Coral Cafe."

Brooke squealed, and she and Ginger threw their arms around her. Marina could hardly believe she'd made it to the final round. She'd thought about reversing the order of her two entries, and actually flipped a coin to decide.

The loudspeaker crackled again. "Let's welcome the first contender in Chef Alain George's Best Beach Pizza Competition." Every hour, a different finalist would compete with the famous chef.

A local chef stepped up to the ring of tables where Alain was working. Perspiration peppered his beefy pink face, and his barrel-chest strained against his chef's jacket. His advance team had delivered portable wood-fired pizza ovens, which Marina found pretty impressive.

In this final round, the rule was that the pizzas had to have at least one ingredient from the sea or an ingredient found on a tropical island. The crowd gathered around, and Alain took the microphone to explain what he was preparing. He might be commanding, boisterous, and elitist, but Alain knew his craft and engaged well with audiences. He was a larger-than-life personality who always delivered.

Kai hurried in through the back of the booth and plastered a kiss on Marina's cheek. "Congrats! I just heard your name called. Sorry I'm late, but Axe and I were talking about the theater and lost track of time. And Carol wanted to talk to me again."

"It's okay." Marina laughed. "Glad you're having fun."

The other contestant was making a thin-crust pizza with pineapple. Marina knew that was a controversial ingredient. Some loved it, some hated it, but properly grilled pineapple could be delicious.

Alain was center-stage now, though plenty of people were still visiting the booths and sampling dishes.

"Do you have everything you need for the final round?" Kai asked. "If you've forgotten anything, I can run back to the cottage for you."

"I have it all."

"Even the cognac?"

Marina nudged her sister. "Especially the cognac."

As Alain and the other chef worked, Marina watched as she handled her dishes. At one point, she was so engrossed that when one of her toaster ovens binged, she nearly jumped.

Pizza was fairly easy to make, but as with any dish, the art was in using the finest ingredients, knowing how flavors would blend, cooking to perfection, and creating a beautiful presentation.

When the pizza pies were ready, a panel of judges—other Southern California chefs and television celebrities that Alain had recommended—each received a slice. They were grading on presentation, adherence to the theme, and, of course, taste. Each of them made their notes on a scorecard.

Kai folded her arms. "The judging panel is so obviously stacked in Alain's favor."

Ginger shrugged. "We fully expect him to win, not because he would have the best entry, but because of his ego. As Poppy said, what's important are photographs and the promotional value of cooking next to Alain. Marina can use that for the cafe. Alain agreed that participants could have that right. Carol made sure of that. Each restaurant has spent a lot in food costs for this event."

Marina nodded at that comment. "I'm glad the two of you worked on that. And that Carol donated the legal fees." As much as Marina would like to win, she understood the purpose of this event and competition.

Their purpose was to promote Summer Beach restaurants and build an annual affair that would position the community as a destination for great food. To that end, Marina would be happy—win or lose.

When Marina looked up from her work, she realized Vanessa was standing in front of her. But her friends weren't around.

Vanessa looked concerned. "Can we talk for a moment?"

"Can it wait? I have to cook with Alain shortly."

"I checked the schedule." Vanessa smiled again. "You have an hour. This won't take but a few minutes." Vanessa glanced behind her. "Everyone hovers around me, but we're alone now. Please."

Marina glanced at Ginger, who nodded. "This way," Marina said, motioning for the other woman to meet her behind the tented booth.

21

"*L*et's walk around to the rear of the house," Marina said. All the ingredients for her pizza were ready, and she had at least an hour to spare until her turn.

Walking beside her, Vanessa took small, anxious breaths. The sun illuminated the reddish tips of Vanessa's short, dark brown hair. The style emphasized her dark, expressive eyes.

After they turned the corner and were out of sight, Vanessa motioned toward a garden bench. "May we sit? I still get very drained."

"Of course," Marina said, feeling for Vanessa and her health challenges. They sank onto the bench.

Vanessa rested her hand on Marina's and began. "I want you to know that Jack is the best father I could want for Leo. No one is perfect, but he's right for my son."

All Marina could do was nod in agreement. "I can see that."

"Perhaps Jack has mentioned it to you, but I happen to know that he plans to ask me to marry him."

Marina felt a sharp pain in her chest. She wished Vanessa hadn't chosen this time before her cook-off to tell her. However, she supposed Vanessa suspected that she cared for

Jack and was trying to lessen the blow. She appreciated that. "I'm very happy for you," she managed to say.

"Jack asked Denise and John to take care of Leo next weekend," Vanessa said. "It's thoughtful of him."

Marina swallowed. She couldn't bear to hear the details. "Thank you for telling me." Abruptly, she stood. "I have to go back."

"Please, wait just a moment."

Marina felt like racing to the beach, running until her heart gave out. But that was no way to react. She'd known this was coming, yet she had no regrets. What she had done was for Leo—and Vanessa. Who would want harm to come to such a gentle woman? Instantly, Marina felt guilty for her moment of jealousy. She sat down. "I still have a little time. What else did you want to tell me?"

Vanessa twisted the edge of her skirt. "It's ironic, isn't it? Jack is probably the best-looking, most intelligent, compassionate man I know. And yet, I never had any romantic feelings for him. Oh yes, I know. We had one night, but that wasn't about love. It was a last desperate act of consolation because we didn't know if we would be alive in the morning. That was my last dangerous assignment. I quit when I returned."

"I didn't realize that." Marina listened.

"At that time, I had no intention of ever marrying. I never wanted to be married and yoked to a man for the rest of my life. I had watched how my mother had catered to my father —and they had a good marriage—but that role simply wasn't for me. As an only child, I knew I would care for my parents; I didn't want to have to look after a demanding husband, too. Not everyone in my culture is as progressive as you might be."

Marina took this in, but she still didn't understand what Vanessa was getting at. "You've been through a lot these past years. Have you had a change of heart now?"

"My perspective has changed in many ways." Vanessa

214 | JAN MORAN

smoothed her flowing skirt. "You see, when I discovered I was pregnant, I decided to keep Leo. I couldn't give my parents the wedding they had dreamed of for me, but I could give them the grandchild they wanted. Fortunately, they had the joy of knowing Leo before they died. They finally accepted that I refused to marry anyone." Vanessa paused and looked up. "I haven't changed my mind on that."

Marina tried to squelch the glimmer of hope she felt. "Is Jack aware of this?"

"He is. But Jack is one of the good guys, the one who is always looking out for people. As a reporter, he investigated treacherous situations—drug cartels, political corruption, espionage. He's merely shifting that sense of being the good guy to Leo and me. For my son, that's what I had hoped. But for me…" She shook her head.

"So you don't plan to accept his proposal?" Marina held her breath.

"I will not. I am quite firm on that." Vanessa took her hand. "Even if I did, I couldn't marry a man who is so obviously in love with another woman."

Marina blinked. "We haven't known each other very long. We haven't even dated."

"That's why I want to talk to you. You seem to care for him, too. A few weeks ago, when I was making my final preparations, it gave me satisfaction to think that you and Jack might get together and you would be looking after Leo."

Marina smiled. "That's a little premature."

"I know, but I've had to think so far ahead to plan for Leo. For his college, my grandchildren. And that's what I saw. And if not you, then someone like you. With your characteristics. But I know in my heart that you would be so good for Leo, and he adores you."

Marina wiped the corner of her eye. Woman to woman, she couldn't imagine saying these words about her children to another. Vanessa had more strength and courage than Marina could fathom. "Leo is so precious," she choked out. "Such a wonderful boy."

"Yes, he is." Vanessa squeezed Marina's hand. "Now, I know Jack isn't perfect. He has always had a case of wanderlust, though it seems to have lessened. And he can be very driven and tenacious about things he is passionate about. All I'm asking is that you understand why he intended to propose to me. As much as I have tried to discourage him, I think he feels he must make an effort now that I seem to be on the mend."

Marina nodded. Though she had known, she still couldn't tell Vanessa that.

"I will nudge him in your direction, and it's up to you whether you want to do anything about that. While I intend to make a home here for Leo and stay in Summer Beach near our dearest friends, I'm setting Jack free."

Relief flooded Marina, leaving her weak with joy. As tears welled in her eyes, Marina embraced Vanessa, holding the woman's thin frame with care. "Thank you for sharing your story. You have no idea how much you have lifted my heart. And I will always look after Leo, even if Jack and I aren't together. Although I hope you aren't going anywhere for a long, long time."

Vanessa pressed her hand against Marina's cheek. "Not many of us realize that we truly only live one day at a time. So live today." Vanessa pulled away, and her face was wreathed with a sweet smile of relief. "Now, it's time we sent you back to work."

The two women stood and started back. At the booth, Vanessa said, "I'd like for us to keep in touch."

"So would I," Marina said, and she truly meant it.

When Marina stepped back into the booth, Ginger looked at her curiously. "Is everything all right?"

"I've never been better." Marina gripped her grandmother's hands and smiled. "I'll tell you after I show that chef who's really the boss up there."

"My goodness, I haven't seen you this fired up since..." Ginger gazed after Vanessa, who turned around and gave Marina a good-luck thumbs-up sign. Ginger chuckled. "Heavens alive, I think I know what just occurred."

Marina hugged Ginger. "And I'm going to make sure everyone knows about the Coral Cafe."

Marina and Ginger continued serving guests while the next contestant competed against Alain. After a while, the chef's team wheeled a cart over to collect the supplies Marina had brought. It was growing late in the day now, yet Marina still had to give her best performance. And if anyone in the audience even mentioned the word *meme*, she would ignore them. This time, she was prepared for anything. She secured her hair, smoothed her jacket, and she was ready.

The cameras were rolling.

Arthur Ainsworth winked at her as she gave him the description she'd written. She took her place in the competition circle. "And the final challenger today is Marina Moore, proprietor of Summer Beach's newest restaurant, the Coral Cafe, right on the beach and open for lunch and dinner. She's also the person responsible for putting together our first Taste of Summer Beach. Let's hear it for Marina."

Applause spread across the crowd, and Marina dipped her head in acknowledgment. As she did, she saw Jack. Instead of averting her gaze, she looked straight at him and smiled.

From the corner of her eye, she saw Ginger cutting through the crowd toward Jack with a determined look on her face. When she reached him, he leaned down, and she whispered to him. Jack jerked up his head, and Ginger nodded in the direction of Charles and Anne.

It seemed odd, but Marina couldn't think about that now. She turned to Alain and shook hands.

Alain looked at her hand and raised his brow. "You're injured."

"That won't slow me down," Marina said.

A slow smile spread across Alain's reddened face. "Let's cook."

Arthur set the timer and called out, "Go!"

Marina and Alain turned to their stations. Immediately, Marina switched on a burner and tossed butter into a skillet. She placed the cognac nearby.

She saw Alain watching her, clearly interested. Turning back, she tossed flour over the stainless steel work area. Quickly, she reached for a ball of dough she had prepared beforehand and pressed her palm into it. She had used a recipe of flour, olive oil, kosher salt, yeast, and honey. Working the dough, she stretched it by hand and smoothed it on the floured counter, leaving the rim a little thicker.

Next, she brushed a white sauce made with dry mustard and a pinch of cayenne onto the dough and sprinkled her cheese—fontina and parmesan with bits of mozzarella.

From the corner of her eye, she could see Alain working feverishly. She spied a container. *Duck confit. Caviar. Wild mushrooms. Mango sauce.*

She gulped. The man was indeed a pro.

Shaking off her lapse, Marina refocused on her work. She had to execute to perfection. She quickly arranged shrimp and porcini mushrooms around the edges, forming a wide well in the center. She slid a paddle under the pizza and placed it in the pizza oven.

While that baked, Marina continued working. She could feel Alain's eyes on her, but this time, she didn't look up. He continued his playful banter, cajoling the crowd, but Marina only smiled and continued working.

She arranged the next round of ingredients she'd prepared earlier. *Rosettes of smoked salmon, perfectly curled and trimmed. Plump tiger prawns with tails, chunks of lobster.* She quickly sautéed the shrimp and lobster in the butter, added a generous pour of cognac, and cooked until the sauce bubbled and reduced. Still running ahead of Alain, she pulled the pizza from the oven and began to arrange the final presentation.

Racing against the clock, Marina fashioned a circle of tiger prawns around the interior bowl with the tails standing jauntily upright. The savory lobster was next, and she filled in the entire remaining area before sweeping drizzles of herb aioli over it. At last, working with care, she arranged the salmon rosettes in the center like a crown.

Quickly, she shaved Italian white truffle and sprinkled basil leaves on the lobster and shrimp with a flourish. Finally, in the center of the smoked salmon rosettes, she cradled an enormous scoop of Russian beluga caviar, compliments of Anne and Charles. They had given it to Marina after she had finished the party on the yacht.

Marina stepped back just as Arthur called time and threw up her hands. She had done her best, but was it good enough?

Arthur tapped the microphone. "There you have it. Duck Confit with Mango Pizza by Chef Alain George, and Lobster Thermidor Pizza by Marina Moore, inspired by Chef Julia Child."

Media photographers gathered around to snap photos. Marina stood behind her creation, proud of her achievement. Kai and Heather and Jack were also taking photos.

Next, they presented their work to the judges and sliced their pizzas for them. Marina stood waiting while the judges tasted and scored their efforts.

Alain turned to Marina. "That was quite an ambitious creation."

"Yours looked amazing, too." She received his words as a compliment, even though he hadn't exactly said he admired it.

"It is on your menu?"

"It's pretty costly for a beach cafe. Maybe by special order. I'd like to taste the duck confit."

"We will trade tastes." Alain sliced a piece for her, and she did the same.

Marina took a bite and rolled her eyes. "This is utterly delicious."

Alain inspected her creation before working his way through the slice. "This is a feast on a pizza."

Marina laughed. "I suppose it is." She had been going for presentation, but perhaps it had been over the top. *Too much?*

The judges tallied their scores and handed them to Arthur.

"Ladies and gentlemen. Let's congratulate all the contestants and restaurant owners on their efforts here today."

Alain posed for photos with the contestants. Marina knew these images would be priceless mementos for her fellow chefs, and the media coverage would be extremely valuable. A woman from Alain's team asked the final contestants to wait by the stage. Marina took her place and waved at her family, who were in the front.

After the applause and cheers subsided, Arthur went on. He called the third-place winner, the Chicago Deep Dish Pizza—a traditional style fused with spinach and seaweed. The Island Pineapple Pizza took second place.

And now, it was between Marina and Alain.

"For the final competition…"

Marina held her breath, hoping against the odds.

"For the Duck Confit with Mango Pizza, Chef Alain George."

Cheers swept across the crowd. Alain stepped up to the microphone and thanked everyone for participating. Marina was a little disappointed, but she had to keep her perspective. Besides, had she actually expected to win against a seasoned chef? She had to laugh at herself for even dreaming about it. *Maybe in a few years.* She started toward her family.

"Before I finish, I must say a special thanks to my fellow chef, Marina Moore," Alain said. "To find such creativity here in Summer Beach—from the entire restaurant community—is such a welcome surprise and the reason I am here today. Little did I imagine that I would be outdone by a woman who has just opened her first restaurant, the Coral Cafe."

Had she heard correctly? Marina turned to see Alain beckoning her to join him.

"In this case, the judges were clearly biased," Alain said amidst gasps from the crowd. "I know a masterpiece when I see it—and taste it. Marina deserves this award."

Above the cheers, Marina heard Kai and Shelly yelling in unison. "Woo-hoo!"

Jack charged to the front, snapping photos. Ginger beamed and waved.

Marina's knees felt weak as she made her way to Alain.

"You won this fair and square." He extended his hand to congratulate her. "You're very talented. Mind if I call on you? We have guest spots on my show, and I would like my viewers to see who beat me in the Beach Pizza Competition. Well done, indeed."

As Marina shook his hand, she felt as if the world were spinning around her. "I'd be honored, thank you."

After more photos, the pizzas were sliced and shared. Ginger, Kai, Heather, Ethan, and Brooke and her family gathered around her to congratulate her. Kai whispered, "I have to run. Don't go anywhere."

Marina wondered what Kai meant by that. More people came to congratulate her—Colette from the Starfish Cafe, Mitch from Java Beach, and Rosa from the taco stand. They were all so pleased that one of their own had unseated Alain George, and they were all talking about what they could do the next year.

Marina saw Jack approaching and waved him over. He hurried toward her and clutched her hands.

"That was incredible," Jack said, reaching down to kiss her cheek. "You're quite a woman."

Just then, music blasted through the crowd, and Carol Reston took the stage. Everyone began clapping and whistling.

She began to sing one of her most popular songs—a duet— and suddenly, Kai stepped onto the stage, her voice lifting over the crowd.

Whistles and cheers broke out all around Marina as their friends and family cheered Kai on. Marina knew this was one of her sister's dreams, to sing on stage with the legendary Carol Reston. Kai was giving the song everything she had, and media were taking photos and video. This was her sister's moment, too.

"Isn't Kai fabulous?" Marina said to Jack, but when she turned around, he was gone.

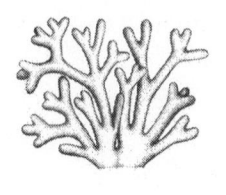

22

"You should have stayed and celebrated your win with everyone," Ginger said as they walked into the cottage. "I could have returned on my own."

After the close of the inaugural Taste of Summer Beach festival that evening, the owner of Spirits & Vine on Main Street invited all the restaurant participants to join them for a celebration.

Marina dropped her purse onto the sofa, stepped out of her clogs, and circulated her aching ankles. "Honestly, I was glad you wanted to go home. The event was incredible, restaurants will see a lift, and we've started a new tradition—but I'm exhausted." Her cell phone binged, and Marina pulled it from her purse.

She checked her phone and held it out for Ginger to see. "That reservation app Kai set up has been lighting up all day. People think they need reservations." She was amazed and filled with gratitude.

"I daresay everyone will need to reserve a table during your busiest hours soon." Ginger squinted at the phone. "Why, that's impressive. Well done."

"It's interesting that many people attending the event were

unaware of the variety of restaurants in Summer Beach." Marina flopped back against the couch, turned off the ringer, and shoved the phone back into her purse, eager for a respite. "Everything can wait until tomorrow."

Kai had gone with Axe to Spirits & Vine to represent the Coral Cafe. She was thrilled to have shared the stage and a song with Carol Reston, whom she had long admired. Throngs of event attendees filled Main Street, and most of the shopkeepers were staying open late to serve them. Heather and Ethan had gone out with friends, and Brooke had joined Chip and the boys at the village arcade. The Coral Cottage was uncharacteristically quiet.

Ginger put down her purse. "We'll all sleep well tonight."

"I'm so thankful we don't have to unpack," Marina said.

That morning, Ethan and his roommate had helped Marina load the tables and appliances for the booth into the friend's van, and they also disassembled the booth after the event. Not a speck of food had been left. The boys promised to deliver everything in the morning, and Marina would make breakfast for them while they unloaded.

While most of Marina's family and friends were out celebrating, Marina needed to unwind and relax. Comfortably nestled in the living room, she stared at the old stone fireplace and the glossy green peace lilies with white floral spikes clustered around it. A warm sense of accomplishment suffused her aching limbs.

Ginger turned to her with a triumphant smile. "Congratulations, my dear. Today proved that great results require bold ideas and thorough planning. And above all, execution."

"I couldn't have done it without everyone's involvement. Yours, in particular."

"No one person could have done it all. But you led the effort and saw it through. You chose the right people to help you. And your creativity and courage proved you're a worthy contender, even at the top level. I must say, well done."

Marina smiled and wiggled her toes. "It feels good to know that I could manage all this—from the cafe to the event. What's more, I like knowing I can make my way without having to depend on the Hals of the world." Even better, she was bringing all her new friends and restaurant owners along in her success as well.

Ginger sat beside Marina and put her arm around her shoulders. "Why don't we open a good bottle of wine to mark this occasion and celebrate? We can sit outside on the patio, listen to the ocean, and enjoy the serenity."

Stretching, Marina said, "Sounds heavenly. Let's turn on the firepit. I hardly ever have time to sit down and enjoy it." The firepit had a clear view of the ocean and the marina, where guests could watch boats coming and going.

"The evening is sublime. Let's turn on those magical fairy lights, too." Ginger stood and held her hands out to Marina to help her up. "Enjoy your moment. I'm sure you'll be very busy tomorrow."

They strolled toward the guest cottage.

Marina was happy. All was right with the world, and the future seemed as bright as it had ever been.

"If you turn on the firepit, I'll bring the wine," Ginger said. "I left a partial bottle on the chef's table." She looked up at a glow emanating from the cottage. "Looks like we left a light on."

While Ginger stepped inside the guest cottage, Marina started toward the fire pit. Suddenly, she heard a scream, a scuffle, and a resounding thunk. Marina raced toward the open door, her heart in her throat. As she did, she saw a dark figure running toward the road. Terror shot through her.

"Ginger!" Marina sprinted toward the guest cottage, dreading the worst. "Ginger!" A surge of adrenaline powered her through the door.

Ginger whirled around. "There are two of them. Did you see the other one?"

Her grandmother stood over a large man laid out on the tile in the hallway in front of the private dining room. Dark liquid oozed around him. In her hand, she held the neck of a wine bottle, its contents dripping from the jagged glass, its cork still in place.

Marina grabbed Ginger. "Get away from him."

"He's not going anywhere. That's what I told him, but he didn't believe me. I wouldn't have whacked him if he hadn't physically threatened me." She held up the remains of the broken bottle. "Waste of a good wine."

Marina rushed Ginger outside. At once, the screech of sirens split the night, and flashing lights illuminated the patio. Several police cars turned in, and Chief Clarkson stepped out of one of them. "Are you ladies okay?"

"One perpetrator down inside, Chief," Ginger called out. "Not dead, just knocked out. He still has a pulse."

"Another went that way," Marina added, pointing in the direction where the other man had bolted.

The Chief gave the order for his team to search the property.

"Why didn't you call for me?" Marina demanded. She was still shaking, though Ginger seemed calm and even more emboldened.

"You weren't the only one who took self-defense classes." Ginger kissed Marina's forehead. "It's not the first time I've surprised an intruder, although this is the first time in Summer Beach. Why, did I ever tell you about the time I encountered —" Ginger stopped. "From the tragic look on your dear face, I'll save that story for another time."

"I appreciate that." Marina was still trying to catch her breath after the shock of fearing that Ginger had been harmed—or worse.

After the police officers made sure that no one else was on the property, they stashed the young man that Ginger had knocked out in the back of a police car. Chief Clarkson called Ginger and Marina into the cottage.

"Don't touch anything," Chief Clarkson advised. "We'll have a team here in the morning to go over everything for evidence."

"Will we be able to open at noon?" Marina thought of the pending reservations.

"We can use the kitchen in the main house to cook," Ginger said. "As long as we can serve on the patio."

"That should be fine," Chief Clarkson said. "They'll start early."

"And we'll have breakfast ready for them," Ginger added.

The chief smiled. "That's kind of you, but not necessary."

"I'll decide what's necessary to make sure your team is properly fueled to do their best. And I have my suspicions on who might be behind this."

"Yes, ma'am. Jack shared that with me."

Marina gaped at Ginger, wondering how Jack had gotten involved and what Ginger knew about this. Then she recalled that Ginger had rushed to talk to Jack just as Marina was going into competition against Alain.

The police chief stepped toward the private dining room, where the vintage chandelier was still on, though dimmed. He pointed toward the safe near the rear door. "This is what they were after."

The closet had been forced open and the safe dragged across the floor, leaving scratches on the Saltillo tile.

Chief Clarkson motioned toward the open door. "Looks like they couldn't get it open, so they were trying to take it with them. My hunch is that they had a third party bringing a truck. We also had a report of a stolen vehicle."

"Who would do this?" Marina couldn't imagine who might have even known about the safe. Except for Jack. But no…surely not. "And how did you know to come so fast?"

Chief Clarkson shot a look at Ginger. "Your grandmother

and Jack can explain that. He called in a tip and told me he was calling to alert you to avoid the cottage. I take it that neither of you received his calls."

Reflexively, Marina looked for her phone. She'd left it inside in her purse on the sofa.

"No, but I was on guard," Ginger said. "Jack shared his hunches with me some time ago. Tonight, I asked him to warn you, Chief."

Just then, another police car pulled up. Jack got out and pounded across the lawn toward them. He met Marina and folded her into his arms. She had never been so glad to see him and melted into his embrace.

"So glad you're safe," he said. "And Ginger? How are you?"

"She's doing better than I am." Marina was still shivering from the ordeal. "But I have a lot of questions for you two." She should have gone with Ginger into the guest cottage. Or when Ginger saw the light, they should have called the police right away. If Ginger had any inkling of trouble, why did she go in?

Because she didn't want you harmed. Her grandmother was fearless. But this situation could have gone terribly wrong. Marina would talk to Ginger about this, although she knew it wouldn't do much good. Her grandmother was as hard-headed as…well, as she was. Marina sighed and shook her head. She would have done the same for Heather and Ethan.

One of the police called out, and Jack whirled around. In the distance, Princess Anne was pulling away from the marina.

"We'll alert the Coast Guard," Chief Clarkson said. "They won't get far."

"I wish someone would tell me what's going on," Marina said.

"We will." Ginger rubbed her shoulder. "This calls for Julia's favorite wine."

"Finally," Marina said.

Jack chuckled. "I heard that once when a sommelier asked what her favorite wine was, she told him it was gin."

"That's my Julia," Ginger said with a fond smile. "She might say the evening called for a Brut Champagne even a Château d'Yquem, but she enjoyed her reds and whites from Bourgogne—what we call burgundies. Unless you feel like a gin and tonic."

Jack shook his head, and Ginger returned to the house with an officer. Marina stared in amazement; Ginger was sharing the finer points of wine with the officer as if she had not just vanquished an intruder. Ginger's let's-get-on-with-it attitude didn't allow others to rob her joy—even if they had tried to rob her home.

Jack motioned toward the Adirondack chairs surrounding the firepit. "Why don't we sit there?"

"That's where we were heading when Ginger confronted the burglar." Marina eased into a chair while Jack turned on the gas. Flames leapt eagerly into the night air, and Marina shivered. Jack shrugged out of his denim jacket and draped it over her shoulders.

"You don't have to—" Marina stopped. In a flash, she realized that her automatic denial of small courtesies had once been tied to her self-worth. Even Ginger had admonished her, advising her to be straightforward. Accept compliments and assistance with grace, my dear. Then, if you really don't want help, people will know. Marina lifted her chin. "I appreciate that. And everything you've done for Ginger —and me."

"Goes both ways," Jack said, easing into a chair beside her. "Leo liked the pizza you brought over. So did I."

Marina's chest warmed with that thought. "I like doing things for those I care about." There, she'd said it.

Jack reached for her hand, but just then, Ginger returned with a dusty bottle of Saint-Émilion. "With this June chill in the evening air, I'm sure Julia would excuse a fine Bordeaux."

Jack opened the bottle for her and poured three glasses. Behind them, Chief Clarkson was still talking with his officers.

"Chief, I would offer you a glass," Ginger began, "but I know you'll decline. Do return for a meal one evening, though. And bring that lovely woman, Imani Jones."

Marina smiled and caught Jack's eye. "Are you match-making again, Ginger?"

"Why, I seldom do that," she retorted, her eyes twinkling above her glass in the firelight. "After I introduced Anne to Charles—not their real names, by the way—I vowed to stop." She shrugged. "Old habits, though…"

Marina sat up. "You introduced them?"

"It was years ago while Bertrand was stationed in Europe. Charles was a young protégé of my husband's during the Cold War. Neither are they Americans, my dear." Ginger raised her glass to Jack. "That yacht was suspicious right away. Large vessels are generally owned by heads of state, wildly successful business people or their heirs, or those with shady business."

"Charles presented himself as a stock investor," Jack said. "However, he wasn't up on the latest investment news."

Ginger nodded. "Slippery, they were. I don't know why they're here, but when I spotted them at the food festival, I recognized them from years ago. Jack had already shared his suspicions of the couple, so I told him to call the police chief to watch them."

"But how did you know there might be trouble here?" Marina asked.

"I didn't know for sure," Jack replied. "At the food festival, Charles asked me if Ginger still lived in the Coral Cottage. After speaking to Ginger, I wasn't comfortable with that."

The couple's inconsistencies now made more sense, but Marina was still confused. "What do you think they were doing here?"

Chief Clarkson turned around. "Higher authorities also alerted us to their interest."

"From my research, my guess is drugs," Jack said. "Aiming to distribute along the coast. I did a lot of research. Whether Charles and Anne were part of this, or something else, remains to be seen."

After being on board and overhearing the couple's argument, Marina could imagine that. "But why break in here?"

Ginger sipped her wine and nodded. "Bertrand once had incriminating evidence on Charles. They knew he had passed away; they probably thought I had, too." Ginger arched a brow. "Do you know that Charles and Anne once had dinner here, several decades ago? I vaguely recall that Bertrand and Charles spent time in the guest cottage, where my husband did a lot of his writing. Perhaps that young man saw the safe then. He might have assumed that Bertrand had evidence there. Or perhaps he was after some of my former work product. But it was never there." Ginger tapped her temple and smiled.

The codes and keys. Marina was almost afraid to ask. "Is any old evidence against them in the safe?"

Ginger laughed. "Not anymore. But it's so dreadfully heavy that it's almost impossible to move without the proper machinery. I kept my stories in there so they wouldn't be misplaced."

"You don't have to tell us what's in there," Jack said, holding up a hand.

Ginger rose, and Jack stood with her out of courtesy. "I'll wrap this up with dear Clark and his team, and then I'll turn in. As fine as this wine is, a few sips are I all can manage tonight. Good night, my dears."

After Ginger left them, Jack leaned forward, resting his forearms on his knees. "If you want to stay out here a little longer, I'll sit with you. I don't want to leave you alone."

Marina considered Jack over the rim of her glass. She could follow Ginger in, or she could take a chance. Firelight flickered, warming Jack's face. "Stay. But not because you think you're protecting me."

"If there's one thing I've learned, it's that the Delavie-Moore tribe doesn't need protecting. The bad guys should be afraid of you all."

"Especially Ginger, as it turned out." This evening would undoubtedly become part of the family lore—retold and laughed about over family holiday dinners. Growing warmer, Marina touched her wine glass to Jack's and sipped. Tonight, she was too tired for games, yet empowered by what she had accomplished. "I used to think you were one of the bad boys some women fall in love with. But now I think I miscalculated."

"I won't lie to you; there were times I should have been more considerate in relationships. I was too quick to chase a story. That's one of the unfortunate demands of the job."

"Still, that was your profession," Marina said. "And you excelled at it."

Jack laughed softly. "I always pictured myself as a super-hero with a pen."

"This is such a lifestyle change for you," Marina said thoughtfully. "A new son, new house, new career…"

"You left out a new dog." Jack grinned. "It's a change, for sure, but one I welcome. How do you feel about your new life here?"

"Since spring, I've gone from anchor lady to meme star to cafe owner. That was quite a challenge, but I couldn't be happier now. Sometimes, when your world blows up, you discover sparkly bits among the debris." Marina tucked her hair behind her ear and studied Jack, weighing the options before her. "Like you."

Swirling his wine, Jack laughed. "I've never heard myself described as a sparkly bit before, but I'll take it." He shifted in his chair. "There's something I need to tell you."

Marina heard a note of angst in his voice, and she thought

about what Vanessa had told her. She tightened her grip on her glass, steadying herself to hear his story. "Go on."

"You know that Vanessa has been responding well to the new treatment. I've also missed so much of my son's young life. As you can imagine, there's nothing I wouldn't do to try to make it up to him." Rocking slightly, he gazed into the fire.

Marina watched him and waited. He seemed to be struggling with a decision.

Raising his brow, he said, "I thought I could give my son something he's never had. A home with two parents."

Ruminating on this, Marina swirled her wine, listening to the sounds of the nighttime beach. Crickets in the distance, rustling palm trees, endless waves. She would have loved nothing more than to have had Stan by her side, but she was proud of her children—and the job she had done raising them alone.

Finally, she said, "While that's an admirable ideal, many parents rear children on their own—for any number of reasons. What's important is that children are cared for and feel loved."

"I'm sorry, I know you didn't have a choice," he said quickly. "Heather and Ethan are great kids and a testament to your parenting ability." He paused and ran a hand through his hair. "I thought for a wild moment of asking Vanessa to marry me—for Leo's sake. She's an admirable woman, but…" He hesitated. "I can't marry someone I don't love, not when…"

As Jack touched her hand, Marina held her breath.

"Not when I feel such a strong attraction to you," he finished. "I'm taking a chance here, and you can tell me to go jump in the ocean anytime you want."

Threading her fingers with his, she asked, "Did Vanessa decline your offer?"

Jack shook his head. "In one regard, it's the right thing to do. However, I should think that most women want one-hundred percent of her husband. Same with us guys."

"The good guys, right?" Marina smiled.

A gust blew between them, nearly extinguishing the fire, yet it rallied back, stronger than before.

Jack's eyes glistened in the flickering firelight. "I thought about the kind of woman Vanessa is and what she would want. She doesn't want pity. She never wanted to marry—me or anyone else—so I have to respect that." Hesitating, he brushed a finger along the back of her hand. "And I'd never want you to think that you were my second choice."

Marina felt a catch in her throat, and she blinked back sudden tears.

He held his hand out to her. "Would you take a walk with me on the beach, like we used to do?"

Marina pulled his jacket around her and rose. Jack lifted his arm across her shoulders, and Marina warmed to their closeness.

As they strolled toward the beach, she glanced over her shoulder at the cottage. She thought she caught a glimpse of shadowy movement through the kitchen window, but now there was nothing.

Except, perhaps, Ginger ducking away from the window, smiling to herself. Marina took a few steps and glanced back again.

Ginger lifted her hand and blew her a kiss.

Marina's heart filled with gratitude—for the devotion of her grandmother and her safety tonight.

They reached the beach, where the waves raced in, and foamy saltwater chased their steps.

Mesmerized by the sea, Marina thought about the constancy of the ocean and that of real love. Each might have its ebbs and flows, but the power of constancy outweighed such vicissitudes. She thought about Ginger's love for Bertrand and the love she still had for Stan.

Could such a love develop with Jack? She leaned toward him as they walked, satisfied to be alone together.

Jack turned to her, his face shadowed in the faint light of a new moon. "What if I promise to call this time?"

Marina squeezed his hand. "Actions speak louder than promises," she replied, teasing him.

"I deserved that." Jack winced and grinned sheepishly. "However, I would like for us to get to know each other better this summer—if you want, of course. And not just this summer, but I hope for a long, long time. Marina Moore, I'm yours—if you will only give me a sign."

Before Marina could respond, an electric-blue glow shimmered on waves rushing toward them. With each sweep of the tide, the mysterious illumination disappeared and reappeared. At once, the phenomenon rippled across waves on either side of them, lighting the shoreline with breathtaking brilliance.

Jack caught his breath. "What's that?"

"It's called bioluminescence. A rare miracle of nature."

Awestruck, Marina clasped Jack's hand, and they stood together, entranced.

"When tiny plankton are disturbed, they emit this radiant, bioluminescent light." She smiled at him. "There's your sign."

Laughing, Jack brought her into his arms. She could feel his heart pounding in rhythm with hers. Raising her face to his, Marina closed her eyes as their lips met. This time, their connection was solid. This was the man she wanted—intelligent, compassionate, kind, and so much more.

All around them, the ocean glittered and glowed as if celebrating the magic between them. When Marina finally took a breath, her heart filled with an exquisite feeling that she'd known only once before in her life.

"This view is even more spectacular than the one out there," Jack murmured, caressing her cheek.

Marina laughed softly. "Are you comparing me to a force of nature?"

"There's no competition," Jack said. "Poor Mother Nature."

Marina kissed him again, and then, holding each other, they stared into the inky-black night and across the shimmering ocean, spellbound by the dynamic luminescence of the sea—and their growing love.

The End

AFTERWORD

Author's Note:

Thank you for reading *Coral Cafe*, and I hope you enjoyed sharing the debut Marina's new cafe. Join Marina and Kai and the rest of the Delavie-Moore family as the cafe expands and the performing arts center debuts in *Coral Holiday*.

If you've read the *Seabreeze Inn* at Summer Beach series, you're also invited to a wedding in *Seabreeze Wedding*, the next in that series.

Keep up with my new releases on my website at JanMoran.com. Please join my Reader's Club there to receive news about special deals and other goodies.

More to Enjoy

If this is your first book in the Coral Cottage series, be sure to meet Marina when she first arrives in Summer Beach in *Coral Cottage*. If you haven't read the Seabreeze Inn at Summer Beach series, I invite you to meet art teacher Ivy Bay and her sister Shelly as they renovate a historic beach house in *Seabreeze Inn*, the first in the original Summer Beach series.

You might also enjoy more sunshine and international

travel with a group of friends in the *Love California* series, beginning with *Flawless* and an exciting trip to Paris.

Finally, I invite you to read my standalone historical novels, including *Hepburn's Necklace* and *The Chocolatier*, a pair of 1950s sagas set in gorgeous Italy.

Most of my books are available in ebook, paperback or hardcover, audiobooks, and large print. And as always, I wish you happy reading!

CORAL CAFE RECIPES

Since *Coral Cafe* centers on food, I wanted to share some favorite home-cooked recipes that I wrote into the book, many of which are inspired by the nearly year-round fresh produce and seafood found in California. The state is also home to noted chefs Alice Waters and Wolfgang Puck, who popularized the gourmet pizza trend in California with all manner of toppings. Such pizzas and flatbreads are nearly endless in their variety.

Included are three of my home-cooking recipes you might like to try: a caramelized onion vegetarian pizza, an easy smoked salmon pizza, and a decadent seafood supreme pizza. Also included is a pizza crust recipe similar to one Wolfgang Puck popularized at Spago in Los Angeles. Any of these may be made just as easily with flatbread or gluten-free pizza crust alternatives.

For pizzas with light-weight fillings, puff pastry can be a delightful alternative that elevates a meal. I like to fill mine with a simple brushing of olive oil or *crème fraîche* with mushrooms, caramelized onions, spinach, and ricotta or shaved Parmesan.

For a new twist on pizza night, pass out individually-sized

flatbread or pizza crusts, organize toppings, and let each person build their own. This approach is a great way to get kids into the kitchen to learn to cook or share an enjoyable evening with friends.

∼

Vegetarian Supreme Pizza

Sweet-and-savory caramelized onions are the key to the vegetarian pizza that Marina makes in this story. The process of transforming sweet onions into a tasty garnish might take between 30 to 60 minutes, depending on the sugar and water content of the onions. The good news is that caramelized onions may be prepared ahead of time and will keep in the refrigerator for three to five days.

Caramelized onions are also delicious in French onion soup or as burger toppings. Make a larger batch on the weekend to have it ready to go. When shopping for onions, remember to look specifically for sweet onions, as these are best for caramelizing due to their high sugar content.

People are often divided on pizza sauces, so I suggest you use what you like. Here, I've recommended pesto or marinara, but if desired, you may omit sauce entirely and simply brush the crust with a generous amount of olive oil to crisp the bread. As to cheese, while the traditional mozzarella is easy to melt, Gruyère is a rich, nutty flavor alternative. Rosemary pairs well with Gruyère, too. Or opt for fontina or Parmesan.

Vegetables are another area of potential contention. Try mushrooms—white button, portobello, porcini, or a wild mushroom mix. Load on sliced zucchini and artichokes with Roma, heirloom, or halved cherry tomatoes—or whatever catches your fancy.

Enliven your pizza with pinches of your favorites fresh or

dried spices. Sauté your garlic before adding to your pizza for a sweet, mellow, nutty flavor.

For the meat-eaters in the family, simply add sliced Italian sausage, prosciutto, or pepperoni to their side of the pizza pie. Above all, use your imagination, and cook what you enjoy eating.

Makes: 1 large or 2 small pizzas or flatbreads
Preheat oven: 450 F (225 C)
Ingredients:

- 1 10-inch pizza crust or flatbread (homemade or store-bought)
- 6 ounces (170 grams) fresh mushrooms, your choice, sliced
- 1 zucchini (small or half of a larger one)
- 6 ounces (170 grams) artichoke hearts (canned, drained)
- 1 to 2 medium sweet onions (Maui, Vidalia, Walla Walla, or other sweet yellow onion)
- 6 ounces (170 grams) sliced mozzarella or grated Gruyère
- 1/3 cup (80 ml) pesto or marinara sauce (store-bought or homemade)
- 1 tablespoon extra-virgin olive oil (15 grams)
- 1 tablespoon butter (15 grams)
- Pinch of fresh or dried spices to taste: oregano, parsley, garlic, rosemary
- Kosher salt and pepper to taste

Garnish:

- 1 bunch of fresh basil leaves, sliced or torn

Instructions:

To caramelize sweet onions: Slice onions in thin, 1/8 to 1/4 inch (5 mm) slices (round or lengthwise for different variations). Heat olive oil and butter in a large, wide skillet. Add sliced onions to cover just the bottom (but not packed tight). Sauté over medium-high heat for 10 minutes. Reduce to medium-low heat and cook until onions are soft and browned, stirring frequently for approximately 30 to 40 minutes. Season with kosher salt and pepper as desired. To keep onions from drying out, add a little water or stock to deglaze the pan as needed. Finished onions should be soft and amber-brown in color, but not mushy. To aid in the caramelization process, add a teaspoon of sugar if needed. Remove from heat and let cool.

Slice mushroom, zucchinis, artichoke hearts, and other vegetables as desired. Sauté mushrooms in a little olive oil to remove excess moisture, add dried or fresh spices. Set aside.

Spread pesto or marinara sauce as desired over uncooked pizza crust or flatbread. Sprinkle sliced mozzarella or grated Gruyère on crust. Scoop caramelized onions over cheese. Arrange sliced vegetables on top.

Bake at 450 F (225 C) for 8 to 10 minutes (or 5 to 6 minutes if using prebaked crust) or until cheese is melted and crust is a golden brown. Allow to cool for 2 to 3 minutes before slicing.

∼

Chilled Smoked Salmon Pizza

For seafood lovers, pizza was once bleak territory. I still recall the first shrimp pizza I had at a beachside cafe in San Diego. It was a simple concoction of pesto sauce, sautéed shrimp, mozzarella cheese, and fresh basil. In the *Coral Cafe*, Marina adds this dish to the menu. It's a light beach alternative, especially when prepared with a puff pastry.

One of my favorite easy summer dishes is a simple smoked salmon recipe inspired by the popular pizza originally served at Wolfgang Puck's Spago restaurant. This is especially light and flavorful for summer fare. This recipe is quick and easy to make—especially with store-bought flatbread or pizza crust.

This smoked salmon pizza pairs well with one of Julia Child's favorite lightly chilled white burgundy wines or a glass of champagne, Italian soda, or sparkling water. If you like, toss a little arugula on top and drizzle with balsamic or serve with a salad. Who said fast food has to be dull?

Makes: 1 large or 2 small pizzas or flatbreads
Ingredients:

- Baked pizza crust or flatbread (homemade or store-bought)
- 8 ounces thin-sliced smoked salmon (225 grams)
- Cream sauce (below) or 1/2 cup of *crème fraîche* (100 ml)

Cream Sauce:

- 1 1/2 cup sour cream (350 grams, 12 ounces)
- 2 tablespoons shallots, minced (6 grams)
- 2 tablespoons fresh chives, chopped (or parsley or dill) (6 grams)
- 1 1/2 tablespoon lemon juice (22 ml)
- Dash of white pepper

Garnish Options:

- 1 ounce caviar, hackleback, or roe (30 grams) (or less)
- Bunch of chopped or torn basil leaves
- Arugula with balsamic drizzle

Instructions:

Mix ingredients, cover, and chill. Spread over baked pizza crust or flatbread. Place thin-sliced smoked salmon over the cream sauce.

Garnish with caviar or roe as desired. May also garnish with fresh basil leaves—or arugula finished with a light balsamic drizzle.

Alternate shortcut: May also substitute 1/2 cup of *crème fraîche* (100 ml) for the cream sauce. Add spices, chives, or dill as desired.

∾

Seafood Supreme Pizza

For Marina's pizza cook-off against a top chef, she needed a spectacular dish, such as the Lobster Thermidor for which Julia Child became known (along with many other dishes).

In my kitchen, I opt for an easier method of simply brushing olive oil with garlic over the crust to let the seafood shine, though I bring in the flavors of Lobster Thermidor to add character. This is a pizza to impress. Add a salad, candle-light, and wine—and enjoy.

If you wonder why the dish is so named, Thermidor referred to a French play, and it was created at Maison Maire restaurant by Leopold Mourier, an assistant to renowned chef Auguste Escoffier in Paris. It's an interesting bit of 19th-century food history.

Lobster Thermidor is a decadent blend of lobster meat, egg yolks, mustard, and cognac—a very rich French concoction. Traditionally served scooped into lobster shells or gratin dishes, Gruyère or Parmesan cheese is melted on top. Thermidor is a somewhat more laborious recipe, but there are plenty of Thermidor recipes online to adapt and reduce for a deliciously different pizza sauce.

Makes: 1 large or 2 small pizzas or flatbreads
Preheat oven: 450 F (225 C)
Ingredients:

- 1 large or 2 small pizza crusts (homemade or store-bought)
- 2 cloves garlic, minced
- 4 tablespoons olive oil (60 ml)
- 8 ounces porcini or small portobello mushrooms, sliced (225 grams)
- 1/2 cup Parmesan cheese, grated (100 grams)
- 1/2 cup fontina cheese, grated (100 grams)
- 16 shrimp, medium, tail off
- 8 tiger prawns, tail on
- 4 to 6 ounces lobster, cut into chunks (150 grams)
- 2 tablespoons butter (30 grams)
- 1/3 cup cognac or brandy (75 ml)
- Pinch of dry mustard
- Pinch of fresh or dried spices to taste: oregano, parsley, garlic, rosemary
- Kosher salt and pepper to taste

Garnish:

- 1 ounce of smoked salmon, sliced and curled into a rosette (30 grams)
- Bunch of chopped or torn basil leaves
- Optional: 1 ounce of caviar (30 grams)

Instructions:
Sauté minced garlic and pinches of desired spices in olive oil in a large skillet on medium heat. Brush half of oil and garlic over pizza crust or flatbread.
Sprinkle Parmesan and fontina cheese over crust. Slice mushrooms, sauté lightly to remove excess moisture, and

246 | *Coral Cafe Recipes*

drain. Arrange around rim, leaving 1/2 to 1 inch (15 to 15 mm) for crust as desired.

Sauté shrimp in remaining olive oil and garlic on medium-high heat until cooked. Let cool 1 to 2 minutes. Inside the mushroom perimeter, place sautéed shrimp, approximately 2 per slice (for a pizza cut into 8 slices), or 1 per slice on a small pizza.

In a large skillet over medium-high heat, combine 2 table-spoons butter (30 grams), dry mustard, and white pepper to taste. Add prawns and lobster and sauté. Add cognac, bring to a boil, then reduce heat and cook until sauce is reduced and prawns and lobster are cooked. Let cool 1 to 2 minutes.

Arrange prawns, tail up, within the ring of shrimp. Arrange lobster chunks within ring of prawns, clustered in the center.

Bake at 450 F (225 C) for 8 to 10 minutes (or 5 to 6 minutes if using prebaked crust) or until cheese is melted and crust is a golden brown. Remove from oven. Let stand 2 to 3 minutes.

Roll sliced salmon into rosette. Use as garnish in center of pizza. Optional: scoop caviar or roe into center of rosette. Sprinkle with basil. Slice, serve, and enjoy.

$\sim$

Gourmet Pizza Crust

If you have the time and inclination, this is a fairly easy crust recipe that pairs well with most any pizza. It can be made one or two days ahead.

Makes: 2 6-ounce or 1 large crust (175 grams)
Preheat oven: 450 F (225 C)

Ingredients:

- 1/2 package dry active yeast or fresh yeast (or 1/8 oz. or 1 1/8 tsp.) (10 grams)
- 1/2 teaspoon honey (3 ml)
- 1/2 teaspoon kosher salt (3 grams)
- 1/2 cup warm water (105 to 115 F; 40 to 45 C)
- 1 tablespoon extra-virgin olive oil (15 ml)
- 1 1/2 cup all-purpose flour (180 grams)

Instructions:

Begin by dissolving yeast in 1/4 cup (60 ml) of warm water in a small bowl. Add honey.

In a separate bowl, mix flour and salt. Add yeast and honey mixture, olive oil, and remaining water. If using an electric mixer with dough hook, mix on low for about 3 to 5 minutes until dough forms around the hook. Dough should pull away from sides of bowl when ready.

On a floured surface, knead dough until smooth, about 2 to 3 minutes. Form into a ball, place into a bowl, and cover with a damp towel. Put in a warm location and let rise for 30 minutes.

Separate dough into 2 balls. Work dough again 4 to 5 times, and roll on counter until smooth for about a minute. Return to bowl to rest for 15 minutes.

When ready, spread dough on surface, leaving a slightly thicker edge if desired to hold toppings. Add toppings and bake at 450 degrees F (225 degrees C) until cheese is melted, about 8 to 10 minutes depending on firmness of cheese and toppings.

If using only 1 ball of dough, extra dough will keep in the refrigerator for up to 2 days.

I hope you enjoy these recipes, and I would love to see your photos online. *Bon appétit*, my friends!

ABOUT THE AUTHOR

JAN MORAN is a *USA Today* bestselling author of romantic women's fiction. A few of her favorite things include a fine cup of coffee, dark chocolate, fresh flowers, laughter, and music that touches her soul. She loves to travel, and her favorite places for inspiration are those rich with history and mystery and set against snowy mountains, palm-treed beaches, or sparkly city lights. Jan is originally from Austin, Texas, and a trace of a drawl still survives, although she has lived in southern California for years.

Most of her books are available as audiobooks, and her historical fiction is translated into German, Italian, Polish, Dutch, Turkish, Russian, Bulgarian, Portuguese, and Lithuanian, and other languages.

Visit Jan at JanMoran.com. If you enjoyed this book, please consider leaving a brief review online for your fellow readers where you purchased this book, or on Goodreads or Bookbub.

Made in the USA
Coppell, TX
03 March 2021

511321 92R00152